Marta Acosta

IS

"HILARIOUS."
—*NATIONAL EXAMINER*

"WICKEDLY SNARKY."
—*EL PASO TIMES*

"CLEVER AND AMUSING."
—*SAN FRANCISCO CHRONICLE*

Praise for the work of this award-winning author

"Ultra-hip and very now. . . ."

—*BookPage*

"The characters pop off the page and the dialogue crackles with good lines."

—*Orlando Sentinel* (FL)

"An addictive combo plate of romance and vamp satire."
—*Publishers Weekly*

"Stephanie Plum meets *Sex and the City* in this stylish, hilarious novel."
—Jennifer Cox, author of *Around the World in 80 Dates*

"Quirky, surprising, and cinematic."

—*Star Democrat* (Baltimore)

"Intelligence and fabulosity mixed into a delicious cocktail."
—Marcela Landres, *Latinidad*

"An elegant vampire tale."

—*Oakland Tribune* (CA)

Haunted Honeymoon is also available as an eBook

Also by Marta Acosta

Happy Hour at Casa Dracula
Midnight Brunch at Casa Dracula
The Bride of Casa Dracula

As Grace Coopersmith

Nancy's Theory of Style

Haunted Honeymoon

Marta Acosta

GALLERY BOOKS

New York   London   Toronto   Sydney

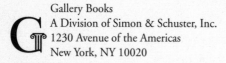

Gallery Books
A Division of Simon & Schuster, Inc.
1230 Avenue of the Americas
New York, NY 10020

First Gallery Books trade paperback edition October 2010

GALLERY BOOKS and colophon are trademarks of Simon & Schuster, Inc.

For information about special discounts for bulk purchases, please contact Simon & Schuster Special Sales at 1-866-506-1949 or business@simonandschuster.com

The Simon & Schuster Speakers Bureau can bring authors to your live event. For more information or to book an event contact the Simon & Schuster Speakers Bureau at 1-866-248-3049 or visit our website at www.simonspeakers.com.

Manufactured in the United States of America

10 9 8 7 6 5 4 3 2 1

Library of Congress Cataloging-in-Publication Data is available

ISBN 978-1-4165-9887-9
ISBN 978-1-4391-1580-0 (ebook)

To my brother
Marlo
with love and affection

Haunted Honeymoon

Prologue

The next time a sex toy sales consultant offered to teach me how to unlock handcuffs with a paper clip, I would accept.

Alas, hindsight is easy when one has both wrists cuffed to a metal chair bolted to a cement floor. But, necessity being the wacky aunt of improvisation, I could surely figure it out. Perhaps there was a paper clip in the desk.

A cat, one of dozens of identical striped cats here, gazed at me from atop a console across the room.

I said, "We're both screwed, aren't we, *gato*?"

If I could pull the metal chair from its bolts, I could drag it to the desk and use my teeth to open the drawers to rummage through the office supplies. I'd always been fond of office supplies and had liberated many pens and notepads during my years of temp work; office supplies should repay the favor and liberate me.

I was yanking my arms upward to test the cuffs when I heard the *sssh-sssh* of corduroy and squeak of crepe-soled shoes. My interrogator walked to the desk and sat on it.

The others called him the Professor, and he had that neglected look of abstracted academics. His shaggy graying hair was unbrushed, and he wore a misbuttoned argyle sweater. He placed a thick manila file on the desk and opened it.

"Here we are again," he said flatly.

"I assure you that I wouldn't continue to bore you if I had a choice," I said. "Why not let me go?"

When the Professor looked at me, I saw impatience in his hazel eyes. He said, "Your resistance is unreasonable and exasperating. You know we won't consider releasing you until you tell us who you are and why you killed Ford and Cricket Poindexter, yet you continue to whine about it."

"I've told you what I can. There's no more I can say."

"There's no more you *will* say. Try to be precise."

"I heard a scream. I went to see what it was. I came across the accidents. Please note that I am once again demanding my right to speak to my attorney. Kidnapping and confinement is a felony."

"Only when humans are involved, not creatures. But the law is a distraction," he said with a frown. "You were carried away in your bloodlust. Things got out of control—all that blood and you couldn't help yourself since you're a vampire, after all."

"There's no such thing as vampires."

He stood up and reached for a button on the wall. The blinds opened and light flooded in. It was day. How long had I been here? I blinked to adjust my eyes.

My interrogator was staring at me. "Aren't you afraid of the sun?"

"I'm totally freaked out about global warming."

He leaned over the desk and banged on it, a man of thought being reduced to physical acts. "Here are the facts. Fact: Ford Poindexter called nine-one-one and said that a vampire had killed his wife, Cricket. Fact: the call ended abruptly. Fact:

you were discovered at the scene, covered in blood, with blood on your mouth, by the bodies of the Poindexters. Fact: Ford's phone had been crushed."

I was too exhausted to cry anymore for poor Ford and Cricket Poindexter. "I'm sorry, but I've told you all I can. I came across the first accident and witnessed the second."

The Professor opened the desk drawer and pulled out a ruler. I hated the ruler. He said, "Do you expect me to believe you when you can do this?" He came to me and struck me hard across the face. The metal edge cut into my skin and I tasted blood on my mouth, but the taste of my own blood didn't do anything to sate my craving. Then my skin mended over smoothly.

"How do you do *that* if you're not a vampire?" the Professor asked, his brow wrinkled in puzzlement.

I could have told him things. I could have told him that I had been a normal human *chica* until I'd gone to a party and met a rather fabulous man. A moment of passion with Dr. Oswald K. Grant, certified plastic surgeon and vampire, had infected me, but my own freakish immune system kicked into high gear and fought off death.

I could have explained that I was the only known Normal— well, *normalish*—survivor of the infection, which caused a craving for blood and had given me the ability to heal quickly from minor cuts. Unlike born-vampires, I could enjoy daylight without sunblock.

A second infusion of blood by a more powerful vampire, Ian Ducharme, had saved my life after an attack by a rogue vampire. But the cure had been almost as deadly as the injury. When I'd finally recovered, I was unusually strong, able to heal from serious injury, and I could see in almost total darkness.

Ian's blood had also transmitted a condition he had that was rare even among vampires: when I touched someone, skin to skin, I got a delicious buzz. The sensation almost compensated for the fact that alcohol and drugs didn't affect me.

I got a rush from drinking blood. Now, blood *and* sex . . . that was a thrill.

I could have mentioned that I'd been engaged to Dr. Oswald Grant, but so many forces had conspired against our marriage that our relationship shattered like a thin crystal goblet on a stone floor.

I could have relayed my adventures with heiresses, tabloid writers, has-been actors, shapeshifters, and the nutcase who'd hired me to ghostwrite his memoirs, which became an international bestseller, but my interrogator seemed tragically humor-deficient.

If I felt confessional, I might have shared my inability to stay away from goddamn Ian Ducharme, a man with too many secrets who also believed he was exempt from the law. A man who would kill for me and might kill because of me.

The Professor asked, "Where are you from? Whose orders are you following?"

"I'm under no one's orders. I don't know what you think I am, but I'm an ordinary human girl."

"No, no matter what the DNA testing says, you're not ordinary. I always find out what I want to know. You're going to tell me why you murdered the Poindexters. You're going to tell me who you are and *what* you are."

Then he struck me again and again with the ruler, repeating dispassionately, "Who are you? What are you?" until his arm got tired.

I hurt so badly that I was sobbing, but I could and would endure his blows rather than give up the people I loved, or anyone else for that matter.

The Professor breathed heavily with his exertions. He leaned forward, looking like a depressed middle manager. I imagined that his blood would taste thin and unsatisfying, of salads with no-fat bottled dressing, frozen fish, and intellect.

I spit out a mouthful of blood and said, "Do you want to know who I am? I am a Miracle of the Saints and if you don't let me go, you will pay for it, I promise you, you crazy mad scientist. Did I mention crazy?"

The Professor went to the door and spoke to the beefy guards outside. Their blood would be deliciously thick and salty, like the greasy burgers and fries they ate every day.

He told them, "Do whatever you have to do to find out who she is. And *what* she is."

It was at times like these that I wish I'd exhibited a little more self-control. Some judicious restraint and diplomacy. And yet I never did. Which brings us back to hindsight.

one

Love to Blood You, Baby

It was a marvelously sunny April day and I took a minute to admire the dignified bumblebees hovering like stripy zeppelins over the lavender hedge, and inhale the scent of freesia and narcissus before I packed my gardening gear into the back of my small green pickup. Since no one was around, I tossed a thirty-five-gallon bin of green recycling into the truck bed without my usual pretense of effort.

The garden had once been formal and restrained, with perfectly trimmed boxwood hedges; the sort of landscape my father, who had a landscaping company, installed. I'd transformed it into a place bursting with color and texture by adding interesting plant varieties and flowering shrubs.

As I swept the debris from the path, my brown dog, Rosemary, tap-danced by my side, and I told him, "We'll go in a minute. Thank you for your patience."

I leaned on the handle of my broom and looked up to see Gigi Barton, my client and friend, coming toward me. The heiress to the Barton tissue fortune ("It's not worth sneezing at if it isn't

Barton's!") was dressed in a bold geometric print wrap dress over skinny pants and heels with a dozen tiny buckles. She worked the path like a runway and held out one arm to display a small silver package.

"Milagro, are you talking to that dog?"

"Yes, I am. The majority of pet owners talk to their pets. Did I tell you that I'm freelancing for *Paws to Reflect,* a newsletter for canine companions?" I had a degree in creative writing from a Fancy University (F.U.), but I hadn't been able to sell any of my fiction.

"You have the oddest ways of amusing yourself," Gigi said, "but the garden looks gorgeous. I love the urns."

The magnificent terra-cotta urns contained hundreds of deep purple and lemon yellow tulips, pansies, and freesias. "Thanks. I layered the bulbs, so you'll get a long succession of bloom."

"Wonderful!" She held the silver package toward me and said, "Would you give this to Lord Ian? I finally had the chance to have the mug shot framed from my arrest at our scavenger hunt last summer."

Gigi ran in the same circles as my boyfriend/lover/whatever, Ian Ducharme, who had one of those suspect European titles. Of course, I thought all titles were suspect unless they were on the covers of books.

I pulled off my grimy goatskin gloves and took the package. "I'm sure you look stunning."

She laughed. "I've learned a thing or two about getting a good mug shot over the years. The trick is to soften the lights with a scarf and have the photographer work with you. A girl like you shouldn't have any problem doing that. Just flash a little tit . . . or, in your case, a lot."

"Thanks for the tip, but I'm not planning on getting arrested anytime soon."

"That's what's fun about arrests, so spontaneous!" she said. "Oh, and tell Lord Ian that I'm taking his advice and looking into a summer house in Lviv."

"Where's Lviv?"

"Oh, it's the new Warsaw, Milagro. *Everyone* knows that."

"I'll pass along the message. See you soon, Gigi."

"Ciao, sweetie," she said, and returned to her house.

I finished sweeping, put away the broom, and then my dog and I got in the truck. I started the engine, cranked up the music, and considered my options. I hadn't planned on driving to see Ian, but the heat of the day had made me amorous, and I knew he was returning from one of his mysterious trips.

I'd never been able to stay away from him even when I was engaged to Oswald Grant, a much more admirable man, a good man, a principled man.

I joined in the traffic speeding out of the City and across the bridge, enjoying the sight of the rich orange cables and spires contrasting against the glimmering silver-green water and the azure sky.

On days like this, it was easy to convince myself that all was well with the world. I was grateful that I could not only endure the sunlight but enjoy it. There were few benefits of being the only hybrid (vampire-normal/whatever) alive, and this was one of the most important.

Once over the bridge, I took a boulevard that led to low hills and then exited onto a street that wound through expensive neighborhoods, each more wooded and exclusive than the last. I hated showing up anywhere empty-handed, so I stopped at the posh market in town.

Everyone here had that trust-fund look of studied casualness as they parked luxury cars with bike racks, drank organic soy chai lattes, and jogged in gear designed by NASA scientists.

My mutt barked at a dog walker with a trio of pewter gray Weimaraners.

"I agree," I said. "But it's rude to say so aloud."

I left Rosemary in the truck and went inside the market, conscious of my dirty jeans, sweaty T-shirt, and work boots. You'd think I'd get over my discomfort in these places, but I always felt like the scholarship girl who didn't fit in anywhere.

The difference now was that I wanted others to see me as an ordinary *chica,* instead of what I'd become.

It was warm enough to grill tonight. I tried not to look obvious as I lingered by the butcher counter, before picking out two strip steaks dripping with glossy garnet juices. As the butcher wrapped the meat, I caught a reflection of myself in the mirror behind the counter.

Strands of long black hair had come loose from my ponytail and my damp T-shirt clung to my bounteous *chi-chis.* When I wiped at smudges of dirt by my eyes, I smeared my mascara.

I bought a bottle of pinot noir, radicchio, two baskets of blackberries, sourdough bread, and a Nylabone for Rosemary. While I was waiting for my turn at checkout, I picked up a copy of the latest *Vogue* and flipped through it.

I stopped at a page with an ethereally beautiful blonde modeling boots and little else. Her name was Ilena, and I'd met her when she was with Ian. She'd called me a "pretty chubby little pickle," and I was fairly sure she meant "pretty chubby," not "pretty and chubby." Either way, the insult still rankled. I shoved the magazine back in the rack.

Once in my truck, I gave the chew toy to my dog, who let it drop to the seat.

"Don't be like that. I'll share my steak with you later."

I drove on a series of twisting lanes up a wooded hill. Most of the houses were hidden from the street. At the apex of one turn, I made a sharp right into the driveway of a belligerently modern house. The real estate agent had called this ugly arrangement of turquoise and peach blocks a West Coast Tuscan, but I thought of it as a California Crapsman.

There were no other car here, meaning that my boyfriend/lover/whatever hadn't returned yet.

When I opened the car door, Rosemary leaped out and ran around to the back of the house. I grabbed the groceries and Gigi's gift and followed my dog to the backyard, a plateau of grass with a small oval pool and a fantastic view of the wooded hills beyond. It was private here and serene, so long as I kept my gaze averted from the house.

I left the packages in the shade of a patio umbrella and stripped off my clothes. When I dived into the pool, Rosemary jumped in, too. I swam a few laps, enjoying the weightless sensation, and then I got out and looked for a stick to throw for my dog.

I spotted one of Rosemary's tennis balls in the shrubbery border. When I bent to pick it up, I heard, "Ah, a glorious full moon in broad daylight."

I grabbed the ball, jumped, and turned.

My boyfriend/lover/whatever, Ian Ducharme, let out a sexy, rumbly laugh. He was wearing an ivory long-sleeved shirt and navy slacks. His deep brown eyes glinted in the shadow of the Panama hat that was tipped forward to shield his face from the sun.

He had dark curly hair, an aquiline nose, hooded eyes, and a Cheshire Cat grin. He wasn't tall and he wasn't markedly good-looking, but he had charisma, which came from the Greek *kharisma*, meaning "gift," and that charisma made me distrust my attraction to him.

I said, "Don't do that!"

"Do what? I was merely admiring the sumptuous vista." Ian and his crafty sister, Cornelia, had been hauled around their family's properties when they were young, and they spoke English with a Continental accent: some words had a clipped British pronunciation and others were rolled luxuriously.

"Don't sneak up on me like that. I'm going to sew tiny bells onto all your clothes so that I can hear you coming." I threw the tennis ball in the pool and Rosemary paddled after it.

"Aren't you going to welcome me back?" Ian took a step toward me, and I suddenly felt both shy and thrilled.

I walked in the other direction, putting the pool between us. "I don't want to muss your clothes. You dress so flawlessly that I'm abandoning all efforts to keep up with you. I'm going to stay naked from now on."

"A laudable policy."

Ian moved toward me, but I kept stepping away. Despite all the times we'd been together, he could still make me feel wary; and, yet, I trusted him implicitly, inexplicably. I trembled with anticipation.

I said, "I only came here to deliver a package from Gigi. It's on the table. It's a framed mug shot."

"How thoughtful. I'd like to have a photo of you now, my raven-haired Venus rising from the waters."

"I bet you would."

He feinted a move left and I took a step right.

"Hellooo!" came a woman's voice.

As I looked to see who was calling, Ian moved swiftly to me and grabbed my wrist. I yanked hard, trying to throw him off balance, but I was distracted by the woman who appeared around the side of the house.

She was a pretty honey blonde with hair below her shoulders and a golden tan. She had the look of the wealthy women here, from her neatly arched brows to her narrow nose to her perfectly polished toenails in chic sandals. She wore a gauzy sleeveless shift and her arms and long legs were toned. She seemed to be about thirty, but it was hard to tell.

"I hope I'm not interrupting anything," she said cheerfully.

"Not at all," Ian said with a smile as he let go of my wrist.

It's amazing how accurate those dreams of being naked are: you think that if you act normal, no one will notice. I held my hands demurely in front of my hoo-ha.

She said, "I saw your Jag here and thought I'd introduce myself. I live next door."

Her eyes were hidden behind sunglasses and I couldn't read her expression as she took in my nakedness. I stood straight and pulled my shoulders back, although parts of me continued to point forward. "Do excuse me for being underdressed." And overfleshed.

"What's the good of having a pool if you can't skinny-dip?" she said, and turned her attention to Ian. "I'm Christine Poindexter, but everyone calls me Cricket."

"Delighted. This lovely young woman is Milagro de Los Santos and I'm Ian Ducharme."

Cricket tilted her head in a way that her first boyfriend probably told her was adorable. "*Lord* Ian Ducharme? You're a friend of Gigi Barton's, aren't you?" Her smile broadened, showing lots of straight white teeth.

I said, "Yes, Gigi's fab. I just came from her place," but Cricket wasn't asking me.

"Milagro redesigned Gigi's garden to reflect her vivid personality," Ian said, gazing fondly at me. "Milagro has a talent for bringing out one's essential character."

I liked that he never left me out of conversations even when he dragged me naked into them.

13

Cricket gave me another look. "Oh, is that your truck out front? I was wondering why it wasn't parked in the service lot down the street. I just lost my yard man."

"I'm a garden *designer*," I said, even though I was wild about double-digging and weeding. "I'd be happy to recommend someone to do maintenance."

"Would you? That would be great."

My dog dragged his soggy self out of the pool, dropped the tennis ball at my feet, and stared at me. One of the great things about dogs was that they didn't care what you wore, or didn't wear.

I said, "Very nice to meet you, Cricket. If you'll excuse me." I picked up the ball, aware of my boobies swaying with the movement, threw it in the pool, and my dog and I jumped back in the water.

While we splashed about, Cricket and Ian spoke for a few more minutes. I submerged so I wouldn't have to hear her giggle and flirt with him. Women were prone to giggle and flirt with Ian, and then they were prone to get prone with him.

When I came up for air, she was gone and Ian was standing at the edge of the pool.

"You stayed under for a very long time," he said.

"I've been practicing holding my breath in case anyone tries to drown me."

Ian was a member of the quasi-governmental Vampire Council, and my only ally in the secretive organization. Throughout my life, people had frequently wished I was dead, but only the Vampire Council and my mother Regina had ever taken the initiative to do anything about it.

"Why don't you learn self-defense, Milagro? I can recommend an excellent instructor."

"He'd probably tell me to shoot anyone who looks at me sideways. I'll manage on my own, thank you."

"And yet you thought you needed to attend university to read novels," Ian said. "I invited Cricket for drinks later."

"Cricket," I sneered. "Letting her see me naked was hilarious. Ha, ha, and ha."

"You could have jumped in the pool, or run into the house, or hidden behind me if you were so concerned."

"I have nothing to be ashamed of. Besides, Nancy told me that naked is the new black," I said, referring to my friend from F.U.

"I have long considered Nancy Carrington to be one of the great thinkers of our time. Come inside. I have something for you."

"Is it in your pants?"

He laughed and strolled toward the door at the back of the house.

I threw the tennis ball for Rosemary for a little longer, but curiosity won over and I got out of the pool.

Ian had placed thick Egyptian cotton towels on a chair. I dried off, wrapped a towel around me, and gave Rosemary a vigorous rub. His short fur was shiny and smooth, the color of semisweet chocolate, and he had a snowy white chest. We'd found each other on a city street and been together ever since.

I left my Rosemary lolling in the sun and went inside to the not-so-great room. The orangey brick floor and brick oven of the kitchen carried on the misguided Tuscan theme. On the other side of the room, a mirror ball hung over a varnished parquet dance floor. Oversized turquoise leather furniture had come with the house.

Ian was in the master bedroom, which had beige "texturized" walls, ridiculous white marble columns, and an ostentatious stone fireplace. I perched on the king-sized bed and watched Ian unpack his accessories from an overnight case.

"I am still baffled that you actually bought this house," I said. "It's beyond hideous."

"You like the disco ball."

"Well, that *is* fabulous. Who wouldn't want a disco ball in their house? No one worth knowing. However, one could easily buy a disco ball and install it in a less hideous house, or even in an attractive house."

"The location suited me. There's room enough for you to live here."

"I am happy, ensconced as I am in the City."

"My invitation is open." Ian took out a small brown cardboard box. "This is for you."

My mother Regina had ignored my birthday every year except my eighteenth, when she told me she had fulfilled her legal duties to me, and I was still excited by gifts. I opened the box and lifted a bit of crumpled tissue to see small plastic mirrored globes dangling on silver-tone chains.

"Disco ball earrings, how fabulous! Thank you." I put them on and looked up to catch my reflection in the ornate mirror on the ceiling.

"I saw them at a market stall and thought of you."

"A market stall in Marrakesh, Paris, Florence, New York, Shanghai?"

"Yes," he answered with a grin.

"I can never find presents for you. I can't give you anything that you can't buy for yourself, and better."

"Yes, you can, *querida*," Ian said, and in a moment he was on me, pressing me back against the bed, and I could smell his cologne, spice and leather and wood smoke. His warm mouth was on mine and all my wariness vanished because his touch was enough to bring out the instincts that I kept hidden from the rest of the world.

He was strong and I was strong.

Ian's well-tailored clothes hid a powerfully built body. I couldn't remember the moment when I'd begun to see him as beautiful, but now he was beautiful to me. I loved his broad chest and muscled legs, his jawline, his strong hands, the curve of his ass.

I impatiently pulled off his shirt and scraped my teeth over his shoulder as I fumbled with his belt buckle. He snatched away my towel and then reached for the gold penknife that he kept on the bed table.

Ian flicked the knife open and took my hand in his. My blood rose toward him, wanting release. Although I felt the blade slice into my palm, it never hurt when he cut me. Ian licked at the blood that spilled from the cut, and the prodding of his tongue sent delicious tremors into the gash and through me.

A few seconds later, my skin had healed and was smooth again.

I took the knife and pressed the tip against his chest, forcing the cut to stay open long enough for a crimson rivulet of blood to run down through the dark hair toward his firm belly, and then I was licking and sucking, intoxicated by the incredible taste, pleasure thrumming through me, every nerve alive to the slightest touch of his fingers, lips, body.

He painted a line on my skin with blood, his tongue and lips following it until pleasure grabbed me like a riptide, dragging me so deep that I thought I wouldn't surface again, and when I finally did, I had bitten deep into the flesh on Ian's leg.

And then things got fiercer. A chair was broken and sheets were flecked with scarlet. Feathers from a torn pillow floated in the air and stuck to our bodies.

We fell back on the floor, our sweaty limbs intertwined, and let our wounds heal and our heartbeats slow to normal.

Ian said, "We should be able to rid ourselves of all the furniture this way." He turned on his side toward me and leaned over to lick a last drop of blood from the hollow of my neck.

"You could just donate everything to the Goodwill."

"I wouldn't wish such ugliness on anyone."

I ran my hand over his thigh before I slipped my arm around his waist, pulling closer to him. I had a smooth pink scar on my inner arm from the time I'd been slashed and he'd transfused his blood into the wound to save me, and now it throbbed warm in response to his skin. I said,

> "'Let us roll all our strength and all
> Our sweetness up into one ball,
> And tear our pleasures with rough strife
> Thorough the iron gates of life.'"

Ian kissed my temple and said, "You were the one being coy, mistress."

Pleased that he'd recognized the Andrew Marvell verse, I said, "Have you used that poem to seduce virgins?"

"Generally a limerick will suffice." He grinned and stood, then offered me a hand up. "I'm happy to be with you again, Young Lady."

Young Lady was my nickname with his family and my ex-fiancé's family. Hearing it made me feel nostalgic for the Grants and for Oswald's wine-country ranch, which had been my home for almost two years. "I'm happy to be with you, too. What time is Cricket coming? Do you think she was named after the sport or the insect?"

"The latter, I should think. She has something of a voracious crop-devouring quality. She's bringing her husband."

"He'll probably drone endlessly about cars or technology or the stock market. Promise to prop me upright if I begin to list."

"Perhaps he'll be a handsome gigolo and you'll exchange erotic innuendos."

"Oh, Ian, why must you get my hopes up?"

"We've just time for a shower."

"That shower is the only good thing about this house. And the disco ball. And the view. And Rosemary likes the pool."

After we showered, I massaged multispectrum sunblock all over Ian's body, and was getting distracted again when he asked about my newsletter.

"The latest brouhaha is between the pit bull people and the Chihuahua people. They're waging a bitter nature-versus-nurture battle and submitting dozens of frothing-at-the-mouth letters and columns. Circulation has tripled."

"I'm very proud of you, but I hope you'll have time for your own writing."

"All I get are rejections from agents," I said with a sigh. "I can't tell myself anymore that the literary world isn't ready for my stories. It's me they don't want. They want a crafty little bastard like *Don* Pedro."

I'd ghostwritten a bestselling book, a fantastical memoir of a man who claimed to be a shape-shifter. I'd been paid a pittance and *Don* Pedro was internationally lauded as a spiritual leader.

"Is it the money or the fame you desire?"

"I want to be taken seriously for my craft."

Ian tweaked my nipple and said, "I take you seriously. Now, if you don't want Cricket to think you're predictable, you may want to wear clothes."

"Cricket. It's onomatopoeic, isn't it? Cricket, cricket, cricket."

"I'm looking forward to your veiled insults already, darling."

"I will be the epitome of charmishness," I said as I went to the walk-in closet where I kept a few of my things. I dressed in a tiered lavender silk flapper dress and silver metallic flats, brushed out my hair, and stroked on shadow, mascara, and lip gloss before going to the kitchen.

I sloshed together a pitcher of martinis and put out Fra' Mani salametto, Humboldt Fog cheese, pears, almonds, and a baguette. I hoped the sausage wouldn't give Cricket ideas.

I heard the doorbell ring, and a minute later Ian escorted his neighbor and a younger man into the not-so-great room.

Cricket had changed into a black-and-white polka-dot skirt and a little white lace-trimmed cotton blouse that rode up to show the diamond that glinted on a hoop through her navel. Very sexy soccer mom.

Her husband was young and gawky, his manner at odds with his well-shaded auburn hair and professional tan. His nose looked as if it had been broken at least once, and his hands and feet were too large for his skinny frame.

"Milagro, this is Ford Poindexter," Ian said. "Ford, my friend Milagro de Los Santos."

Ford reached out to shake my hand. His grip was firm and slightly damp, and I got a nice warm zizz from the contact. He grinned. "Milagro de Los Santos? Does that mean anything?"

"Miracle of the Saints," I said. "Ridiculous, I know."

He laughed a nice laugh. "People ask if I'm named after the car, or related to Henry."

"Or Ford Maddox Ford,"

"Close, well, not really," he said. "Ford Prefect."

"From *Hitchhiker's Guide to the Galaxy*! Seriously?"

"Seriously. My father's a sci-fi freak."

Ian poured the martinis and handed one to Cricket, who said, "Really, Ford, you make him sound like a geek. He's a genius, a visionary."

"Does he write science fiction?" I asked.

"Good God, no," Cricket said with a laugh. "He works on research projects, whatever inspires him."

Ford said, "He's got multiple degrees in bioscience, physics, chemistry, and engineering, and the corporation that employs him lets him do whatever he wants."

"I'm impressed. I tried to go to grad school for a teaching credential, but got detoured to the landscaping department."

Cricket turned back to Ian. "Where is your family home, Lord Ian?"

"I'm a citizen of the world, Cricket," he said, which was his usual cagey vampire response.

I ignored the flirty way she was smiling at him, and I asked Ford, "Does your father work on any fun projects?"

"I'm not sure. He's very secretive about his work and my mom kicked him out of the house because he 'accidentally' ran over her cat. She's the only person he listens to, and she says he can't come back until he clones it and brings her a robot maid, too."

"Color me fascinated. *Could* your father clone a cat?"

"He said cloning is for schoolchildren," Ford said. "He took Señor Pickles's body and went to his lab eight months ago. We haven't seen him since."

"You haven't seen your father or the dead cat?"

"Either of them. It's not unusual. He works for this military contractor and it's all top secret," he said. "I can tell by your expression that you don't approve."

"I've had a few unpleasant experiences with groups more interested in profit and power than ethics," I said. "But if your dad's a sci-fi fan, I'm sure he's pro-humanity. Sci-fi is all about the individual's ability to overcome adversity, particularly fascistic forces."

Cricket rolled her eyes to indicate that she was officially over me at this point. Which was fine, since I was over her the moment we met.

She looked around the room. "This house looks exactly the way I imagined it. You know about the previous owner? He was a cocaine kingpin."

"He was a real estate developer," Ford said.

"He was supplying three counties," Cricket continued. "At the time, everyone thought it was cool to be friends with a drug distributor, and he was so generous with his merchandise that they let him build this eyesore."

"Cricket, some people may like this house," Ford said politely. "It's all subjective."

"We think it's gruesome, too," I said, sure that Cricket would attribute any tackiness to me. As I nodded my head, I felt the plastic mirror-ball earrings bobbing against my cheek. I tossed my hair just to feel them swing again.

"Will you be doing a remodel?" Cricket asked Ian. "I can recommend a wonderful design team."

"Milagro likes the disco room, so I think I'll keep it as is for now."

Cricket looked at him sympathetically. I wanted to smack the both of them, but Ford said, "It's an awesome party house."

His wife sighed. "That's why I make all the aesthetic decisions in the relationship." She spoke as if she was teasing, but I got the feeling that it was true.

Rosemary, always on the lookout for food, came into the kitchen, tail wagging. Ford bent over to scratch his back, setting off paroxysms of butt wiggling. "What's your dog's name?"

"His name is Rosemary."

"That's a girl's name," Cricket said slowly, as if I was an idiot.

"Rosemary is for remembrance," I answered. Ford gave me a quizzical look and I said, "I had a wonderful dog who died." Ian was watching me, so I didn't mention that the name also represented everything else I'd lost: my fiancé, my home at his ranch, my almost normalness.

We stood around the massive kitchen island and finished off

the martinis. Cricket focused her attention on Ian and brought up all her travels and her recent vacation in Lviv. "We stayed at a ski chalet near the Carpathians," she said. "I do hope Lviv won't be discovered. The chalet next to us had just been rented by a stunning model, Ilena, who had us over for drinks."

I glanced at Ian, but he didn't change his expression at the mention of his ex-lover, who was also an expert in international economics, and made me feel insecure on a number of levels.

I turned back to Ford, who told me, "Come over some night and we'll have a film festival in the screening room. I've got original Hammer and Castle films and old projectors that go *tick-tick-tick*. I mean, if you like horror."

"I write horror stories," I said casually, hoping he wouldn't think I was too weird.

"Really? I've tried to write. I got two hundred pages of a time-travel story done, and then I got stuck. Do you write about monsters?"

"Mine are political allegories, more like the original *Frankenstein,* so, yes, I write about monsters."

"My father used to read *Frankenstein* to me at bedtime."

Cricket shook her head and said, "You really are making him sound like a kook."

She returned to her conversation with Ian. I went on to discuss scientific developments that science fiction had successfully predicted, and it seemed natural for the Poindexters to stay for dinner.

Ian pulled bottles of a spicy, smoky cabernet franc from the cellar, and we grilled vegetables and juicy filet mignons that were in the fridge. I put away the steaks I'd bought.

Ian and I shared a resistance to the effects of alcohol and other drugs, which was unusual even among vampires, and I felt a little envious of Ford, who got more and more sozzled and expansive as we finished our meal with glasses of cognac outside in the dark.

Cricket just got flirtier, but she was careful to touch and smile at her husband, too, keeping him off guard. It was close to midnight when she teasingly unbuttoned her blouse and said, "Since we're all friends here and I already saw Milagro . . ."

Ford watched goggle-eyed and adoring as Cricket did a striptease on the lawn, and Ian smiled at her bump-and-grind. She had a svelte body, and my ex-fiancé, whose career was perfecting breasts, would have admired the craftsmanship that had gone into her full, perky set.

Cricket dived into the pool and Ford quickly stripped to his boxers and jumped in. His wife floated on the surface and laughed. "Come in! The water's fine."

Ian said, "Another time," but I took it as a dare.

"Why not? We're all friends," I said, and pulled off my dress. Although Ford was besotted by his bride, he wasn't unimpressed when I undid the hook on my ivory lace bra. I let him get a good look before jumping in the water.

Ford did cannonballs, Cricket displayed a smooth side stroke, and I tried to see how long I could swim underwater.

After the night got chilly, we got out, wrapped ourselves in towels, and said shivery good nights. Cricket promised to have us over soon, gazing at Ian the whole time.

When they had gone, I said, "I'm surprised you didn't jump in the water. Cricket was totally sexing you up with her eyes."

"It would have made Ford nervous, and I liked him quite a bit. He's a charming young fellow, isn't he?"

"Yes, he's fabulous."

"He enjoyed your many charms, my dear."

I gave Ian a stern look. "I like him and he likes me. It's clear that he loves his wife."

"You, my dear girl, always interpret everything as sexual. I meant as a friend."

"Oh. It's so hard to tell with you and your too sophisticated Euro vampire values."

"You know that you're the only one for me, *querida*," he said as he stroked my cheek.

We never used the word "love" with each other. Our very avoidance of the word gave it power and substance.

I looked into Ian's dark eyes, searching for goodness, but all I saw was desire, and I wasn't sure who had inspired it. "I have to finish my newsletter."

two

Good Help Is Fine to Bite

I took Rosemary with me to the schlocky master suite. When I turned on the light, I saw a package on the bed, wrapped in plain white paper with a red satin ribbon. A small card said, "To My Own Girl."

When I opened the package and unfolded the tissue inside, I saw three books bound in olive leather and blue and olive marbled board with gold lettering on the spines. They were first-edition volumes of *Jane Eyre,* and I couldn't believe I was holding them. Running my fingers over the old typeface, I felt connected to the past, to Charlotte Brontë, and even more to Jane Eyre.

The character was more real to me than most people. She'd been my friend ever since I was a lonely girl shut away in my bedroom a million years ago. I saw Jane small, plain, and watchful, wearing her simple governess dress, yet equal to anyone.

When Ian came in an hour later, his dark curls wet from a swim, I placed the first volume carefully on the bed table and smiled. He knew exactly those things I loved.

I said, "I was happy enough with the earrings, but this . . . Thank you, Ian. It is the best present anyone has ever given me."

"I have another gift to give you now."

"Is it in your pants?"

"As a matter of fact . . ."

He was strong and I was strong.

Rosemary woke me early by whining forlornly at the bedroom door.

No matter how quietly I got up, Ian always opened his eyes. I liked him this way, drowsy, warm, and affectionate.

He smiled and said, "My own girl."

"We're going out for a run," I said, and leaned over to kiss his cheek, deliciously rough with morning beard. He reached out for my hip, but Rosemary was waiting, so I pushed Ian's hand away.

I dressed in shorts, a tank top, and running shoes. I caressed the covers of *Jane Eyre* on the way out, the very sight of the books making me smile.

The hill was extremely steep and there were no sidewalks, so I kept to the far side of the road and enjoyed the challenge of avoiding branches and patches of loose rocks. It was going to be another sunny day, and I breathed in the resin-scented dew evaporating off the redwoods and firs.

My dog and I explored a few trails and I spotted the glossy dark leaves of a madrone and lacy fronds of wild ferns.

Rosemary began lagging, so, after checking to see that no one was around, I picked him up and began the journey uphill to the house.

I came in the opposite direction that I'd left. As I got close to Ian's house, I put down Rosemary. I saw the service parking lot that Cricket had mentioned. A stand of gorgeous black bamboo blocked it from view, which was why I hadn't noticed it before.

I stepped into the driveway of the lot and saw a middle-aged couple getting out of a new Volvo wagon.

He was tall, with graying brown hair cropped close to his head, wearing a black suit and a white shirt. She was nearly as tall, with a neat brown bob, a black dress, a white apron, low-heeled shoes, and a black leather handbag.

When they saw me, I smiled, said "Hi!" and gave a wave, and they smiled and nodded at me.

I continued on my way back and slowed to look at the Poindexters' house. A drive of old granite bricks led between dense privet hedges. I could see the corner of a roof, but nothing else.

I heard footsteps and glanced back to see that the man and the woman were a few steps behind me. I wondered where they worked and was surprised when I turned right at Ian's courtyard and they followed.

Turning to face them, I said, "Hi, can I help you?"

"Morning, miss. We have an appointment with Lord Ducharme."

Their complexions were normal; I surreptitiously took a sniff but I didn't smell the herbal-scented sunblock many vampires used.

"I'm Milagro. I'll take you in."

The woman and man looked at each other with delight and then grinned. She said, "Miss de Los Santos, what a tremendous honor to meet you!"

Their enthusiasm and attire clued me in that they were thralls, normals who subjugated themselves to vampires. I had achieved some fame among them since I'd managed to do what they could only dream of doing: become a vampire. Or vampirish. Whatever. "So you're here to visit Ian?"

"We're here to work, Miss de Los Santos," the woman said. "I'm Anna and this is Cal Kogalniceaunu. At our last position, they called us Mr. and Mrs. K, but please call us whatever you wish."

As we came to the front of the craptastic house, their eyes widened.

"Such an impressive estate!" Mrs. K said.

Thralls lived to serve. Some believed in the vampire myth (undead vamps with supernatural powers), others were role-playing in what they thought was an S and M game, but the most trusted were those whose families had been allied with the vampires for generations.

We went into the house and were met by Ian, who was wearing a navy silk robe open over his bare chest and drawstring pants. I supposed this was proper attire for interviewing feudal staff.

"Look who I found out on the street," I said. "Mr. and Mrs. K."

"Lord Ducharme," they both said, and Cal took Ian's hand and bowed.

I shot a look at Ian, who was, as always, annoyingly comfortable with people falling all over him.

"Welcome," he said, all lord-of-the-drug-king's-manor mannerish. "I trust your trip was pleasant."

"Yes, sir," Mrs. K said. "Our hotel was very comfortable and our things are being delivered later this morning."

"Wonderful. I'll show you your rooms."

Ian led them down the hall and I heard them going downstairs. I took Rosemary with me to the not-so-great room and scooped kibble into his bowl. "Someone has earned my displeasure," I told my dog. "Not you. You're an excellent dog."

There was a bottle of dark crimson calf's blood in the fridge. I poured about a quarter cup into a tall glass, filled the glass with icy water, and squished in some lime juice.

I was thirsty and the drink was cold and mineral and savory.

As I tipped back the glass to catch the last drops, warmth suffused my body, making me feel both relaxed and revived.

It was tasty, but animal blood didn't have the effect on me that Ian's blood did. Nothing did.

As I was pouring coffee beans into the grinder, Mrs. K came into the room. "Please allow me to take care of that for you. Would you like espresso or filter coffee?" She glanced around at the appliances as she came to stand beside me.

I held on to the canister of coffee beans. "I can make it myself."

"Miss de Los Santos, it's my pleasure to help."

I sighed and let her take the canister. It was no use arguing with someone determined to serve. "I'll have a cappuccino, please."

I got my laptop and went outside to the bulky stone table and adjusted the white canvas umbrella over it to shade my screen. There were dozens of new letters from *Paws to Reflect* subscribers on the current controversy. I began choosing those to be included in the next issue of the newsletter, and Mrs. K brought my frothy drink out to me.

Ian came out a little later, now dressed in slacks, a French blue twill shirt, and a Panama hat.

Looking up from my work, I said, "You could have told me you were hiring thralls."

"Have you forgotten that I said I would have household staff?"

"I thought you meant a cleaning service. The kind that comes in once a week and vacuums, not indentured servants."

He had the nerve to laugh. "Really, Young Lady, they earn far more than you do and are assured lifetime employment with many benefits."

"I *would* earn more at my writing if that sneaky little nut job Don Pedro had paid me properly and given me credit for my fauxoir. Which is beside the point, because I love what I do."

"As do my employees." Ian reached out to cover my hand with

his own. "Milagro, I may disagree with some—or many—of your decisions, but they are yours to make. Let others decide how they want to live their lives."

"It's the duty of those who think clearly to protect the vulnerable against self-destructive behavior."

"Spoken like a benevolent dictator, which I believe you are at heart. Thralls would find it insulting that you think yourself more capable of determining their lives than they."

I closed my laptop and said, "I've got to get back to the City. Thanks for every—" I began, and then remembered the beautiful books and the delightful earrings. "I'll consider what you said. It just goes against my ideas of an egalitarian society. I know you think it's silly that everyone should be treated equally."

"Everyone should be treated well, but many don't want to be treated equally and some don't deserve it."

I kissed him and just the taste of him made me want to stay.

"I don't see you enough." He ran his fingers along the inside of my thigh and upward. "I'll be here for a few days. Come back tomorrow. Mrs. K is a graduate of the Cordon Bleu."

"I'll try. I really do have work." My girly parts were clanging as madly as wind chimes in a storm. "Bye, Ian."

"Adieu, Young Lady."

I got my things together, and Rosemary and I headed back to the City. Once we got to the bridge, the fog began rolling in. The day was gray and chilly by the time I arrived at my place.

My fourth-floor loft had been one of the early conversions in the eighties. I liked the cheesy pink, gray, and black color scheme and the glass block partition by the kitchen space. The pièce de fabulousness on my pink granite counter was a professional-quality, lime green Margaritanator 3000.

Nancy, my best friend from F.U., had given me her old furniture: a shocking pink velvet sofa and armchair, a rose-colored shag carpet, and a variety of froofy throw pillows. It was flagrantly feminine and silly, just like Nancy.

I went through my mail, hoping for a response to the query letters I'd sent out on the novel I'd written. I read a form rejection letter, then tore it up and tossed the pieces in the recycling bin. Then I saw the thin envelope from my co-op association and was filled with dread.

My ex-fiancé had given me the loft as a wedding present, hoping that I'd want to renovate it and start a career in real estate. I hadn't. When we'd broken up, I repaid him with a settlement that I'd received from the Vampire Council after one of their members had tried to kill me. Though I owned the loft, I couldn't really afford the property taxes and monthly condo fees.

I opened the letter and my eyes went directly to the large sum in bold type in the middle of the page. It was a bill for my share of upgrading the electrical work, a sum roughly double my annual income.

My eyes fell on the *Jane Eyre* volumes. Ian had given me many gifts, but I couldn't bear to think of selling any of them.

I set aside this problem and finished my newsletter, e-mailed it off, and took Rosemary on his afternoon walk. When I returned, I phoned Gabriel Grant, my ex's cousin, who was also a security director for his family.

"Young Lady! I've been thinking about you."

"Nice things, I hope. Want to have a drink tonight, or dinner? Maybe I can make dinner for you and Charlie." Charlie Arthur, his vampire beau, was a hotel manager. "I can fire up the Margaritanator 3000 for strawberry margaritas."

"Charlie's at a conference, but I'm free. Can we go shopping first? I need new shirts."

"You are a dream date," I said, and we arranged to meet at the mall downtown.

I put on a dress, a jacket, and cute flats, and walked on the gusty, busy streets to the mall. I rode the dizzying circular escalators up to the top floor and waited for Gabriel.

I liked watching the crowds. Frequently I saw girls who looked like me, curvy brown-eyed girls with dark hair and olive skin, gossiping with their girlfriends and wearing sexy outfits. I imagined being with them, talking about normal things like how we hated our jobs and cool clubs and hot guys.

I spotted Gabriel's pretty copper-gold hair as he rode the escalators up, and then he got off and saw me.

"Hey, gorgeous," he said, giving me a kiss. He was a small, lithe man with fine features and green eyes. "I envy that tan."

"I've been swimming stark nekkid at Ian's new place."

In unison we said, "The Dark Lord!" The nickname was the sort of joke no one was brave enough to say in front of Ian. Gabriel claimed not to know Ian's full role with the Vampire Council, and Ian claimed that all he did was attend meetings.

Gabriel and I walked into a favorite department store, and I said, "The Dark Lord hired a married couple of thralls to work as his butler and housekeeper."

"You sound annoyed." Gabriel took my hand, and we strolled toward the men's department.

"I'm annoyed to the nth degree."

"You don't expect him to do his own mopping and scrubbing. He probably needs a full-time person just to care for his suits."

"He's got a place in town that does that for an astronomical fee. You know I have Major Issues with thralls. It seems so exploitive. You should have seen them kissing his ass." I saw Gabriel's expression and said, "No, hold that thought."

We laughed and he said, "It sounds as if your problem is with their desire to please, not the work they do. Most people don't want to be in charge."

34

Gabriel pulled a vintage-style slate blue polo off a rack and showed it to me.

"Love it," I said. "Ian told me it's insulting to assume that the thralls aren't capable of self-determination." I considered my ex's ranch hand, Ernesto. "I always thought of Ernesto as Oswald's buddy, but . . . but is there an emotional master-servant component to their relationship that I didn't see?"

"If you asked Ernie that question, he'd laugh in your face. Did you hear that he just bought twenty acres of old cabernet vines?"

"Ernesto's going into winemaking? I feel so left out of family news." I sorted through a pile of graphic print Ts so Gabriel wouldn't catch my expression.

"Sorry, babe, I'll try to share more." While we chose two more shirts, he filled me in on the health of the horses, his niece's tumbling class, and his grandmother's latest cookbook project, recipes that used local wines.

"Do you know that your grandmother hasn't answered my last phone call?"

"She's in a tizzy."

"Edna? She is the most tizzyless person I've ever met." I loved his snarky grandmother so madly that Ian had accused me of wanting to marry Oswald just to be near her.

"Well, you should see her now. Oswald has been in contact with our grandfather and he's coming out to visit. He's spending time with all the grandkids and then he's going to stay at the ranch."

"What! What!" I said, and grabbed Gabriel's arm. "That's what you should have opened with, Gabriel. The mysterious AG Grant at Casa Dracula," I said. "Spill the frijoles. What's he like?"

"I've only met him twice in the last ten years. He's . . ." Gabriel squinted and thought. "He's a cool old dude. Old-school, for sure, obsessed with all of us producing children, and he looks, um . . ."

"Like Oswald. I know. Why is everyone so afraid to mention Oswald in front of me?"

"Because you don't seem to be over him. You idealize your life at the ranch and you've *always* idealized Oswald. I don't want to feed the delusion."

"It's not a delusion. It's the realization that we could have done better. We should never have let the Council dictate the conditions of our marriage."

Gabriel gave me a skeptical look and then said, "But were you two ever such a terrific match, Mil?"

"It's normal for couples to have problems, isn't it? We could have worked them out if only so many people hadn't interfered with us."

"Oswald blames in large part, as he puts it, *goddamn* Ian Ducharme."

"Ian didn't break us apart," I said uneasily.

Gabriel touched his fingers to my hand and said gently, "Word got around that you and Ian were seen leaving Bar None together when you went by yourself to check out the hotel for the wedding."

Guilt squeezed me harder than a vise. Bar None was a vampire bar in the foggy coastal resort town where Oswald and I were going to be married. "Does Oswald know that I ran into Ian there?"

"If by 'ran into' you mean 'spent the night with,' Oz suspects, but he doesn't ask directly, and we don't say anything. I'm not judging you, babe, but wasn't that a sign that you weren't ready to get married?"

It was too complicated to explain that I'd slept with Ian to get him out of my system and to prove that I would be able to do for Oswald what a vampire expected his wife to do: to exchange blood while making love. I asked, "Is Oswald dating anyone?"

"He isn't interested in dating. He wanted to be married by now," Gabriel said. "I don't think he's gotten over you either. He still feels guilty about bringing you into our world. He worries about you."

"I kept telling him not to feel guilty—if it wasn't for the infection, I wouldn't have met all of you," I said, but I was relieved Oswald wasn't seeing anyone yet. "Back to your grandfather. Think of all the things he could tell us about Edna when she was young and behaved badly."

"I think she's afraid of just that. Granddad and Oz are talking all the time. They've bonded over being workaholics who fell for party girls."

"What's he going to think about your grandmother's addled young lover?" I asked, referring to the actor Thomas Cook, who adored Edna almost as much as he adored himself.

"Thomas is hanging around Grandmama so close that he's crowding out her shadow. I think she's looking forward to his next movie, when he'll be on location in Miami."

As we talked, I felt an aching homesickness.

"I'm making you sad," Gabriel said.

"I just miss it all. Oswald and the whole family gathering in the evenings as the sun set. Our conversations, the laughter, the warmth . . ."

"What you used to call *espíritu de los cocteles*," he said, "the spirit of cocktail hour."

"Yes, that," I said. "And I think about my dog being buried in the field with no one to visit her grave."

"I'll put some flowers on Daisy's grave the next time I visit," he said. "Let's play a surveillance game. Ten points for spotting shoplifters and fifteen points for store dicks, and the first one to fifty points pays for dinner. I'll spot you twenty points to start."

"Then all I need is two dicks to win."

"If only. We'll rendezvous here in thirty minutes."

I raced across the mall to a teen shop and right away I saw two kids switch out their old shoes with new ones. I surreptitiously snapped a photo of them with my phone. Only ten points to go.

I went to a department store's perfume department and followed a customer for ten minutes as she walked around with a sample bottle of expensive eau de parfum half hidden behind her Hermès handbag.

I was crushed when she returned to the counter and told the clerk that she wanted to buy a bottle.

My phone rang and when I answered, Gabriel said "I just scored fifty points" at the same time that a man's hand came on my arm and the man said, "Miss, may I have a word?"

The man was dressed in a track jacket and jeans.

"Are you a store dick?" I asked him, and held the phone out for his answer.

"I work for the store," he said grimly. "Can you step aside with me for a moment?"

I put the phone back to my ear and said, "Store dick! Fifty-five points. I win!"

Gabriel met me in the hallway outside the mall's security office. After briefly arguing my case, I finally conceded that he had won on time, if not on points.

We meandered until we found a bistro with a dark, empty section. We asked for a table in the corner.

"You should have noticed the dick tailing you."

"I was focused on the potential Mommy-is-a-klepto. Generally I'm hyperaware of dicks."

"Don't I know it," Gabriel said. "Seriously, Young Lady, girls are raised to ignore attention, and you're not just any girl. Keep an eye on your surroundings."

"I'm practicing holding my breath underwater."

"That's good. I'd like you to take self-defense classes."

"Ian suggested the same thing, but I can kick anyone's ass. Well, except his, even though I frequently want to."

"There's more to self-defense than physical strength. It also teaches you awareness, taking the time to think, and knowing how to take and keep control of a situation."

"I've learned all I need to know from *The Hitchhiker's Guide to the Galaxy:* Don't panic." I was all set to tell Gabriel about Ford and Cricket Poindexter when a heavenly waiter came over and it became urgent to ask, "Do you have anything *sizzling* on your menu?" while Gabriel said, "I want something *saucy*. What are your *sauciest* suggestions?"

When we both were sipping spicy tequila cocktails, I said, "Ooh, this is a party in my mouth."

"Speaking of which, how are things going with Ian?"

"Oh, you know. He asks me to move in with him, but he still won't tell me what he actually does for the Council. I want to know, but on the other hand, I may run away screaming."

"But how do you feel about him?"

"Like I'm fighting an addiction, but still want one last high," I said. "How did you know that Charlie was the one for you?"

"He fit all my requirements—hefty, hairy, gay, and having the family condition," Gabriel said. The Grant family avoided the *V* word as if terrified it would bite them. "But he's also very sweet."

"He's the whole hefty, hairy package," I said. "I never told anyone else this, but do you know that when I was engaged to Oswald, Ian tricked me into reciting the vows of an ancient wedding ceremony? The words were in that awful language of yours and I didn't know what I was saying."

"Well," said Gabriel. He nervously played with his cocktail napkin, folding it into a tiny diamond shape. "Don't toy with him, Milagro. You know what he did to someone who hurt you—what would he do to someone, even you, who hurt him?"

I cringed as I thought about the vampire that Ian had cut one hundred times for the one cut I'd received.

Gabriel said, "He's not called the Dark Lord because of his hereditary title, Mil. The Council sends him to deal with intractable problems and people have mysteriously vanished, their bodies never found."

"I know. I heard that Ian was supposed to get rid of me."

"That may not be true at all. Besides, he wouldn't have done anything while you were at the ranch with us."

"It's a comfort knowing that one's boyfriend/lover/whatever wouldn't have disrespected your family by killing me on your property," I said. "I could never care for someone who's capable of terrible things."

"Milagro, *you're* capable of terrible things, but you don't do them," Gabriel said. "Are you sure you don't feel something more for Ian?"

"I don't know. My hormones always hijack my brain every time I'm around him," I said. "Enough about me. How are things going with you and Charlie and your parents?"

Gabriel raised his eyebrows and looked up, an expression that reminded me of his grandmother. "His mom and mine have bonded over the fact that we won't produce grandchildren. We're both feeling the burden of our kind's crappy fertility rates."

By "our kind" Gabriel meant vampires, who had such low birth rates that they used dating services to make matches that had better chances of bearing children.

I said, "Let's go out to My Dive on Friday."

My friend Mercedes owned the club where I spent many of my evenings. She was the only one who knew about my vampire associations and she'd become friends with the vamps.

"Wish I could club it with you," Gabriel said. "But I've got to head to HQ for a confab. The Council's riled up about an activist in England, Wilcox Spiggott, who's trying to organize a movement for our kind to come out."

"Wilcox Spiggott," I said. "Wil-*cox* Spiggott."

"I know—it's so fun to say. Wil-*cox*. But the Council isn't laughing, especially since he's never gone to them for approval."

"Shouldn't someone be setting the groundwork for eventually coming out? Like sometime in the next century."

"You're still hopeful that we'll be accepted despite all you've been through," Gabriel said with a grin. "The Council is happy in their dark coffins, and I'm concerned that Spiggott might be a loose cannon."

"It would be nice not to have to be careful all the time."

"We'll get there eventually, *chica*."

When I went home, I got online and tried to find information on Wilcox Spiggott. The name came up only once in the UK. I cross-referenced the address and found dozens of businesses at the location, including something called Crimson Leasing Agents & Realty.

Vampires were wild about real estate. I wrote down the address and the phone number.

The next day, I awoke to my phone ringing. The *Paws to Reflect* editor wanted a special issue dedicated to an upcoming public meeting about dog park restrictions after a child had been bitten by a bad-natured sharjackanoodlese (shar-pei, Jack Russell, poodle, and Havanese).

I became caught up in interviewing the yapping factions and wasn't able to see Ian before he left on one of his mysterious trips.

"I'm quite disappointed," he said when I called him.

"Gabriel said he's going to a meeting with the Council about

Wilcox Spiggott's vampire rights movement. Is that where you're going?"

"Milagro, if you want to know where I'm going, come with me."

"You're trying to manipulate me by baiting my curiosity. Promise me that you won't let those vipers lock up Spiggott. I still have nightmares about their underground lair."

"No doubt you're terrified of being forced to attend another tedious meeting there," he said. "Why are you interested in Spiggott? Attractive young fellow, but insubstantial."

"How can someone organizing a liberation movement *not* be substantial? It is by its very nature a serious activity."

"My meeting shouldn't take long. If you come, I'll spend most of my time with you. We can get married all over again."

"Ha, ha, and ha," I said. "How's everything working out with your serfs and your new neighbors?"

"Splendidly. Mrs. K's cooking is as delectable as promised, and Cricket is especially attentive to me."

Jealousy embraced me with the excessive enthusiasm of a drunken frat boy. "I bet she is. She's probably talking to her divorce attorney and ordering new monogrammed linens so she can trade up. Too bad Ford seems to be in love with her."

"Ah, but we all choose the partner who gives us what we need, not what we *think* we need, or *want* to need."

"While that sounds insightful, it may just be glib, so I'm not going to read anything into it."

But after we said good-bye, I did think about it.

I'd believed that Oswald was the right person for me, and I wanted to be the right person for him. Our breakup had been engineered by others: Ian's crafty sister, who'd been assigned as our vampire wedding consultant; the vampires' Council, who would have preferred me dead; and Oswald's parents, who detested me. There was also a friend's bat-shit-crazy jealous ex-girlfriend, who'd mistaken me for a romantic rival.

And there was me, too. When I remembered how I'd betrayed Oswald, I felt sick with shame and remorse. If I could do it all over again, I wouldn't make the same mistakes.

three

Once Bitten, Twice Snide

I finished the story for *Paws to Reflect* in time to go to Mercedes's nightclub, arriving before the small red neon MY DIVE sign was turned on. Ian had invested in my friend's business, allowing her to do a remodel and add the My Dive Annex, a tiny shop that sold *cafecitos* and Cuban sandwiches.

Lenny, the house manager, was hurrying through the lobby as I came in. He gave me a pat on my bottom and said, "Sugar, do me a favor and help the bartenders. One of the girls is running late tonight."

"Sure, Lenny. I could waitress if you need me."

That sent him into convulsions of laughter, bending his skinny torso over and holding his arm across his waist. After he'd finished, he gasped, "I remember when Mercedes hired you."

Chagrined, I said, "Who knew that balancing a tray of glasses was so hard?"

After helping the bartenders stack barware and tote supplies from the storeroom, I went to Mercedes's office and stretched out on the grubby brown sofa that had survived the remodeling.

We could hear the new house band, Juanita and the Rat Dogs, rehearsing. Oswald hadn't liked their klezmer-Cuban music, but Mercedes and I agreed that they were brilliant. "I love Juanita's percussive right hand," I said as the musician ripped through a piano solo.

"Me, too," Mercedes said, turning her head from her computer screen to listen.

My friend was a sturdy woman who'd inherited her Cuban mother's cocoa complexion, her Scottish father's freckles, and both parents' immigrant work ethic. She'd shared her passion for music with me, introducing me to dazzling bands and genres, and she'd taught me how to salsa dance.

Her short dreads were pulled back with a headband and she wore a black T-shirt with a purple graphic that said *Attack of the Rat Dogs,* the title of the album she was producing with the band.

"Can I have a few of those T-shirts?" I asked. Oswald had always liked funny T-shirts. Maybe I could give Gabriel one to pass on to him.

"You have to pay for them."

"*Serio,* Mercedes, I work here for free all the time."

"You drink and watch shows here for free all the time." She wasn't smiling, but her brown face had an affable, intelligent expression that I loved. She kept pulling off her new glasses, rubbing the bridge of her nose, and putting them on again.

"I contribute substantially to the ambiance," I said. "I just got hit with a monster fee from my co-op. They've got to do electrical work."

"*¿Cuanto cuesta?*"

When I told her the amount, she let out a whistle and then said, "You can't keep living off payoffs for failed murder attempts.

What would you do if no one ever tried to kill you again? *No cojes los mangos bajitos.* If you had a regular job, you'd qualify for loans to pay for the assessment."

"I love that so many Cuban aphorisms involve food. Now I want a mango daiquiri. Anyway, writing takes up all my time."

"I have a problem believing that you're slaving away in front of your laptop when you're so tan in April. You should consider writing something marketable."

"Like stupid stories about stupid girls and their stupid obsessions with stupid boyfriends and stupid handbags? Bitch, puhleeze. I'm dedicated to my craft, to literature." I lifted my leg to show Mercedes my rocker-girl heels with silver stud details. "Do you like my new shoes? They make me four inches taller. I'm practically Amazonian."

The corners of her mouth twitched upward, but she was already focusing on solutions to my problem. "If you got a room-mate, you could use her rent to pay for the assessment, or maybe you should expand your gardening business full-time."

"Your suggestions are shockingly soulless for the daughter of musicians." I reached into my handbag to pull out a bottle of red-black nail polish.

"Real musicians have day jobs, which is why my parents still teach."

"What I need is corporate funding. Ian's neighbor's father is a sci-fi geek who has multiple graduate degrees in science, and all he does is hang out in a lab," I said, dabbing polish over the chips on my nails.

"No one just 'hangs out' in a lab."

"He won't clone his wife's dead cat, Señor Pickles, or build her a robot maid, which seems like a very churlish attitude. If I was a scientific genius, cloning pets and building robot maids would be on the top of my to-do list."

Mercedes knew I still missed my old dog, so she was silent for a few seconds and then she said, "If you got a Daisy clone, you could give me Rosemary. He's a great dog and I've been thinking I could use a pet. I could also use a few robot bartenders."

"If I ever meet the scientific genius, I'll get him right on that," I said. "Gabriel and I went shopping and had dinner this week."

Mercedes and Gabriel had bonded over their enthusiasm for computer hacking. "How's he doing?"

"He's going to a Vampire Council confab about someone who wants them all to come out. I think Ian is perfectly happy living in a crypt. Thus *cryptic*. Cryptology. Cryptography. Those are all excellent words."

"So is crap," she said. "Milagro, I know you want to talk about what's going on with you and Ian, but I can't get involved, because he's my business partner. Please don't ask me to play sides, because I like you both."

"But you like me better, right?"

Now she laughed and said, "Don't try me when you know Ian paid for the club's renovation. If you go to the corner store and pick up two jumbo bags of M&Ms for the Green Room, I'll give you a T-shirt."

"Fine," I said, swinging my legs over and standing up. "Peanut or regular?"

The show was great and afterward I went home and took Rosemary out for his last walk of the day. He was a good dog, but I still didn't love him the way I'd loved my first dog. Even now I noticed that Rosemary didn't perk his ears the way Daisy used to perk hers.

I felt so guilty about my ambivalence that I gave Rosemary a splash of my chicken blood nightcap before bed.

During the next few days, I caught up with my Stitching & Bitching group at the Baltic, a German bar with a delightful

Mexican owner named Carlos. He let us use the stage to have an impromptu poetry slam on knitting and politics, and then my friends tried to help me with my latest project. I was trying to knit a scarf with a bluish gray alpaca-wool-silk blend that matched Oswald's eyes. I didn't know if I'd ever give it to him.

Early one morning I drove north to the posh wine country town where Oswald had his plastic surgery office, offering succor and sutures to the wealthy and imperfect.

As I went past the hillside winery with a funicular, I thought ruefully of a disastrous lunch there with Oswald's parents.

I parked my truck a few blocks away from Oswald's office and snuck into a café that had a good view of his parking lot.

I nursed a double latte for an hour and had started on my second when I saw Oswald's dark blue Lexus drive into the lot. I slunk low in my seat, the latte halfway to my mouth, as I watched him get out of his car.

Oswald's chestnut hair was longer and brushed back. His expression was solemn and he wore a gray suit and pale blue shirt. There was the broad brow that I'd kissed. There was the lovely mouth that tugged up in a crooked smile. There were the marvelous long-fingered hands that had cared for me when I was ill and delighted me when I was well.

I stared at the building's back entrance long after Oswald had gone inside. I was fumbling in my handbag for a tip when I heard someone say, "Hi, Milagro."

I looked up to see Vidalia, the doctor who'd joined Oswald's practice. She was a petite woman with tiny hands that did precise work. Seeing her in her prim suit, most people would never believe that she'd been the bat-shit-crazy scorned woman who'd tried to kill me.

"Hi, Vidalia," I said cautiously.

She sat down. "I'll wait here while they're making my protein shake. We've got a long day ahead, and I'll need some energy."

"You're acting very nonchalant for someone who cut the wires in my car, buried my engagement ring, dragged my wedding dress through the mud, and attacked me in wolf form."

She shook her head and smiled regretfully. "I was out of my mind with jealousy and I really believed that you were having an affair with my ex. Of course, the drugs I took to shapeshift messed me up, as did the transformations. I wanted to be a she-wolf, but just became a megabitch."

"I never even kissed your ex. Oswald thought I was losing my mind because of your sabotage."

"I'm really sorry about that, Milagro." She glanced through the window and across the street to the parking lot.

We watched as a van turned into the lot and parked in the shade. The side door slid open and two young men and a woman got out. One was leaning on a cane. Another's empty sleeve was pinned to his shoulder. The woman's face was a rough, red mass of scar tissue. The driver and passenger got out and helped them to the building's entrance.

"Your patients?" I asked.

She nodded. "We're doing their evaluations this morning for surgery on the weekend. Oswald and I are spending most of our free time with wounded vets. Most of them need psychiatric counseling, too, though, because they've got post-traumatic stress. But we do what we can."

My feelings softened a little. "I'm glad you're helping."

She smiled and said, "It's funny how things turn out. If I hadn't been stalking my ex, I wouldn't have come here and learned that Oswald was looking for an associate. If I hadn't attacked you, I wouldn't have been forced to do this pro bono work. It's been the most rewarding thing in my life."

"A happy chain of incidents," I said, half sarcastic and half serious.

"I don't think so," she said. "So many things happen around you."

"I didn't ask you to be a crazed stalker. You made those decisions all on your own."

"True, but I think you're a catalyst for things happening. I think that there is individual choice in our lives, but we operate in a larger framework. Within that framework, there are certain pivotal people, and you're one of them."

"Vidalia, if it makes you feel better about your behavior, go ahead and think that," I said. "But I'm not going to accept that it was okay for you to do what you did because of bigger forces. You were one of the reasons my relationship with Oswald ended."

The waitress brought over Vidalia's protein shake. The doctor popped a straw in the top and took a sip. She stood up and said, "Milagro, it tears Oz apart every time he sees you. Sometimes you have to let someone go."

"Our feelings for each other were real," I said. "I'm not like you, Vidalia."

"Then why are you stalking Oswald?" she said. "'Bye."

She'd been wrong about me before. She was wrong about me now.

The next day, my *amiga* Nancy Carrington and I went to an Yves Saint Laurent exhibit at the museum and then for a lunch of salads and rosé. Nancy looked like a privileged, chic girl about town, which she was, but all you had to do was peer into her twinkly blue eyes to see her essential wackiness.

She tossed back her golden blond hair and said, "I went to a blow job class. Isn't my hair fabulous?"

"A blow *what* class?"

"I learned all the tricks of professional stylists. You must take one. As Sun Tzu says in *The Art of War,* know thyself, know thy hair type, and you will have naught to fear in a thousand fab 'dos."

"I love that you can draw fashion tips from ancient military strategy."

"It's one of my talents. I spent my entire senior seminar on Adam Smith thinking of ways to apply his economic theories to skirt trends. If you start seeing wool dirndls, invest in new technology," she said. "Do you ever think about your old beau, Oscar, the plasma sturgeon?"

"Oswald, and, of course, I still think of him, and I prefer to experiment with my hairstyle." I tossed my head to swing back my hair. "Our relationship feels unfinished. It didn't die a natural death, beaten lifeless by a million arguments, or mutual animosity, or boredom. It was that damn wedding."

"How tragic, because that flip is trés Farrah, may she rest in peace, without the crucial new millennium update. You know, you've never quite explained how you met him."

"Didn't I?" I said. "My hair is post-new-millennium, and I met Oswald at that party for Sebastian Beckett-Witherspoon."

"Your first love," she said. "Go on."

"Sebastian was awful when he saw me, and Oswald was so fabulous, but he was engaged." Oswald had neglected to tell me about his fiancée or his vampirism when we'd lip-locked and I'd accidentally been infected.

"You home-wrecking bitch," she said as she waved to the waiter for refills of our water.

"Oswald's first engagement was not a love match. They were marrying to please their families, like you and Todd."

"Honey-bunny, I loved Todd, as implausible as you think that is," she said. "Orville is kind of a wiener for getting engaged if he wasn't in love."

"That's why Oswald ended it. But while he was engaged I met Ian and had a brief, torrid tryst." I'd walked out on Ian when he tried to give me a willing thrall as an after-dinner mint.

"Lord Lustalicious," she said. "When he looked at me, I swear I could feel my panties magically evaporating. I have a theory that he can make a girl orgasm by uttering some seemingly banal phrase, like 'What a lovely basket of bananas.'"

I started laughing. "Ian thinks that you are one of the finest thinkers of our time."

"He's a perceptive man," Nancy said. "But why did you bring Ian as your date to my wedding if you were living with Orwin?"

"Ian wasn't my date. He was my escort. I told you that Oswald was away on his annual vacation repairing cleft palates for children, but you didn't believe me." That night was as indelible to me as the scar on my arm where I'd been slashed. Afterward, no matter how hard I tried, I'd been unable to let Oswald taste my blood.

"Milagro, you with a plastic surgeon is unbelievable, since you have Major Issues with your mother, Regina's, makeovers," Nancy said. "Will you ask Ogden if he'd rent his ranch to me for one of my parties?"

"Not a chance. Oswald needs time to get over me."

"That's why I adore you. You're as mature as an excellent wheel of Parmigiano-Reggiano," Nancy said. "How are things going with Sir Sexalot? Is his new house party-worthy?"

"It would be excellent if you were throwing a *Scarface* party," I said. "It has a mirror ball and a pool. Ian is . . ."

"Sexeriffic?"

"Yes, but also too much the continental roué, I think. All mysterious and imperturbable and debauched and pleased with being Ian Ducharme."

"I've never heard you be so critical about anyone in possession of a penis."

"Oswald raised my standards. Now I have higher expectations of those in possession of a penis."

"Osgood was *nice,* but are you really a *nice* girl, Milicious?" Nancy narrowed her blue eyes.

"I think we should marry someone we admire, someone who brings out our best qualities," I said. "Do you ever miss Todd as a friend?"

She considered before speaking. "Actually, I do. I spent so long with him and we really grew up together. It's almost as though the memories of your life are less real because you can't share them with someone who was there. I miss Todd's family, too."

"I'm still friends with most of Oswald's family, but they're careful not to mention certain things."

"*C'est la vie,*" she said. "I wish you'd marry Ian because I bet his mother has a tiara she could give you as a wedding present, and I think a tiara would be wonderfully sparkly against your hair."

"You are quite inspirational, you know, Nancy."

"Yes, I know."

Although Ian must have returned, he hadn't called. When I thought about him being close by, I felt like a junkie trying to ignore a poster for free heroin on a liquor store window. And, like a junkie, I gave in to my desire.

Since Ian often saw me in my gardening clothes, I decided to wear something special. I changed into a black silk bra and thong, a garter belt and stockings, a lace-trimmed black slip, a clingy wrap-around plum-colored dress, and black heels.

I put my hair up to expose my neck and wore dangling Victorian garnet and gold earrings that Ian had given me. I stroked on dark eye shadow, layers of mascara, and glossy plum-red lipstick. As I got ready, I became aroused as I imagined how Ian would undress me and the many interesting ways I'd let him violate me.

I didn't call him first in case I came to my senses at the last minute. It was likely that I'd stay the night, so I took Rosemary with me so I wouldn't have to return to my loft early in the morning.

When I arrived at the California Crapsman after sunset, cars were in the drive. I rang the doorbell and a moment later Mr. K answered the door.

"Good evening, Miss Milagro."

"Hi, Mr. K." Rosemary scampered by me into the house, but Mr. K didn't open the door farther. I could hear music and voices from inside. "Ian's back, isn't he?"

"Yes, miss. If you would wait a moment, I'll announce you."

"No need for us to be so formal," I said, and stepped by him.

"Miss," Mr. K said, but I was already through the foyer and then I turned toward the sunken living room.

It took me a moment to register the scene. A three-piece jazz band played while people chatted. A few had the too-smooth color of spray-on tans as they quaffed dark red drinks. Among the others, I saw bruises and scabs, the marks of blood tastings.

Ian wasn't in the room. Someone whispered, "That's Milagro," and someone else said, "Mmm, mouthwatering."

I ignored the comments and walked out of the room.

Mr. K said, "Please, Miss Milagro, allow me—" He tried to block my way and I moved around him, heading to the master suite.

The door was ajar and I pushed it open, saying, "Ian . . ."

He stood by the stone fireplace, facing out to the room, and Cricket was in front of him, her back to him, in a filmy pale yellow spring dress. His mouth was on her shoulder, his hands gripping her arms.

Cricket's head was thrown back and her eyes were closed like a martyr in spiritual ecstasy, the thin straps of her dress falling off and exposing most of her breasts. Her hips were pushed back against him, moving in a slow grind.

Ford sat in an armchair, clutching a tall cut crystal tumbler, transfixed.

I felt as if I'd stepped off a cliff.

I wanted to kill Ian and I wanted to cry, but I was paralyzed, telling myself, *This isn't happening.*

Ian lifted his mouth from Cricket's tan shoulder, showing a red gash on her golden skin. He licked a spot of blood off his lip.

"Hello, darling," he said, and gently urged a dazed Cricket toward her husband.

She fell into Ford's lap and took his drink from him.

Ian came to me and I stayed stiff in his embrace, just as he remained stiff from Cricket's friction. His warm lips nuzzled my cheek, my neck, and I could smell the blood on his breath, his subtle spicy cologne, and the scent of his flesh.

I knew he drank from people, from women, but I hadn't witnessed him doing it since we'd been together. Although we never discussed it, I'd hoped he'd stopped. I thought I would be enough for him.

A stray blond hair was on Ian's dark shirt, and I felt queasy. "You're busy," I said. "I should have called."

"You're always welcome. Let me introduce you."

"No thanks. I'll leave you to your friends." I turned to leave and Ian grabbed my wrist, sending unwanted sensations through me. I stared at his hand, and he let go.

"Milagro, tell me why you're angry."

"I'm not angry." I heard the words as if at a distance, spoken by someone calmly, yet all I felt was rage and hurt. "How you convinced them to do this . . ." *His mouth on her, his hands on her, her ass rubbing him, her body open to him.*

"Come now, Milagro, you've had sufficient time to accept my nature, *our* nature. You can see that we're *all* enjoying this." He glanced back at Ford kissing his wife as she snuggled against him.

Yes, that was the problem: they were all enjoying it too much.

Ford smiled goofily at me and said, "I like to watch." He ran his hand down his wife's arm, and I saw the bruises and scabs there. Ian must have been drinking from her for days. What else had he done to her, *with* her?

Cricket's eyes flicked to mine and she gave me a confident, bold gaze, a "wouldn't you like to know?" look.

I walked out of the room as fast as I could, needing to get outside and away.

Ian caught me in the foyer. "Milagro!"

"What?" I snapped.

"Don't run away, *querida*," he said quietly. "Cricket means nothing, but can't you see that Ford is special? He's very fond of you. He would be thankful to be your thrall."

"Why do you keep pushing me toward him? Maybe it's you who wants to watch. I don't want a thrall." I was mesmerized by the gold hair on Ian's charcoal shirt.

Cricket and Ford came into the foyer. She rolled a scalpel in her manicured fingers. Oswald had used a scalpel on me and I associated the surgical instrument with his affection, with the happiness I'd once had.

Ian said to Ford, "Milagro doesn't believe that others take pleasure in offering what she craves."

The gawky young man stepped to me and put his hand on my shoulder, sending a warm fizzle through me. "Milagro, I'd really like it if you, um, *vant* to suck my blood. It would be totally awesome for someone who grew up on Bela Lugosi flicks."

"Those are pictures on a screen," I said. "Cuts hurt."

"I know, but only for a second, and you're a lot cuter than Lugosi," he said.

Then Cricket lifted Ford's hand and deftly slashed his palm with the scalpel, making him wince before he gave me an abashed smile.

She held Ford's hand out to me and the cut filled with glossy red blood. "Be my guest," the bitch said, daring me.

She had taken something from me and now the copper tang of fresh blood and the eagerness on her husband's sweet face muddled my thinking even further.

"Please, please, please," he said playfully.

I took Ford's hand in both of mine and put my lips to his palm. I looked up at Ian, but I couldn't read his expression, and then I licked Ford's blood. It was mild, yet delectable, a healthy-young-man's blood.

Ford was gazing down at me. I gently moved my tongue along the cut. My mind was clouded, but my body hummed with pleasure and Ford sucked in his breath and then said, "Oh, yeah, harder," and I nipped gently to increase the blood flow.

When I saw the corner of Ian's mouth twitch upward in a smile, I dropped Ford's hand.

"Holy shit," Ford said, and laughed. He glanced around at his wife, who looked pleased. "That was so cool!"

"I told you," Cricket said. She handed the drink back to him. "Let's find Mrs. K and have her clean that up." She led him back toward the party.

Ian spotted the blond strand on his shirt and plucked it off, letting it drift to the floor. "You see how pleasing it is to have an eager friend. Come join the others. They're dying to meet you."

"'Dying' being the operative word. If you'd wanted me here in the first place, you would have invited me. Instead you were drinking from Cricket, and I can imagine what else you were doing, although the thought of you and her . . .'"

He stood as close to me as he could without touching and said in a low voice, "I am not doing this for my pleasure alone, Milagro, although I'm not going to deny that, yes, I like drinking fresh, warm blood."

"That's not all Cricket was giving you."

"She's a novice putting on a show for her husband's pleasure. For me, it was a garnish on a cocktail."

"Emphasis on the first syllable."

"If you want to know if I had sex with Cricket, then ask me."

If I asked and he said yes, I wouldn't be able to endure it. If he said no, I wouldn't believe him. "I don't want to know. I don't care what you do, or *who* you do."

Ian stared at me with his languid, hooded eyes and said, "You're very conflicted about who you are, what we are, as you've always been. But what is amusing in a girl becomes tiresome in a woman. Grow up."

"So says a man who spends every waking hour in pursuit of pleasure."

"Remind me again, Milagro, what it is that you do to contribute to society, besides your decorative value, which is considerable."

His criticism burned like salt in a wound. "I don't do enough, and I don't think I ever will if I keep seeing you. I compromise myself every time I'm with you, Ian." I stopped speaking because he looked as if he was going to hit me and I realized that I wanted to brawl with him. I wanted an excuse to strike him and bite him and tear his flesh.

Ian and I stared at each other for long moments and then I saw him relax fractionally.

"My voluptuous beauty," he said as he put his fingertips to my jaw and ran them along my throat, sliding underneath the neckline of my dress, touching the lace trim of the slip against my breast, making me tremble with desire and rage.

For a moment I thought he would at last tell me that he loved me, but he said quietly, "Stay and destroy the furniture with me."

His hands on Cricket, his mouth on her. I shook my head.

He put his face beside mine and I felt his breath on my ear as he said, "I would never do anything to hurt you, my own girl."

I jerked back, away from him. "Not intentionally, Ian, but you do hurt me." Before I started crying, before I put my arms around him, before I gave in to him again, I turned away and left the house, Rosemary at my feet.

I got in my truck, gunned the engine, and drove too fast down the hill and away from my own awful lust for blood and Ian and blood and Ian.

I stopped at the market. I bought juicy steaks and a bottle of Russian River zinfandel.

When I got to my loft, I tore into the packages, devouring the raw meat and sucking at the juices in a frenzy while Rosemary greedily chomped down a ribeye. I drank the wine from the bottle, the dark liquid spilling down my lips and throat, staining my dress red-black.

The blood was still roaring through me when I looked at the ripped packages and mess around me. I threw everything in the trash. I went to the bathroom and turned the shower on as hot as I could stand it. As I pulled away the shower curtain, I caught sight of my blood-smeared face reflected in the mirror before steam saved me from looking at myself.

But nothing could save me from my own circular thoughts about Ian and Cricket, about sweet Ford and savory blood, about

Mr. and Mrs. K, about my own monstrous appetites. Why did I feel so betrayed when I knew what Ian was, what he did?

I'd walked away from him before and it hadn't hurt like this. Yet I still wanted him too much to think that our relationship was over.

I tried to expend my energy by cleaning the loft, until my neighbor banged at the wall while I was running the vacuum cleaner. I looked at the clock and saw that it was almost four in the morning.

My mind was still replaying the same agonizing scenes of Ian and Cricket when the phone rang at seven o'clock. I thought it must be Ian and grabbed it up so I could scream at him.

"Is this my pretty little bat?" asked an accented voice in chipper tones.

Only one person used that endearment and his accent was as fake as his name and his memoir. "*Don* Pedro Nascimento," I said, using the honorific as sarcastically as possible.

"I am not forgotten!" he said happily. "I hope I am not calling too early, but I had a dream about you. You were in a field of flowers, drinking nectar from a lamb who was your friend."

Don Pedro's bag of con-man tricks included dream-telling, and he was especially gifted at inventing dreams that were easy to misinterpret as prophetic.

I said, "I'm not likely to forget the man who sold my manuscript for seven figures and goes on talk shows pretending to have written it himself."

"I am terribly sorry that you have misunderstood events." *Don* Pedro never used contractions in his speech, and I assumed he thought this made him seem more exotic and foreign than the SoCal car mechanic that he'd been. "I was most astonished when a publisher heard of my humble memoir . . ."

"It's not your memoir. It's my *fauxoir*. I made it all up, thus the faux."

"And told me he wanted to publish my book. I thought of how joyful you would be for me, but knew you were establishing your own writing career and would not want your serious work associated with my small tale of spiritual growth."

"You ripped me off totally. You told me the book was only for your family and students."

"So it was, lovely girl! The world turns in fantastical ways. On the day I was born, a jaguar was seen in the village by my family's hut . . ."

"You were born in Chula Vista, California." Mercedes had investigated *Don* Pedro's background more thoroughly than did his publisher or the reviewers who raved about him. "I concocted that jaguar story. Everything about you is a lie."

He made a *tch*ing sound and then said, "*Mi amor,* what terrible thing has happened to make you so unhappy?"

"Gee, I don't know, *Don* Pedro, maybe some two-bit con artist took advantage of me, causing me to become bitter and cynical."

"Milagro, I am shocked that you think I planned this happenstance of success! My life's work is to help others find their calling."

"Speaking of calling, why did you?"

"I hoped you would want to collaborate with me again."

I burst out laughing. "Are you out of your twisted corkscrew of a mind? Why would I ever, *ever* want to see you again, let alone work with you?"

"My publisher wants another book. It could be a quite enriching project for you, not only as an artist, but as a fellow soul who is responsive to our animistic nature."

"Nothing you can offer me would ever convince me to help you with fauxoir *dos,* the sequel."

"Are you sure?" he said, and then he named a significant sum, a sum that surprised me, and added, "Cash. I will be in London for a week, and I can fly you there to meet with me and explore our second adventure together, my little bat."

A trip to London would get me away from Ian. I'd be able to meet Wilcox Spiggott and he would show me another way, a *better* way, to live with this condition. "Okay, *Don* Pedro, I'll meet you to talk about the book, but you have to fly me out first-class."

I called Mercedes before noon to tell her what I was doing.

She said, "I can't believe anyone is paying you that much to write. You can pay off your assessment fee."

"Exactly. It's too bad my only success is with loony nonsense. It's a sad comment on society and the literary world."

"I can watch Rosemary for you."

"Fabulous. Do you think you can dig up anything about that vamp I told you about, Wilcox Spiggott? I think I'll drop in on him while I'm there."

"Why don't you ask Gabriel? He'll have the inside scoop."

"I don't want the Vamp Council to hassle Gabriel because of me. Not that anything *will* happen, but you know the Council has a problem with me already."

There was silence on the other end of the line, and so I said, "And, no, I haven't told Ian I'm going. I need to get away from him and clear my head. Sometimes I think that he could convince me to do anything."

I heard Mercedes sigh and she said, "Seriously? Because the only time I've ever seen you make compromises was when you were with Oswald."

"That time I was *too* compromising. Trying to please others made me vulnerable to their machinations. You're the only one I really trust to look out for my best interests."

"That's not true. There are others who love you and want the best for you."

"Do you mean Ian?"

There was a pause, and she said, "I meant your dog."

People who said you couldn't run from your problems had obviously never flown first-class to London seated in a private pod with their own movies, luxury gift bags, and a super-cute flight attendant who gave a great minimassage.

After a tasty Bloody Mary, I put on my complimentary terry slippers, eyeshade, and headphones, and tried to sleep.

four

An American, a Broad

I jauntily wheeled my chartreuse zebra-striped suitcase through the airport and to the stairs that led to the trains. Although I'd repaired one of the case's broken wheels with a piece of wire coat hanger, it still looked very stylish.

I liked the hustle and bustle of big-city public transportation, and I liked grabbing a window seat on a train and seeing billboards and scenery flashing by.

Mercedes had recommended a hotel in Kensington that was close to the Tube. The hotel was a well-kept, renovated Victorian with moderately priced rooms, just the sort of comfortable, convenient place Mercedes would stay while checking out bands.

My junior suite was a medium-sized room with a love seat, a narrow desk, a view to the street, and an all-white bathroom with a deep tub.

I walked to a French café, bought a latte, and took a stroll to the park, trying to remember to look to my right when crossing streets. When I returned to my hotel, I called *Don* Pedro.

"*Don* Pedro, why don't we meet at one of the local attractions so I can sightsee while you tell me whatever?"

"Alas, I have so many followers all over the world, those who come to me for guidance in the ways of the shapeshifter. I fear that we would be interrupted and I want to give you my undivided attention."

"Gotcha, no witnesses." I was tempted to tell *Don* Pedro that I actually knew a *real* shapeshifter—it had something to do with biology and optical illusions—but he'd insist that he was one himself.

"May I come to your room?" he asked.

"Only if you promise not to put the moves on me." I was joking since he was a little bug of a fellow that I could crush between my fingers.

He tittered and said, "I shall treat you with the utmost respect even though you are certainly a most enticing young woman and if I were younger—"

"Stop or you'll give me brain cooties. I'll see you at noon."

There was a knock on my door exactly at noon. I opened it to see *Don* Pedro Nascimento, officially the author of *Spiritual Transformation: Adventures of a Shapeshifter.*

He was a tiny brown man with enormous chocolate eyes behind oversized black-framed glasses. He wore khaki pants, a white shirt with colorful yarn embroidery of birds and flowers, and a brown and white woven jacket with a llama motif and fringe. He carried the same worn leather satchel he'd had when I'd first met him.

"*¡Mi Milagro!*" he said, and reached out to hug me.

I moved away and said, "Come in, *Don* Pedro."

He walked into the room and sat down on the love seat. He smelled of coconut oil, and I had a sudden craving for a piña colada, a sunny beach, and a Rupert Holmes tune playing on a boom box. I turned the desk chair to face *Don* Pedro and sat down.

"Your aura is even more brilliant than when we last met!" he said. "I hope that your journey is astonishing."

"Yes, first-class is definitely the way to go."

"I meant your journey *on this astral plane,* Milagro, exploring and discovering your spirit self. Your power glows from you like the sun rising over the red rocks of Sedona, where I once met a shaman in the form of a javelina—"

"That's utterly enthralling. Let's talk business."

He crossed one toothpick leg over the other and said, "I have watched you in my dreams, and I am both enraptured and fretful."

"That's kind of you. Do you mind saving the *caca* for people who pay for your seminars and private consultations?"

"There are different truths, Milagro. There is the truth that you think you know about me, and there also exists the truth of your book as I lived it."

"How could you live something that I fabricated?"

"It could only happen through the magical meeting of our minds, my Milagro!" he said ecstatically. "This is why you and only you can help write my second book. It explores life in different realms."

"Like the earth realm and space realm? Aliens?" I said, suddenly interested. "I'd love to subvert the clichés of aliens as long-armed, big-headed pixies. What about swarms of nanorobots that can cluster together to mimic any other life-form? I could tie that into your shapeshifter mythology."

Don Pedro held up his weathered hand. "I was speaking of the realms of life and afterlife and most especially the Middle World. Life after life and before deathly death. I traveled to an island in the azure Caribbean, and a tribe gathered to make a feast for me and . . ."

I dazed off at this point, because all of *Don* Pedro's stories followed the same plot: he was treated as a wise elder by indigenous people who had a feast in his honor. They invited him to a ceremony, injested magical potions, had visions, shapeshifted, et cetera. However, the word "undead" caught my attention.

"*Don* Pedro, what exactly do you mean by *undead*?"

"The tribe," he said, and then whistled. "That is how they say their name, the whistle of a bird, because they are as birds, neither of earth nor heaven. Their name means the Caretakers. They showed me how they raise up the dead with their astonishing juju."

"If it isn't astonishing, it isn't juju," I commented.

"I sat with one of these living-dead creatures, and we smoked a bowl of an herb that only grows there in the volcanic soil. He told me of returning to life from the misty swamp of eternity." *Don* Pedro stared at me and said solemnly, "This being was an oracle, and he asked me to give you this gift."

"That's really not necessary . . ." I began, worried that he'd pull a mummified foot or, worse, a dried man-handle from his satchel.

Instead, *Don* Pedro brought out a large clear plastic bag with a folded cloth inside. "The oracle said that you would know how to use it to help those who wish to come back and to guide them to the island."

"Of course. Why wouldn't I?" I took the bag and saw that the material was handwoven of fine yarn. It was white with an intricate border of suns, moons, mountains, and waves. "It's beautiful." I would have to show this to my friends in the Stitching & Bitching group. "The colors are so pretty."

"It is imbued with magical powders that will preserve and revive the dead and was woven by a blind *bruja* whose third-eye guides her. The color is taken from the spring flowers that grow in the soil by a spring of freshwater."

"Organic dyes, then. I thought so."

"By the spring, I saw a monkey, a *mono araña,* with a face as white as a ghost, and a bat flew overhead. The monkey said to me, 'The little bat above must spread her wings or she will fall into the chasm. Her strength and her . . .'" *Don* Pedro paused and wrinkled his brow. " 'Her strength and her *fun* are gifts to be used.'"

My strength and fun? As usual, *Don* Pedro made no sense. I held up the powdery cloth and said, "I'm not going to have any problems getting this through customs, am I?"

"Laws of mortal man do not govern the dead."

"That goes without saying. Now, about the writing fee . . ." I lobbied for twice the amount he had initially offered. Fifteen minutes later I agreed to a sum that would pay for my loft repairs and keep me gainfully underemployed for another year.

Don Pedro agreed to transfer a third of the funds into my bank account, pay another third upon delivery of the manuscript, and pay the balance when it was accepted by the publisher.

I felt somewhat regretful as I signed the release that gave *Don* Pedro all rights to the sequel. But he was the reason for the first book's success: people wanted to read about *his* life and they adored his loony interviews and seminars.

"One more thing," *Don* Pedro said.

"What?"

"It would please me to have the story written by hand," he said, and brought out five standard composition books. He unfolded a sheet of paper from one. "Here is a sample of my writing and you have such a discerning eye, I know you can copy it."

No electronic evidence, I thought. "You're in luck, *Don* Pedro. I happen to be an accomplished forger."

"Oh, no, this is not forgery," he said, shocked. "It is transcribing from my spiritual transmission."

"You say potato, I say fauxtato. Whatever."

As *Don* Pedro left, he said, "You will know how to use the magic of the cloth."

"I don't believe in magic."

"You *are* magic." He put his fine-boned hand on my wrist. "You are Milagro de Los Santos, the Miracle of the Saints. You must trust in yourself, in the role that destiny has written for you. Even though others would put you in a cage, the one who watches you recognizes your true self and loves you still."

I was surprised at the shiver that went through me. "I know you're full of it, but damn if I don't want to believe you."

"Then do," he said, and winked one of his big bug eyes.

After *Don* Pedro left I decided to call Wilcox Spiggott.

Mercedes had been able to find only a few public records on Wilcox and, most interesting, that he participated in surfing competitions. I called the number listed for Crimson Leasing Agents & Real Estate. A receptionist answered with a crisp voice, and I said, "May I please speak to Wilcox Spiggott."

"Might I say who is calling?"

I didn't know if my reputation had traveled here, but I didn't want to scare Wilcox off. "My name is Milly. I'm a journalist writing a story on surfing in the UK."

In a moment he was on. "Wil Spiggott here."

"Aloha, dude," I said in surferese. "I'm doing some research on the best of Brit surfing and I'm looking for someone who's hip to things oceanic and—"

"Who gave you my name?"

"Ahhh, well, I was at Hermosa Beach and this dude, awesome surfer, what was his name? Bitchin' technique, really knew how to drop in late."

"Bodhi?"

"Yeah, I think that was it," I said, wondering where I'd heard that name before.

"Long streaked hair, killer smile, liked to skydive? That Bodhi?"

Wow, that sounded so familiar. "I'm pretty sure he's the one. We were downing some brewskis at a bonfire and I was like, dude, do you know anyone I can interview, and he was like, dude, you totally gotta talk to Wil Spiggott." I wondered if I could expand this narrative as a short piece with a mutated shark that would represent the offshore oil industry.

"Bodhi gave you *this* number?" Wilcox said.

"Uh-huh. Any chance I could buy you a drink today?"

"What do you look like?"

"No one's complained," I said, which wasn't entirely true, since some people didn't appreciate my physical and sartorial extravagance.

Wilcox said he could meet me at a pub after work. That gave me time to go to St. Paul's Cathedral. I cried as I read the memorial to American soldiers who died in World War II, young men long gone but not forgotten.

Then I climbed to the top of the beautiful dome. I stood on the windy parapet and looked at the city below. The sun was already beginning to set and lights began to glow golden.

I wished that I was sharing this with someone else because it was too incredible just for me. I wondered what Oswald was doing now, and I tried *not* to wonder what or whom Ian was doing.

I went to the hotel and changed for the evening. I put on tight black jeans, black boots, and a snug cranberry cashmere sweater that I'd gotten on clearance because the shoulder seam was crooked. But the sweater was low-cut and I thought no one would notice the imperfection, especially if I let my hair fall forward over it. I wore a pink trench and a scarf that I'd knit from chunky violet yarn.

When I arrived at the pub, it was crowded with young professionals. I realized I had no idea what Wilcox looked like. I saw a muscle-bound guy with a bleached buzz cut jostling toward the bar. He smiled when he caught me looking at him.

I grinned and made my way to him. "Wilcox?"

"Sure I will coc—" he said, and stopped and glanced over my shoulder.

I turned to see what he was looking at.

The man behind me was tall and thin, with very fine, messy, streaked blond hair. He had a really good fake tan and nice features, but I focused on his light hazel eyes, lined with kohl.

"Are you Milly? I'm Wilcox."

The first man burst into laughter and said "Who isn't with jubblies like that?" before turning back to the bar.

I shook Wilcox's hand and bopped my head. "Aloha. Cool to meet you."

His coat was open, revealing a black V-neck sweater over a rust-colored crewneck and dark-wash jeans. Around his neck was a thin, worn leather cord with a single shell. He had silver rings on his slim fingers and small silver hoops in his ears.

He was definitely, unquestionably fabulous.

"Call me Wil. Let's get a table outside. If you don't mind the cold and the dark."

"That's fine by me."

Wil led me out to an empty bench by a sidewalk table. A waitress had just finished taking orders at the next table and she stopped by. Wil ordered a pint of bitter, and I said, "Me, too, thanks."

When she was gone, the vampire smiled at me and we checked each other out.

"So, Milagro de Los Santos, what do you want to know?"

I laughed and said, "What gave me away?"

"My bros don't know my work number, and Patrick Swayze played Bodhi in *Point Break*."

I thought for a second. "That's why the name seemed familiar. And Keanu played Johnny Utah. Great movie."

"Agreed, but your story was rubbish. Now, Milagro from California, filthy cute, rep for asking lots of questions, brilliant"—he let his gaze drift downward—"immune system. You know I'm stoked to be sitting here with you. We all know about you. Do you really go by Milly?"

"Milagro or Mil will do," I said. "I lied because I didn't need your coworkers to know we were meeting. I heard that the Council was hassling you, and the Council has some Issues with me."

"I heard they wanted you dead."

"Like I said, *Issues*." I wondered what else he'd heard. "I don't die easily, though. Or willingly. I'm quite reluctant about the whole ceasing-to-exist thing. How about you?"

"Equally reluctant. How did you hear about me?"

"Do you know the Grant family in California?"

He nodded and said, "Never met them, though."

"They're good people," I said. "After I was accidentally infected by Oswald Grant, they took care of me and helped me transition."

"I met your *friend,* Ian Ducharme, last year when I was on holiday in Lviv."

"Lviv is the new Warsaw," I said automatically.

"That's when he was with a gorgeous icy blonde, Ilena, at all the parties."

"I'd rather not discuss Ian if you don't mind," I said, trying to quell the ugly swirl of emotions rising in me. "Anyway, one of the Grant family mentioned that you're organizing a movement to have your kind live openly."

"My kind? Aren't you one of us?"

"They gave me a membership card, but most of the time they

tell me that the club is closed for a private party. I think so long as your kind live in hiding and fear, there will never be . . ."

The waitress came back, and I paused while she delivered our drinks. Wil and I fumbled over who would pay, but he insisted, saying, "You're my guest."

I sipped the warmish beerish drink and said "Mmm" to be polite. "You're lucky our drinks came. I was just about to launch into a speech about human rights for all. I know all the politically correct talking points." I didn't mention that I'd learned many from animal rights activists.

"Before we get into all that, what are you doing tonight?"

"I was hoping to see a play, or see if any museums have evening hours."

"Could I interest you in a special tour befitting a special guest?"

When an attractive and unknown man presented me with a vague offer of a good time, I always had the same answer. "Absolutely."

We finished our drinks and took the Tube to a crescent-shaped block of white terrace houses with graceful black railings and boxes of blooming flowers. "It's an underground restaurant," Wil said, putting his arm through mine in a very friendly way. "It's not in the guidebooks."

"Do we need a secret knock?"

"Fer sure."

"I'm not an expert, but you seem to speak surferese very well," I said as he led me up the steps to the glossy red front door.

"It's one of my languages." He lifted the brass door knocker and tapped it twice, then three more times. After we waited, he looked at me and said, "It gets loud." He banged the door with his fist and yelled, "Open up, you bastards!"

I heard footsteps and then a bulky older man came to the

door. Wil practically tackled him and gave him a smacking kiss on his cheek. "This is Mil, Graham. Mil, this is Graham."

"Hello, Mil," Graham said sternly, and looked me in the eyes. "This is a private gathering. Nothing that happens here leaves."

"She's cool," Wil said. "She's with the Grants in California and Ian Ducharme."

"I know Ian," I said. "But I'm not *with* him."

"Ian Ducharme," Graham said with a cynical smile. Then his expression changed. "A sexy señorita with the Grant family and Ian Ducharme? Don't tell me this is Milagro de Los Santos!"

I was a little annoyed at the sexy señorita description. "Okay, I won't."

"Come in! Come in! Welcome to the Bloody Good Table."

The interior of the house was chic and modern, dove grays, snowy white, and black with red accents. A niche in the long hallway held a tall vase of red ginger, and the dark gray runner was edged in red.

Voices and music came from down the hall. "Everyone's in back," our host said.

five

My Fair Vampire

As we entered the large back room, people turned to look at us and a shout of "Wilcox!" went up. There was a jumble of greetings, backslaps, hugs, and kisses. Graham had my arm and was saying, "This is Milagro from California."

A few guests stared, but other than that they went on with their conversations.

A glass of red liquid was put into my hands. "Wild boar," someone said. Everyone looked at me expectantly, but as I was about to take a sip, I heard someone say, "With bathwater."

"*Whose* bathwater?" I asked, which people found hilarious.

"Water from the City of Bath," Graham said. "Lots of sodium and mineral that stands up to the gaminess of the boar."

So I took a sip and swished it around in my mouth before swallowing. "I get the mineral and salt from the water, and the boar . . . it's fresher than I thought, cleaner."

"It's from a small herd that's taken over an apple orchard," Graham said. "That's the apple you're tasting."

"Like Eve," Wil joked.

While I was introduced, I surveyed the crowd. Only about half were vampires, and the others seemed totally cool with hanging with blood-drinkers. There was a bubbly Indian scientist, a gorgeous Latvian painter, clever and grungy graduate students, and a range of foodies. Some may have been thralls, but I couldn't tell by their manner.

It felt different than Ian's crowd, less decadent, I thought as I sampled a canapé of red caviar and salmon mousse accompanied by an eel's blood spritzer.

The food was prepared for both vamps and nonvamps. We all shared spring lamb carpaccio. The wild boar had been braised in Barolo and herbs until it was tender, but fresh blood thickened the sauce for the vamps.

I was introduced to a zoologist who procured rare animal bloods for his culinary adventures. He was anxious about dessert. "It's something I'm trying out for the first time, Masai trifle, a construction, if you will, of the Masais' diet of blood, milk, meat, animal fat, tree bark, and honey."

"Really?" I said, and smiled as if I wasn't squinging inside. "A construction, not a deconstruction?"

"Their food is already elemental, so I'm constructing. I'm using a zebra-blood jelly that's been sweetened with honey and spiced with cinnamon, a tree bark. The meat and fat component are suet mincemeat with black pudding. All layered with organic Devon cream, of course."

"Mmm, sounds . . . unique."

It was unique. Uniquely bad. I took one small bite of the sweet, greasy, mealy, salty trifle and looked for a place to spit it out. Another guest was ahead of me and pretending to cough as she turned toward a palm in a glazed red pot.

"Hmm," Wil said after a taste.

"A noble experiment," Graham, our host, said as he gathered up dishes of dreadful dessert and passed around packets of chocolate-covered biscuits.

Wil and I left the table and went to sit on a long leather sectional. He pulled me close to lean against him and played with my hand, sending a continual stream of pleasant zings through me in the way that alcohol and drugs could not.

"Wilcox, I've been meaning to ask you, how does a vampire surf?"

He laughed. "Bleak, isn't it, being an English vampire surfer? It's like being a Jamaican bobsledder. I wait for bad weather and there's night surfing. Haul some floodlights on a lorry, position them on a cliff, and let the good times roll."

"If you came out of the coffin, it would be easier to do what you love. Most people have no idea of how everyday life is restricted and limited by others' fears and prejudices."

"Yeah, and there's also sun poisoning." He obviously needed to be cheered from his weighty, unhappy thoughts because he asked, "Do you want to go dancing after this?"

"I'd love to."

Graham put out bottles of icy vodka and a tray with slices of lemon, lime, a mound of sea salt, and sprigs of fresh dill and fennel. "Have you decided who's first?"

"Me, I am," said one of the grad students. "I've only had herb salads for a month. I'll taste brilliant."

She stood up and took off her sweater, revealing a thin wifebeater and lots of skin.

A brawnier guy scoffed, "You're a trinket. There's nothing in you to drink."

"Shut up, you," she answered cheerfully. "You fainted the last time you saw a needle."

More guests advocated for themselves and after lots of competitive insults, three of them were selected. The zoologist/amateur chef brought out a black leather doctor's bag, and Graham placed a silver tray with thimble-small glasses on a tall cabinet.

They offered me the first taste. When I hesitated, Wil said teasingly, "Come on, Eve, you've already had the apple."

I'd already had Ford's blood, and this situation was much more . . . wholesome. I took a small sip. It hummed warmly through me and I could taste the green herbiness of the grad student's blood. Everyone followed me, and Graham said, "I get the fennel up front and there's mint, too. Fantastic."

Another vampire swished the blood in her mouth and said, "I'm tasting lemon in here, with rust and chocolate in the finish."

As the others began discussing food pairings with the blood, Wil said, "Shall we?" and I nodded.

We said good night to the group and thanked our host.

Graham said, "I hope you'll come again. I'll cook if you tell me about how you dismantled Corporate Americans for a Corporate America, exposed the movement for vampire supremacy, and tangled with an angry werewolf."

"It sounds impressive when you say it that way," I said, "but the individual incidents were rather humiliating and involved a lot of sexy costumes, pink fuzzy handcuffs, out-of-control parties, and demented plans for world domination."

Graham laughed and slapped Wil on the back. He said, "Milagro, I think you're underestimating the reality."

"It's probably more amusing for an observer," I said. "Thank you for an extraordinary meal."

Wil and I went out to the dark, cold street.

"I love this time of night," I said, "when most people are getting ready for bed, and party girls are getting ready to go out."

"Did you like the Bloody Good Table?"

"I loved it. Everyone was so friendly and lively. It was completely different than the vampire bars I've been to back home, which have so much attitude, and there's a real class division between vamps and thralls."

"We've had longer to adjust, and we're not repressed like you Americans."

"That's a gross generalization. I'm not repressed."

"Excellent," he said with a smile.

When we got to the corner, Wil hailed a cab and we went into the heart of the city. After we got out, he waited until the cab had left and disappeared into traffic. He said, "Rule number nine, never let anyone take you to the real address."

"What are rules one through eight?"

"You know, don't sink your teeth into your nursery school mates." He took my hand, giving me a warm buzz, and led me down a narrow alley, lined with ancient buildings, dark with soot. "Don't run starkers in broad daylight and fry like a chip. Don't tell your girlfriend that the condom broke and you've filled her with vampire spunk."

I laughed and said, "It's nice to talk to someone who isn't so serious. The vampires I first met, the Grant family, are wonderful, but they won't even acknowledge what they are. They always call it 'a condition' and pretend that they're absolutely normal. When I first came into their lives, they were appalled. Well, I am something of a screwup."

Wil stopped walking and turned to me. A lamp overhead illuminated his sexy, kohl-lined eyes. "Milagro, I don't think you're a screwup. What Graham said is true—we've all heard the stories, and I think you're unbelievable."

It was like a first date before I changed. One of those dates where there's a lot of sexual tension and deliberately accidental touching and I was with some really hot guy, and my engine was revving, and the night was ours and we hadn't fought over something stupid yet.

Wil wasn't some depraved aristovamp and he wasn't a workaholic whose parents hated me. He was just a lovely, lovely boy.

Putting his arms around me, Wil drew me to him. "Am I risking my life by doing this?"

"You haven't done anything yet," I said, teasing, but I was thinking, *Goddamn Ian Ducharme can go to hell.*

Wil's kiss was firm and hungry. His touch was exciting because it was new. I kissed him back, but when his hand went under my sweater, I pushed it away and said, "You're not going to bang me against the wall in an alley, Wilcox Spiggott."

He grinned and said, "Bummer. That's one of my specialties. Let's go dancing." He took my hand and pulled me forward until we reached the rear entrance of a building. Wil looked up and gave a wave. I followed his gaze to see a security camera directed toward us.

There was a loud *click-click* sound and then the huge steel door edged open. A massive bald man dressed in a dark suit said, "Evening, Mr. Spiggott. Who's your friend?"

"Milagro from California and the Grant family. I vouch for her."

The man nodded, opened the door for us, and said, "Good evening."

"Hi," I said.

Wil and I walked into a dingy hall.

"You don't have to tell everyone who I am," I whispered.

"But you're a celebrity."

"Only by virtue of not dying. That's not much of an accomplishment."

Wil led me through carved wooden doors to a luxurious lounge with a vast Oriental carpet, furniture covered in watered yellow silk, and dark green leather armchairs. Pale, elegant people were chatting over glasses of red drinks.

This civilized scene made me deeply regret rejecting a hookup in the alley. "There's dancing here?"

"Downstairs."

We walked through a busy dining room, past the clanging noises of a kitchen, and down narrow stone stairs that were so old the steps were worn concave. When we reached a long, dark corridor, Wil took my arm.

"I can see in almost total darkness," I said.

"Then you can lead me," he said, and pulled my arm closer.

"How old are you?" I asked.

"Twenty-six, though I look twelve."

"You don't look twelve. You look like a really mature eighteen-year-old." I liked that Wil was close to my age.

We reached the end of the hall and I heard the thumping of music. There was the soft whirr of security cameras above the stainless steel double doors. When the door opened, music and heat hit me in a blast. A hulking wrestler of a man in a skin-tight black T-shirt and black jeans stood in front of us. "Wil!" he shouted above the din.

"Jonesy," Wil said, then tipped his head toward me. "This is Mil, my friend."

The doorman waved us into the crowded club. Silver foil wallpaper reflected light from ornate red chandeliers. The band onstage squalled an unholy Euro-emo-electronic pop mix that actually kind of worked. Wil led me through the mass of bodies, yelling out to pals, grabbing a spliff from a girl and inhaling deeply. He tried to pass it to me.

"Don't waste it on me," I yelled into his ear. "I'm immune to altering substances." I was so fascinated by a man sitting on a red velvet throne set on a raised dais that I almost tripped. I was even more fascinated with an eight-foot-wide box half filled with thick, dark red liquid and set atop a tall platform.

We made our way to the other side of the room, where tables lined the wall, and sat with a group of Wil's friends.

"This is Mil," he said.

"Wil and Mil," one said, and waved to the waiter.

"Who's that?" I asked Wil as I looked toward the man on the throne. The man had straight black hair and a look of satisfaction.

"The king." To one of his friends, Wil said, "How'd that wanker get to be king?"

"You have a king?" I asked Wil. "No wonder you're working toward a more egalitarian society. Royalty is so Dark Ages."

Everyone at the table started laughing.

"Excuse me for having a more enlightened view of the class system," I said.

"He's *not* the king of the vampires," Wil said, grinning. "We've got a running lottery and the winner gets to be king or queen for a night and choose the DJ and such. The money goes to a charity of your choice, and that arse is always sending it to the damned Windmills Trust."

"I love windmills. Save the windmills!" a sexy girl with long red curls said. Her name was Nettie, and after we shouted at each other over the music about shops I should visit, she looked at me, winked an eye with silver shadow and glitter mascara, and said, "Would you fancy a blood wrestle?"

Which is how I found myself wearing a too-small flesh-colored bikini in a Plexiglas cube filled with strawberry-flavored fake blood. Grappling with a slick, laughing girl while a club full of vampires and their friends shouted was even more fun than I thought it would be.

And if we yanked each other's tops off, and squished our breasts against the Plexi walls and then seductively licked fake blood off each other, it was because we were, at heart, people-pleasers.

And if the gossipy vampires got word back to Ian that I was having a wild time without him, then all the better. I'd made the mistake of caring for him, but he'd made the mistake of thinking that I would be laissez-faire about his philandering.

After our show, Nettie took me to a gym-sized shower room adjacent to the main club.

"This is a huge shower room for a nightclub," I said.

"We use it for the *Blade* party the first Saturday of every month," she said. "We pass out the X, put mixes of New Order's 'Confusion' on a loop, and dance. The lads in their Speedos are a glorious sight when blood rains down. We got the idea from the movie. You must come."

"I have to get back before that. I've got writing projects and deadlines. But next time I visit, I'll come."

"Cool," Nettie said. "May I ask something?"

"Sure."

"What *are* you? You drank a blood cocktail, but your tan looks as real as those lovelies."

"Oh, I've just got a few quirks," I said. "What about you?"

"My family's been in service to the Family for generations," she said. "My parents are rather stodgy, but there's a lot of fun to be had with the vamps."

"There can be."

"So you and Wil?" Nettie asked, but it wasn't really a question. "I went out with him. Girl of the Month and the occasional boy. Well, that's our Wil. So irresistible."

"I'm impressed by his activism," I said, "but I just met him. He's only showing me the town."

"Well, if anything else should happen, he loves a firm-minded girl who can take charge, if you catch my meaning."

"Sure." I liked Nettie even though she didn't seem to have a grasp of anything more serious than the next party. I knew this because she invited us to hang out with her friends on a houseboat the following night.

She said, "It's my going-away party. I plan to get completely mental. Then I'm off to Canada for an assignment."

My rule was: Always participate in cultural experiences when invited by fun chicks. "Fabulous. I'll tell Wil."

In the club, Wil was on the burnt side of toasted and berating the King of Vampires by the bar.

"Windmills, windmills, fucking, windmills again!"

The king grabbed me, saying, "It's good to be king!"

I pushed him away and Wil said to him, "Shove off. She's Ian Ducharme's."

The king-for-a-night looked as if he'd reached into a mailbox and found a rattlesnake. "Shit! Sorry!"

"Wil doesn't know what he's talking about," I said. "Wil, you're hammered. Time to call it a night."

I dragged my escort up to the main club. A porter asked if we'd like a car to take us home. Wil leaned on me heavily as I helped him down the alley.

It had rained while we were inside, and the air smelled of possibility. But no possibilities with Wil in this condition. An inconspicuous gray Vauxhall arrived at the end of the alley just as we did.

The driver got out and opened the back door. "Where to, miss? Oh, you've got Mr. Spiggott there. Let's get him home."

I folded Wil into the car and got in. I said, "Would you mind dropping me off at my hotel first, or do you think I should go with him and get him inside his place?"

"No worries, miss. It's my pleasure to see that he's taken care of," the man said, making me remember the way that Ian's thrall, Mrs. K, had spoken. "I'll deliver him to his houseman safely."

I wondered if a houseman was the same as a doorman. I gave

the driver my hotel address and gazed out the window at the beautiful old buildings. The shining black streets reflected blue, red, and yellow neon lights.

When the car pulled up to the hotel, I thanked the driver and gave a last look at Wil, who was snoring as he slumped against the door. He was sweet to take me out, but I'd have to tell him that I didn't need babysitting.

I went to my room and stared out the window at the thousands of city lights. Here, across the ocean and a continent, I felt safe from my feelings for one man who had promised to love me forever and another who had offered me only pleasure, never love.

six

Bite Me, Spank Me, Make Me Bite Your Neck

I awoke to the ringing of my phone. I was still on West Coast time and mumbled a sleepy hello.

"Wil here. I'm in the lobby."

"I'll be down in twenty minutes."

A hot shower revived me. I put on a mulberry cotton tunic with a ruffled neckline, black leggings, garnet suede ankle boots, and a clatter of black Bakelite bracelets. I wore my hair loose and finished my makeup with dramatic ruby lipstick.

I took my pink trench coat and handbag in case Wil wanted to go for coffee.

My new friend was standing by the staircase, wearing slim jeans, a gray T-shirt, and a black wool reefer jacket. His hands were in his pockets, and his long streaked hair was wet and brushed straight back. He grinned when he saw me.

"You do realize that it's the middle of the night for me," I said. "You look as fresh as a daisy."

"I've come to take you to breakfast."

"Don't you have to work?"

"I took the day off," he said as we went outside. "I was worried that you might get trapped in one of those dull bus tours. 'Here is where prisoners were hung from the infamous Tyburn Tree! To your left you will see a statue of beloved Peter Pan!'"

Laughing, I said, "But I *want* to see the sights."

"I'll give you a proper tour," he promised. "Do you mind walking?"

"It's one of my favorite things."

Wil did give me a proper tour, pointing out historical and architectural sites. We had breakfast at a bright, light-filled restaurant on the edge of an ancient market by the Thames. The waiter recognized Wil, who didn't look at the menu. "Give us the special and something to take the edge off, would you?"

"I'll expedite your order, sir," the waiter said.

Looking around at the hip clientele, I said, "I thought you were going to drag me to another basement."

Smiling, he said, "Our people could survive underground for years if things go all to shit. One hopes they won't. We've adapted very well within this city, which is why so many of us live here." He tipped his chin toward the glass wall. "These windowpanes filter out UV rays."

"Now you sound like the somber person I expected to meet," I said. "Wil, it was so sweet of you to take me out last night, but I hate to drag you away from your important obligations."

He reached out and twined his slim fingers between mine. I didn't pull away until the waiter returned with tall red drinks.

"*Bloody* Marys," the waiter said, and in a lower voice, he added, "Brown Cow organic beef."

When he'd left, Wil lifted his drink to me and said, "To our friendship, Mil."

"May it last long," I said, and we both sipped our spicy, salty drinks.

His hand went to mine again. "I've wanted to meet you ever since I heard about you. Bonus that you're an exhibitionist."

"I'm not!" I said, and then remembered incidents that might be seen as exhibitionistic if taken out of context. "Not usually."

"I like it," he said. "Lucky Ducharme."

"I'm here with *you* now, Wil." As I looked into Wil's pretty hazel eyes, I wondered if Ian was with Cricket now while Ford watched. "So why is the Council irked with you?"

"If our kind live equally among Normals, the Council becomes irrelevant. Those dusty bastards aren't going to willingly relinquish their power and the wealth that goes with it."

I swirled the carrot stick in my drink. "Are things so different here that you're ready to safely come out?"

"No, but we can organize and establish relationships with key contacts. We do that with the Bloody Good Table, our clubs, our business alliances."

"How fab that you incorporate your activism with your social life," I said. "A lot of activists back home are deadly serious."

"You Americans are like that. Look at the way you treat sex— schoolgirl giggles and Puritan moralizing. Sex is *just* sex."

"Sex is never *just* sex," I said. "Oh, God, did I actually say that? Please ignore it."

The waiter delivered our plates and said to me, "It's an update of the traditional English breakfast with black pudding, what you call blood sausage, free-range eggs with shaved black truffle poached in an heirloom tomato sauce, organic red lentils, and whole grain cranberry bread with red currant jam. Enjoy." He left us to our meal.

I dug in, saying, "Everything is so organic this and heirloom that. I had no idea that you were such foodies." A minute later, I said, "Why did the waiter explain what black pudding is?"

"Word travels fast with our kind, and the thralls have their own network," Wil said. "As to the sustainable foods, we're not the ones living in the Dark Ages."

"Wil, if I wasn't enjoying these eggs, I might have to give you a beat-down."

He laughed and said, "You can do that later." Then he outlined his plans for the day.

"Fine, but there are some things that I want to do." I pulled a *Time Out* from my bag and flipped open to the first Post-it marker. "I must see at least one Shakespeare play and I'd also like to see something utterly new. I've got four must-visit exhibits and a list of places mentioned in some of my favorite books." I unfolded a map that had dozens of locations circled.

When I saw the dismayed look on Wil's face, I said, "It's okay. I can find my way around on my own."

"I wouldn't think of abandoning you. I only hope I can keep up with you."

The day was marvelous. Wil seemed amused by my ecstasy at seeing literary landmarks, and I was delighted when he showed me his five favorite pieces in the National Gallery. We bought leather jackets at a Notting Hill vintage shop, and we had a vampire tea at a private lounge in a posh hotel near Harrod's.

"My mother used to bring me here once a year," Wil said. "It's more of a ladies' place."

"Speaking of ladies, I've heard that you have lots of girlfriends."

"Who told you that? Naughty Nettie? She fancied you," he said. "We can make her bon voyage party *extra* special if you've a mind."

"Yes to the party, but no to the extra-special activities. Girls are pretty, but I'm at the other end of the sexuality scale."

He shrugged. "I'm happy to swing whichever way the wind blows, but I don't like to be tied down. Actually, I do," he said, and we laughed.

He didn't go to the theater with me that night, but I loved sitting in the dark and watching a harrowing *Othello*. During the intermission, as I waited in line for the ladies' room, an older woman asked, "Are you enjoying the performance?"

"Very much, even though I always want to warn Othello not to listen to Iago."

"But he must," she said with a smile. "There's synergy between Othello and Iago. Iago must tell the lie as surely as Othello wants to hear it. His insecurity and violent nature must out."

"Do you think that some people want to be around those who encourage their darkest desires?"

"Most certainly! Who could be more seductive than someone who knows our secrets, yet loves us anyway?" she said, and I was reminded of Ian's claim that we choose our partners because of what we need.

I saw the woman after the play and waved good night, wishing I could discuss the play with her, but Wil was waiting for me at a nearby pub.

We went to Nettie's farewell party. The houseboat was both run-down and lavish, two stories tall with battered antiques, primitive paintings of cows, massive silver candelabras, a kick-ass sound system, and a badass DJ.

We danced, talked, flirted, and there was a lot of booze, smoke, and friendly blood play. Nettie was the center of attention, dancing atop a table in a short silver dress, and I noticed Wil staring at her wistfully.

The main lounge became packed and airless, so Wil and I went to the deck. The noise from the crowd was muffled there, and I could hear water lapping at the houseboat and against the shore. A trio shrieked at the other end of the deck and I heard splashing and laughing.

"What are you thinking?" Wil asked.

"I'm thinking about Dickens and fishing bodies out of the river."

"That really turns me on," he said in a sexy growl. Then he started laughing. "You believed me!"

"I did not!"

"You wondered if I'm a necrophiliac. I tell you in dead earnest that I am not a necrophiliac."

I laughed and said, "I wondered if you're a nitwit."

He wrapped his arms around me. "Come to my place and I'll show you what I am."

I thought of Ian's mouth on Cricket. I thought of the scabs and bruises on her body from the times he'd fed on her. I imagined them having sex and I felt ill and angry and miserable. "Sure, Wil, let's go."

Wil's flat was the top floor of a three-story row house. I barely paid attention to the interior, but my general impression was of a smart dude's place: piles of books, papers, and magazines as well as surf gear and posters.

We made it to the bedroom and fell onto the bed. Wil's elbow jabbed my rib, and then his arm came down on my hair, tugging it. "Ow."

"Sorry."

"It's okay," I said as I tried to pull his shirt off. His torso was lovely, narrow and smooth, and he had a tribal tattoo of a snake on his pec. The scent of his sunscreen aroused me, and when he peeled down his jeans and snug boxers, I was pleased to see how pleased he was.

"Strip for me," he said, and leaned back against the pillows.

He turned on his sound system, and Jimmy Hendrix's "Foxy Lady" blasted out, which seemed really funny.

I gyrated around the bed, slowly taking my clothes off. When I was in only a purple leopard-print bra, panties, and my heels, Wil's expression changed and he groaned and rubbed himself as I teased him by dancing just out of reach.

When the song was over and I stood naked in my heels, he said, "Come here, you," and took my hand.

I tried not to compare Wil to anyone else, because he was wonderful. He was young and single and enthusiastic and fun.

I wanted to be the girl I was before . . . before the vampires, and I was glad I could control my reactions so that I didn't automatically fling Wil across the room when he picked up a small knife.

I took his wrist carefully so I wouldn't crush the bones and pushed his arm back.

"Why not?" he said.

"Too soon."

Wil lay back on the bed, breathing heavily, and I thought I might have hurt his feelings. But he dropped the knife on the floor and said, "Do you want to tie me up?"

We improvised with bungee cords and surf leashes, and I took him at my own pace, for my own pleasure, which was also his. When I was finished, I slid atop his sinewy, sweaty body and said, "Cowabunga, dude."

"Damn, Mil, that was crazy good. I'm totally noodled."

After I untied him, we sat on the bed, ate currant yogurt, and watched videos of Wil night surfing in Cornwall.

He massaged my lower back. "It's a rush knowing that I was snaking the Dark Lord's chick."

"One, I'm not his chick, and we've never made any promises to each other. Two, 'snaking his chick' is not a felicitous turn of phrase . . ."

Wil opened his mouth in an O and made a pumping gesture with his hand. "You said felicitous."

"Why do guys always do that? Three, I wouldn't recommend gloating over Ian. Not that he's jealous." I remembered how he'd acted as if my love for Oswald was a temporary annoyance. "And, four, this is just a travel fling. Nothing counts when you're on a trip," I said, even though this hadn't exactly worked for me in the past.

"It counts to me, cutie," Wil said, and I was touched by his tenderness.

"Do you play Hendrix for all your dates?"

"Advance planning. I'd hoped you'd come back with me," he said. "You're a natural top."

"Thank you." I arched my back to display my ample assets. "They're genuine."

He laughed. "No, I mean sexually. You're a top."

"I don't think so. I believe that relationships should be between equals." I was going to say other things, too, thoughtful things, but then Wil's hand went between my thighs and literary references didn't seem so important.

I awoke in the early morning when I heard the bedroom door open. I pulled up the sheet to cover myself and shook Wil, who put a pillow over his head.

A middle-aged man in a dark suit stood in the doorway. His stern expression and conservative haircut and clothes made him seem as if he was from a different era. "Good morning, Mr. Spiggott. Will you take tea in bed, or the breakfast room?"

Wil took the pillow away from his head and twisted around toward the doorway. "I can get my own tea, Matthews. I told you, just Wil."

"As you please, sir. Would your lady friend like anything?"

"Milagro, this is Matthews. Matthews, this is my friend, Milagro." Wil sat up and asked me, "Do you want toast or eggs or anything?"

The man had entered the room and picked up the plastic snack debris on the table. I didn't want him to see anything else, including the ropes we'd used.

I said, "No, thank you very much, Mr. Matthews. If we could have privacy, please?"

"Certainly, Miss de Los Santos." He left and closed the door.

"So he knew who I was. You were right about word getting out fast. Who is he?"

"My houseman," Wil said. "His family has been with mine forever."

"It's a little creepy."

"I'd rather have his hot bitch daughter, but my parents and Matthews objected, and she wouldn't oppose her father. They thought we were consorting in too equal a fashion."

"Were you?"

"Not at all. She was definitely, as Americans say, the boss of me." He smiled and looked off.

"Do you like having a thrall?"

"I could do without." He rubbed his eyes with his fists, like a kid. "One doesn't throw them out in the street. One tries to empower them. Not that my man wants to be empowered. I tried meeting with the leadership of their association, and they said, 'Thank you kindly, sir, but we are satisfied with our situation.'"

"I didn't know they had an organization."

"Yeah, they've been organized for centuries. Matthews is a chapter leader.'"

"Will he talk about anything he sees here?" I'd been so set on making Ian jealous that I hadn't considered that Oswald might find out about my antics.

"Oh, no, Matthews believes that thralls should be utterly faithful to their masters," Wil said. "Now can I have a cuddle?"

"That's all?" I traced my finger over his tattoo.

"Well, I believe that someone's been naughty and needs a spanking."

"How naughty?"

"Extremely," he said.

"Well, if discipline is needed . . ."

We didn't get out of bed until noon, and then we took a slippery, sudsy bath together that left water all over the marble tiles. When we were mopping up, we started a towel fight that had us sliding on the floor and laughing as we snapped at each other.

After we had dressed and I was putting kohl around Wil's golden-brown eyes, he said, "I think I'll take the week off."

"Wil, you don't have to do that."

"You're on holiday. I want you to enjoy it. Leave your hotel and stay with me."

"You want me to stay with you *and* your houseman?"

"I'll give Matthews the week off."

"Well, okay, then."

Wil took me to clubs, parties, art exhibits, and to hang out with his friends. We wore our vintage leather jackets, shared hair products, danced every night, had enthusiastic bouts of sex, and talked about our ideals for a world in which everyone was treated with respect.

While I kept so busy that it was easy not to think of my life back home, I worried that I was taking Wil away from his important work as an activist.

"Can't I help you?" I asked him. I was trying to sort through the piles of paper on the dining table he used as a desk. "We can draft a mission statement and a rollout plan."

He took the documents away from me and said, "Chillax. If you need to do something with your hands or your mouth, take hold of this."

One morning while Wil slept in, I wrote a plan of action with suggested timelines, talking points for the media, and ideas for a website and social networking.

I was working on this project, sitting with my laptop and stacks of papers at the dining table, wearing panties and Wil's Tuska Surf T, when the door to the flat opened. I yanked down the hem of the T over my bottom just as Matthews came in.

"Good morning, miss," he said glumly.

"Hello, Mr. Matthews." I smiled and said, "Wilcox is still sleeping."

"I came to pick up his clothes for cleaning," he said as he looked around at the mess of empty wine bottles, wrappers from salt and vinegar crisps, and dishes. His eyes went upward, where a cerise lace thong dangled from the mod frosted glass and polished chrome chandelier. Then Matthews looked down to the graphs and charts I'd spread on the table.

"Sorry about the mess," I said. "We'll clean up."

"There is no need, miss. I am pleased to stay and be of service."

I spied a condom box under a chair and said, "I think Wil would rather have you just take his clothes to be cleaned, and I don't need any help, thanks."

Matthews followed my glance and saw the box. "As you wish, Miss de Los Santos."

While Matthews went into the bedroom to collect Wil's clothes, I picked up our trash and tossed it in the kitchen bin. I could hear the clatter of wooden hangers, so I quickly climbed on the dining room table to reach for the wayward thong.

When Matthews cleared his throat behind me, I yanked the thong down, setting the chandelier swinging, and hopped off the table, hiding behind a chair. The man was holding a plastic basket filled with Wil's clothes.

"Yes, Mr. Matthews?"

"Enjoy the rest of your holiday, miss."

"Thank you. I'll tell Wil you came by."

After Matthews closed the front door behind him, I latched the chain lock so I wouldn't be surprised again.

I went to the bedroom, but Wil had slept through his houseman's visit. My handbag, on the dresser, had fallen over, and a few things had spilled out. I put back the lipsticks, pens, and tourist trinkets I'd bought.

Wil got up, drank a pot of tea, and played *Grand Theft Auto* for thirty minutes while I wrote postcards.

Then he said, "What's the real situation with you and Ian Ducharme?"

"I'm a free agent."

"Are you sure? Because as crazy hot as I think Ducharme is, I don't want him showing up to kill me."

I'd checked my messages when Wil wasn't around, and Ian hadn't called me. "Ian doesn't give a damn what I do, and I don't give a damn what or whom he does."

Will gazed at me for a moment and said, "You sound quite angry for someone who doesn't care, and you don't want to do any blood play with me."

I took Wil's hand and turned the silver rings on his fingers. "I'm sorry. I didn't mean to overreact. But, Wil, I assure you, you're safe from possessive boyfriends. As for the blood, I'm not a born vamp, and sex and blood . . . It gets too confusing for me."

"I'd wager that you let Ducharme drink from you. If I was the jealous type . . . but I'm not," he said with a smile. "Are you?"

"Maybe a little," I lied.

"Do keep it in check, cutie," Wil said. "I am what I am."

We stayed out especially late on the night before I left. On the way to Wil's flat, we played on a dark empty street, chasing and tickling each other.

He ran into the street to get away. "Can't catch me!"

"Yes, I can!" When I reached him, he took me in his arms and swung me around in a waltz, singing, "Tah, dum-dum, tah, dum-dum!"

We were laughing so much that it took me a moment to notice a black sedan speeding down the street. There was no time to do anything but grab Wil like a sack of potting soil and run to the sidewalk. But the driver was driving so recklessly that his car veered toward us, jumping the curb, and I shoved Wil against a wall and flattened myself over him.

The car sped off and Wil said, "Shit, shit, shit," and I said, "Are you all right?"

"You just saved my life. You're like a superhero!"

I went on tiptoe to kiss his forehead and inhaled his scent of ale, white musk aftershave, sunblock, hash, and sweat. He was lovely and so I said, "You're lovely. That guy drove like a maniac."

"Probably as drunk as a lord," Wil said. "Or maybe it was a lord—Ducharme."

I'd wondered that for a moment as well, but I said, "One, Ian drives luxury cars, and two, he wouldn't have missed."

Wil borrowed a car and drove me to the airport. We kissed good-bye and kissed again, his mouth tasting like the peppermint he'd just eaten.

"I'm going to come see you as soon as I can," he said.

"Come soon. You can stay with me. I have to spend some

time writing, but I want to show you my favorite places in the City."

"Next week. I'll come next week."

We kissed again, and then parted. I turned back to look at Wil and his long, skinny body, and he waved to me. I'd found someone who was trying to make the world a better place, and who also knew how to have fun.

As I pulled my chartreuse zebra suitcase toward the check-in counter, I knew that now I had to face reality, and that included telling Ian that things between us were over for good.

If he wanted that voracious bitch Cricket as a cocktail, he'd have to do without the main course.

seven

Blood the One You're With

I took the airport shuttle back to my loft and shuffled in my hand-bag for my keys. The key chain had come unlatched. I dumped my entire bag out on the front steps as I searched for my house key, before I remembered that my bag had fallen over at Wil's.

Luckily I kept an extra set of keys with my neighbor, who let me in the building. I had a refreshing blood spritzer as I put away my things. Then I drove to My Dive. It was only five o'clock, and the box office girls unlocked the front door for me.

"Helloooo!" I called into the empty club.

I heard a yelp and then scampering as Rosemary came from the back hall. He wagged his tail and I sat on the floor and rubbed his brown coat.

Mercedes came out a minute later and watched our reunion with a smile.

"*Hola, muchacha,*" I said. I gave her a big *abrazo* and said, "I'd jump around, too, but things on me bounce too much."

"Thanks for not licking my face either. Rosemary thinks it's a great way to wake me up. How was your trip?"

"Fantastic. I nekkid blood wrestled some sexy chick in a vampire club."

"I thought you'd be going to plays and museums."

"I did that, too. I wasn't completely nekkid. I was wearing a bathing suit and it was fake blood, but the effect was riveting. I got the writing job, too. As usual with *Don* Pedro, I can't talk about it, but I demanded and got *mucho dinero*."

"That's good. I was afraid you'd try to incite someone to try to kill you just for another settlement."

"No such luck, although I almost got hit by a car when I was waltzing in the middle of a street one night."

"I hope you're exaggerating. Did you meet Wilcox Spiggot?"

"Yes, and he's fabulous and we had a torrid affair."

"Don't tell me anymore," she said. "You know I have to deal with Ian, and it's upsetting for me even if it's just dramatics for you."

"*Cariña,* I need to share with someone, and I was your friend before he was your partner, so I have seniority." I put my arm around her and leaned my head on her shoulder. "I brought you expensive Scottish tea and jam. I also have the demos of totally bitchin' bands, and they're interested in playing here."

We went to her office and I recited my travelogue. Mercedes shut her eyes during some of the more graphic details.

"And in conclusion," I said, "Wilcox is not only sexy and delightful, but Wilcox is also a deep thinker and open-minded."

"Kinky is not synonymous with open-minded. You say that he's deep without presenting any actual evidence."

"But I *explained* how things like the Bloody Good Table help position the vampire community within the larger community," I said. "The Vampire Council is concerned about Wilcox, which is evidence aplenty, and Wilcox didn't want to drag my vacation down with ponderous matters, because Wilcox is sensitive to others' needs."

"You just like saying his name."

"Well, obviously. Wil-*cox*. So what do you think?"

"Why rush full tilt into a relationship with this vampire–surfer–political activist–sex maniac when you're still involved with Ian and haven't recovered from Oswald?"

It was a real question, so I thought before answering. "I felt different around Wilcox, a little like the way I used to be *before* . . ."

"'Before' you always complained that no one took you seriously. You went through party boys like they had a one-month expiration date and you barely held on to your apartment. Do you really want to go back to that?"

"Not that exactly, but I miss the belief that I'd meet someone who was both fantastic and a good person, someone who made a positive difference in the world. A vampire–surfer–political activist might be just the right kind of dude for me. He's more admirable than a louche continental smoothie."

"I'm only going to say one thing about Ian. I think you are too ready to find fault with him because he's not Oswald." Her phone rang; when Mercedes finished the call, she said, "If you update the club calendar, I'll give you a bowl of peanuts and a Bloody Mary."

While I worked on the My Dive website, Juanita and the Rat Dogs rehearsed the same new song for hours. Each time they played it, I liked it more.

When I went to get Rosemary from Mercedes's office, I saw her taking something out of a small padded envelope and grimacing.

"What's that?" I asked.

She held up a brushed aluminum flash drive. "One of Los Hackeros sent me this as a present." Los Hackeros was her nickname for her inner circle of computer hackers. "He designed a worm that he says can bypass any firewall and implode a system.

Hackers have a strange way of showing admiration." She tossed the flash drive in her trash can.

Before I could say good-bye to her, her soundman came by to talk about equipment. When she got up to talk to him, I reached into the trash can, took out the flash drive, and put it in my pocket. I'd delete the worm file without opening it, and then I could use the drive.

I waved good-bye to Mercedes, and I took my dog and went home.

We walked up the stairs and went to my front door, but when I put my key in the lock, it was already unlocked. I pushed the door open slowly and went inside while Rosemary charged ahead of me.

Ian, wearing a beautiful black suit, sat in a pink velvet chair by the windows that showed the glittering skyline beyond. He was holding a large book, and I saw that it was my annotated collection of Shakespeare's tragedies. I felt as shocked as if I'd gripped a wire with a live current.

"Hello, Milagro."

I couldn't say anything about his unexpected visit because I'd given him a key and I'd always gone to his place unannounced. "Hello, Ian."

His dark eyes gleamed below the hooded lids. "I stopped by on my way to Gigi's. She told me you were coming to her little gathering tonight."

"Gigi *always* thinks she's invited me to things, but she forgets to actually invite me." I sat on the fuchsia sofa.

"I heard that you were in London."

"Yes, I had a business meeting there and got a big writing gig."

"Congratulations. I hope you enjoyed your trip."

"Very much." I tried to sound calm as I said, "I met Wilcox Spiggott there and he acted as my host. Vampire society in London is much more advanced than the backward feudalism here or in other places. I'm going to see Wilcox again. He's visiting soon."

Ian gazed at me, making my every nerve alert.

"Milagro, I waited for you through your infatuation with Oswald, or, more accurately, your infatuation with his grandmother, because I know how important it is for you to have a maternal figure."

"You waited for me by consoling yourself with an anorexic Eurotrash model."

"That's a very impolite way to speak of my friend," he said. "I've made my feelings for you clear, and I'd hoped you returned them."

I stared at Ian, thinking of how his touch made me forget who I was, how his taste made me delirious, and how he'd never told me he loved me. "I knew exactly how you felt about me when I saw Cricket freaking up against you and your marks all over her body."

"You're behaving like a petulant child. I've explained that . . ."

"You've explained that you were just using her and I don't know what's worse—if you're fucking her, or if she's just a meal to you and you're playing with your food," I said, my voice rising in anger and hurt. "I never had sex with anyone else when I was with you! I never even had sex with Oswald after that night when you and I . . ." I hesitated and then said, "And I never let him cut me after you gave me your blood. I lost Oswald because of you."

"Is this the fable you've been telling yourself?" Ian asked scornfully. "I have a reason for befriending the Poindexters, and that's what we are—friends."

"Friends with benefits," I sneered.

"I didn't intend for it to progress as it did, but Cricket was aggressive and I had to steer her attentions."

"Right into your crotch," I shouted, and stood up.

"My association with the Poindexters is more important than you, more important than my personal life."

"But you can't explain it. You never explain anything," I said. "Every time I'm with you, Ian, I feel as if I'm drifting farther and farther from my moorings." I began pacing, walking along the far wall of windows.

"Milagro, why do you grasp so desperately at those moorings? Personal happiness aside, do you really think it is even possible for you to live like others do?"

Then I asked him the question I'd always been too afraid to ask before. "Have you ever killed anyone, Ian?"

He stood and came to me. He ran his finger across my lips and even then I wanted to open my mouth and take his finger between my teeth, but I jerked my face away.

"The difference between us, darling, is that you haven't killed *yet*. But, because of who you are, there will be a time when it's necessary, when you will have to decide between something that is wrong and something that is far worse. Then you'll understand."

"No, because I will never *ever* kill another human."

"I wish it weren't so. I wish you could live a safe and happy life, but I don't think it's possible." He stared at me with his deep brown eyes. "Did you intend for your recent antics to humiliate me publicly?"

Although he didn't raise his voice, he was angry and for the first time, I was afraid of him. "No, my antics were to please myself, just as your antics with our neighbors were to please yourself."

He took my wrist in his hand, turning it to show the blue veins and the pale pink scar on my arm. Then he said, "Are you coming with me to Gigi's?"

"No."

"Very well." He kissed my wrist and then walked to the door.

"Be assured that whatever your intention, you succeeded in enraging me." He turned to look at me. "Milagro, when you're finished with Spiggott and you've disposed of him, perhaps you'll want to come back to me, but don't expect me to wait for you or take you back again."

"So that's it then?" I said. "It's over? Am I finally free of you?"

"I could ask you the same thing," he said. "I hope you get everything you deserve. Good-bye, Milagro." Then Ian Ducharme walked out the door and out of my life.

Perhaps it was jet lag, but as soon as he was gone, I felt shattered. The knowledge that he was amoral and dangerous gave me no solace as I sobbed at the thought that I'd never make love to him again, or see him smile and call me his own girl, or make him burst into that wonderful rumbly laugh.

I thought of all his kindnesses to me, all his attentions, the gifts that were always so perfectly suited, the way he treated me as if I was the most fascinating person he'd ever met, the way he made me feel beautiful, smart, witty, strong, desirable.

I thought about the way he looked at me when his dark eyes opened in the morning, as if I was what he wanted to see most in the world.

But catching him with Cricket had proved that it was all a lie. So why did I feel as if someone had carved away a piece of me so deep that I would never heal from the wound?

I was too upset to sleep so I threw myself into my fauxoir. I began rereading *Othello* and thinking about how I could use themes of jealousy and manipulation in *Don* Pedro's zombie story.

I crashed at some point and when I awoke I was bent over in a chair, the hard edge of the flash drive jabbing into my waist. I straightened up, pulled it out of my pocket, and tossed it into a dish filled with barrettes, makeup, and pens.

The sun rose, staining the horizon the same vermilion as my chaise, when Wil phoned. "It's night here and I'm missing you. Do you still want to see me?"

"Absolutely!" I said in a voice more cheerful than I felt.

"Good, I've booked a flight and I'll arrive midmorning tomorrow," he said.

"That's wonderful, Wil! Bring a wet suit."

"Ooh, kinky."

"I meant for surfing. It's cold and gray, so you should be okay with waterproof sunblock."

"Awesome. I'll buy gear there. One of my bros has a surf shop, and I'll be hanging with him."

"I thought you were staying with me."

"For a few nights, but I don't want to impose the whole time. You'll get tired of me."

Which is what Ian had predicted. "How could I?" I asked. "Wil, I told Ian about us."

"How did he react?"

"Very well, considering," I said, my voice catching a little. "I'm sure he's got hundreds of replacements lined up."

"I can't believe I nicked the Dark Lord's girl!"

"Um, Wil, please don't laugh about it. It wasn't easy for me."

"Sorry," he said. "I love you, Milagro."

It was so easy for some people to say, but I knew he didn't mean it. "You're fantastic, Wilcox Spiggott. Oh, I think my house key fell out of my purse at your place. Could you look for it?"

"Ah, I found a key on the table. Thought you had left it for me."

"We're not at that stage yet. Would you like me to pick you up at the airport?"

"I'll hire an Avis car so I can hit the beach straightaway. How about dinner tomorrow night?"

"Perfect. I know just the place." I gave him the name and address of a groovy restaurant-lounge before we said good-bye.

I had a lot to do before seeing Wil again. I got a mani-pedi with polish the color of crushed blackberries. I went to a fancy butcher shop and bought meat dripping with blood, as well as fresh blood. I picked up deep red California cabernets, baskets of raspberries, strawberries, and loganberries, and bottles of blood orange juice.

I visited the Womyn's Sexual Health Collective to buy "relationship accessories" for Wil's visit. While I waited for a sales clerk, I read over a poster titled "Does It Itch?" for the local free clinic.

A gray-haired sales counselor with a cozy round tummy and little gold-rimmed glasses was happy to give me advice for buying restraints. "For you?"

"No, for my friend. I'm the one in control."

She smiled and said, "Sweetie, the bottom is always the one who controls." She suggested a beginner's kit of soft, black velvet-covered ropes and said, "If you want to stock up, we're having a two-for-one sale on lubricants and all our eco-friendly fetish toys are ten percent off."

"Uh, well, um . . ." I was about to giggle like a schoolgirl when I saw the fuzzy pink handcuffs I'd bought when I was engaged to Oswald. I'd thought the cuffs would prevent me from hurting Oswald when he tried to taste my blood. Oswald and I never got to use them, though.

The sales counselor saw me staring at the handcuffs. "Those are one of our bestsellers in bondage play."

"People never handcuff me for fun. The last time I got cuffed, someone was trying to kill me," I said, finally managing to shock her.

"Oh, dear! I can show you an easy trick to open handcuffs. All you need is a bobby pin or paper clip."

"I don't plan on being cuffed anytime soon."

She laid a hand on my arm. "Not to preach, sweetie, but in my experience, which is extensive, you should learn to be prepared for anything. Why don't you sign up for our BDSM workshop? Everyone raves about it. If you join our Toy Club for fifty dollars, you can attend free and you'll also get fifteen percent off every purchase."

"I'll just take the restraints and the club membership, thanks."

I didn't know how late I'd be out with Wil, so I dropped Rosemary off with Mercedes and told her I'd call her in the morning. When I saw my brown dog run through her apartment, heading for the cat door to go to the backyard, I said, "He loves being with you. I wish my loft had access to a yard."

"He's a good house dog and everyone at the club loves him."

She took off her glasses and rubbed her nose, so I said, "What is it, *mujer*?"

She shook her head, sending her dreads bouncing around. "I'm not getting involved."

"You think I'm going too fast with Wilcox, but you don't know the half of it with Ian." *His mouth sucking on Cricket, her blond hair against him.* "He told me I'd kill someone eventually. That's what he thinks of me. I'm not going to see him again."

She didn't say anything, but the furrow in her brow was still there.

"Mercedes, you're always doing things for me. What can I do for you?"

"Keep me out of this business with Wilcox," she said. "You did something anyway. Those demos you brought back are great. I'm going to contact the bands and see if we can work anything out."

"Anything as in a gig or a recording?"

"I'm hoping. Oh, my mom sent a present for you." She went

to her bedroom and returned with a garment bag. "It was my grandmother's, and Mami thought you'd like it."

I took the garment bag and unzipped it. Inside was a scarlet satin cocktail dress with a lovely low sweetheart neckline and a tight waist. The fabric had a soft luster like old pearls. "Oh, Mercedes, it's beautiful! You can't give this away."

"Can you see me wearing it?" she said, and laughed. "Even if my sisters had the *tetas* for it, they prefer new clothes. You like vintage."

I gave her a *besito* and said, "Thank you! I'll save it for a special night at your club."

When I returned to my loft, I admired the beautiful dress for a few minutes before getting ready for Wil's visit.

I set out beeswax candles, rinsed and polished my best wineglasses, and changed my bed linen. My duvet had smudges from Rosemary's muddy feet and I didn't have time to wash it. On my craft table, I saw the woven cloth that *Don* Pedro had given me.

It was large enough to cover the bed. The yarn was soft and had a delicate floral fragrance, like the powdery scent of plum blossoms. It felt almost as if it had been dusted with talcum. I rubbed my fingertip against the cloth and then touched my tongue. It tasted faintly of dried grass, but not *druggy* dried grass.

I spread the cloth over the bed and then I took the velvet-covered restraints from the plain brown Womyn's Sexual Health Collective bag and looped them around the bedposts. The sales counselor had given me a brochure about attaching the restraints, but the illustrations looked hopelessly convoluted.

If my mother Regina had let me join the Girl Scouts, I would be better prepared to tie up my hunky new boyfriend.

I went to the closet and pushed my dresses on the rack, looking for something pretty to wear. One of Ian's shirts was there. I took it from the hanger and brought it close to my face, inhaling his scent, immediately missing and wanting him. I put the shirt in the back of the closet, where I wouldn't see it.

I decided to wear a cute lemon yellow dress that I bought at a shop owned by a Stitching & Bitching *amiga*. It had a corset-inspired bodice and a narrow skirt. I wore it with a narrow black patent leather belt, black peep-toe patent leather sling-backs, and black rubber bracelets and earrings.

I slicked on red lipstick and liquid black eyeliner for a dominatrix/bumblebee look, but I resisted the urge to cut straight bangs because Nancy claimed that cutting one's own bangs was the first step to madness.

I went to the garage downstairs, got in my truck, and drove to the restaurant, telling myself how much fun it would be to have Wil here and show him my town.

He wasn't at the restaurant yet, so I waited on the sofa by the entrance. After ten minutes, I took the hostess's suggestion and had a drink at the bar.

I chatted with the couple next to me, but kept looking at the mirror above the bar for Wil to arrive.

After thirty minutes passed, I called his cell phone. He didn't answer, and I left a message saying that I would wait another fifteen minutes. The couple next to me went to their table for dinner, and more people came and left the restaurant. Even if Wil was delayed, lost, or having a difficult time finding parking, he could have called.

I nursed my second drink slowly. He was an hour late and I felt stupid staying any longer. I left a large tip and drove home cursing him.

As I walked upstairs to my loft, I thought, *He is so inconsider-*

ate. I went to unlock my front door thinking, *He's flaky and irresponsible*, but the door was already unlocked.

Had I left it unlocked, or had Ian returned?

When I stepped in, I smelled the beeswax candles and froze. I walked inside slowly and called, "Hello?"

The candles were flickering and there was red wine in the glasses on the cocktail table.

Wil was on my bed, motionless on the woven cloth, his wrists and ankles tied to the bedposts with the black velvet restraints. He wore a gray MY DIVE T-shirt I'd given him, and in the center of his chest was a dark wound with scarlet blood blooming all around it like a prom corsage from the devil.

eight

Love Lies Bleeding

There was such a stillness to Wilcox that I didn't need to touch him to know he was dead. But I did. I stroked his fine bleached hair, feeling the grit of sand from a day of surfing. I kissed his cool, smooth forehead, and ran my finger over the well-shaped, narrow lips that had always been quick to smile and laugh and kiss.

My tears fell on the pretty face that had been so full of life and happiness.

I wanted to cut myself, to pour my blood into the deep knife wound in his flesh, to make him heal, whole, well—my laughing, lusty Wil again, but I knew I was too late. The dead couldn't be brought back.

I closed Wil's empty hazel eyes, smudging the kohl, and untied the velvet restraints from his wrists and ankles.

My survival instincts cut through the fog of grief. Someone was setting me up and I had to move fast.

I blew out the candles but didn't turn on the lights. I wrapped the soft woven cloth around Wil's body, and then I swiftly changed into jeans, sneakers, and a sweatshirt. I threw my laptop, wallet, the composition books, clothes, and other necessities into an enormous sports bag.

I tore up the receipt from the Womyn's Sexual Health Collective and shoved the velvet restraints in the sports bag.

I didn't know when I would be coming back so I packed *Jane Eyre* and a leather box that held my most valuable possessions, Ian's gifts to me: ruby necklaces, Victorian garnet earrings, an enamel fountain pen, the mirror ball earrings, gold bracelets . . . The last thing I put in the bag was my knitting project, the blue-gray scarf for Oswald.

Placing the bulky bag over my left shoulder, I picked up Wil's shrouded body and hefted him over my right shoulder. The cloth released a puff of the fine powder.

I balanced Wil's body as I hurried to the stairwell and down to the garage. After placing him in the bed of my pickup, I positioned gardening tools on top to hide his bulk.

I drove out of the garage and into the dark street just as a black car with a long radio antenna pulled up in the red no-parking zone in front of my building.

It was my fault that Wil was dead. I'd used Wil to get back at Ian, even though I knew Ian had no boundaries. I didn't know what I would say or do when I saw Ian, but I needed to see him now, to make him pay for what he'd done.

I tried to drive like everyone else, about ten miles over the speed limit, and I gripped the steering wheel tight to stop my hands from shaking from my sorrow and fury. It was all I could do to function and watch out for cops.

I slowed when I reached Ian's neighborhood and switched off my headlights as I drove up the winding roads, swerving once to avoid a raccoon that turned its masked face with eerily reflected red eyes toward me.

I remembered how Ian had casually said "when you dispose of him" in reference to Wil. I wouldn't give Ian the opportunity to hide any evidence of his crime, so I turned into the service parking lot down the hill.

An extra-long Dumpster had been deposited at the far side of the lot for debris from a renovation project. I drove around it and parked at the farthest edge of the dirt before it sloped down the hillside, so that my truck was hidden from view.

I left the truck without taking anything and kept to the edges of the road to Ian's house. Banging on the ugly tangerine-colored carved front door, I shouted, "Let me in!"

Mr. K opened the door. I shoved him aside and went in the house, screaming, "Ian!"

"Miss Milagro, please." Mr. K followed me as I ran through the rooms, looking for the man who had murdered Wil.

"Miss Milagro, if you would calm down . . ."

I grabbed Mr. K by the lapel of his jacket and Mrs. K came into the room, looking alarmed.

I said, "Where is goddamn Ian Ducharme?"

"Lord Ducharme not here," Mr. K said.

His wife said, "Miss, let's be reasonable."

I gave Mrs. K a look that should have fried her in her sensible heels. "Where is that evil bastard?"

"We are not at liberty—" Mr. K began, and I slammed him against the wall.

Mrs. K cried, "He's across the country at a meeting with the Council! He'll be there for another week."

She had given up too easily. I put one hand around Mr. K's throat and said, "Tell me the truth *now* . . ."

Mr. K. tried to shake his head, but my grip was too tight. His face was turning puce. Mrs. K said in panic, "He's with Ilena at her home in Oslo."

Ilena, Ian's former lover. "When did he go?"

"He went straight to the airport after dinner at Gigi Barton's the night before last," she said. "I booked the flight myself."

I released my grip on Mr. K's neck, and he bent over, gasping.

"I'm sorry. I apologize for hurting you, Mr. K," I said. "It's inexcusable, and I'll make it up to you another time." *Think, think.* "Could Ian have changed his flight?"

Mrs. K shook her head. "When I phoned Miss Ilena's house-keeper today to confirm that his luggage had arrived on the next flight, Lord Ducharme was there. I spoke to him. He said he would be going on to Lviv tomorrow and didn't know when he'd return."

So Ian hadn't killed Wil. I turned and walked away.

Mrs. K asked, "Would you like us to give Lord Ducharme a message?"

"Yes, please tell him that I said he can go straight to hell. I'll probably meet him there."

I walked in a daze back along the dark street toward the service parking lot. When I heard painful sobs, the sound was so close to my own heart that I took a moment to register that the weeping came from Cricket and Ford's house.

I could have walked on and I *should* have walked on, although *Don* Pedro would have made some crackpot claim that I was destined to be there at that moment and destined to follow the sound.

My steps were silent on the granite brick drive as I passed between the dense privet hedges. The Poindexters' house was a beautiful old brown shingle with white trim. A lantern on a post illuminated the glossy green front door. Now I could hear the choking, guttural cries more clearly; they sounded how I felt.

I knocked, and when no one answered I opened the front door and went into the house. I called, "Ford! Cricket! Is everything all right?"

I found them in the elegant farmhouse-style kitchen. Cricket's body was sprawled on the limestone floor and her young husband knelt beside her. I saw shards of broken glass and blood everywhere. An unwanted craving surged through me at the rich, rusty iron scent of blood.

A bloody X-Acto knife had rolled under a butcher block cart.

"Oh, my God, Ford, what have you done?"

It was then that I saw the phone in his blood-covered hand. He held it to his ear and choked out, "Vampires killed her! Vampires wanted her blood!"

I grabbed the phone from him, dropped it on the floor, and stomped on it, making sure it was thoroughly crushed. "What the hell happened here, Ford?"

"Can't you see!" His eyes flitted from me to his wife. He held up Cricket's wrist revealing a deep ugly gash across it and dozens of scabs. "She wanted to give Ian her blood when he came back. She was draining herself every day because she . . ." He clenched his fists and squeezed his eyes shut.

"Breathe, Ford, breathe."

"I told her it was too much, and she just laughed," he said, looking at me. "I told her that he was in love with you, but she thought she could have him. She wanted him because . . . Oh, God, she's my world."

"Ford, did you . . ."

"I didn't! I didn't kill her. I didn't mean to do anything. She asked me to help, to do it with her, and the knife slipped and the blood spurted out." He let out a cry and stood up suddenly. Too suddenly.

Ford slipped on the pool of blood and fell. His head crashed against the stone of the kitchen island with a horrible thud. I caught him before he hit the floor.

"Ford!" I said, but his eyes were rolling up in his head and he took only one more shuddering breath. Oswald had taught me CPR, so I set Ford down on the floor and frantically tried to revive him.

Even though his heart had stopped and blood was spilling from his head, I continued to pump his chest and breathe into his mouth, thinking, *Please, Ford, breathe!*

I was still trying to save him when I heard cars out front. The men in black gear pried me off Ford's body and I started screaming, "Ford, breathe, breathe!"

I stood shaking, covered with blood. I hadn't personally killed Wil, Cricket, and Ford, but they were still dead because of what I did and did not do. My sins were both of omission and commission.

The men in black handcuffed me and yanked me roughly outside. They put a hood over my head and threw me in the back of a black van. Ford's blood had seeped through my sweatshirt, and I was revolted by my loathesome craving.

The men didn't speak, and I bounced around the back of the van as they sped down the hillside. I expected that we would stop at the police station or sheriff's, but they drove many miles and I realized that they hadn't shown badges or identified themselves.

The hum of traffic diminished, and then all I could hear was the van's engine. The vehicle stopped, there was a metal rattling sound, like a large gate, and the van drove slowly and stopped.

The van's door clacked open and I was yanked out. I stumbled, but regained my balance when a hand shoved my back. I walked forward and heard the ding of an elevator. Someone bashed me forward.

We rode up a few floors before the elevator dinged again. The men pushed me forward and jabbed me until I hit a wall. I heard a door click shut behind me. There was a screech of metal on metal as something was moved behind my legs.

"Sit down," a man said.

I sat. The hood was yanked off my head and a light glared in my eyes. I could make out the outline of men with short hair and dark suits in a military stance in front of me.

"Who are you and why did you kill Ford and Cricket Poindexter?"

"She was already . . . she was gone when I got there. Ford slipped and hit his head. I was giving him CPR," I said in a flat voice, stunned by going from one death to two others.

"Ford Poindexter said that vampires had killed her. What did he mean?"

"I don't know." I stared at nothing and caution slapped me out of my shock. "I'd like to talk to an attorney."

The first man said, "What's your name?"

These men weren't law enforcement, nor were they U.S. military. If they had my name, they'd get my address. If they got my address, they could find traces of Wil's blood at my loft and animal blood in the refrigerator. They could find my friends' names and information. They would find the stack of unused wedding invitations in my closet. They would learn about my truck and eventually find the body in the back.

"I have the right to speak to an attorney."

"You haven't been charged with anything. Did you have a sexual relationship with Ford Poindexter?"

"No!"

"Then who are you and what were you doing at the house? Why don't you have any identification on you? How did you get there? Do you work the streets? Is that how you met them?"

"I'm not telling you anything until I talk to my attorney."

"Tell us what we want to know and we'll let you make a call."

"Tell me who *you* are and let me speak to my attorney."

It went on this way for hours. We were like automatronic dolls at a theme park, reciting a limited script on a loop. Ford's blood dried dark brown on my sweatshirt.

Eventually they became impatient. "Tell us about the vampires."

"There's no such thing as vampires. You may as well ask me to tell you about zombies." One man raised his hand and I relaxed so that the slap wouldn't hurt as much, but it still stung so sharply that my eyes welled.

My throat got dry and I stopped talking. When I closed my eyes to block out the harsh light, someone behind me kicked the chair to startle me.

They dragged me down a dark hall with chipped green walls and industrial pendant lights, and shoved me into a cinder-block room. The thick metal door had a slot for them to slide food through.

There was an open toilet in the corner of the room and nothing else except a bolt in the wall. They took away my shoes and socks, and ran a chain through my handcuffs and locked it to the bolt. Then they threw a ratty blanket in the room.

The Vampire Council's dungeon prison was like a luxury rumpus room by comparison. Well, the vampires I knew did everything with more panache, even imprisonment. In fact, when Ian had been under house arrest for cutting the vampire who slashed me, the Vampire Council let him stay in an elegant town house with an adoring housekeeper.

I sat on the dirty blanket and closed my eyes so I could think. Even if Ian was away when Wil was murdered, he could have ordered the murder. Did Wil's murder have anything to do with the Poindexters' deaths? No, except that danger followed the vampires, followed me.

I didn't know if Ian had set me up, or if the Vampire Council had taken advantage of his absence to send me a message in the form of Wil's corpse.

Ford's phone call had summoned the people who now held me. Could these people have something to do with Ford's father, who worked for a military contractor? Was this place his laboratory, and, if so, what the hell was he doing?

I sobbed for poor Wil and Ford, and even Cricket.

That's when the music began blasting in my cell. It started with the Ramones. The three-chord, two-and-a-half-minute songs were the aural equivalent of haiku, expressing so much within strict conventions. The music was my companion and my solace: I wanted to be sedated, too, instead of being consumed by sorrow and guilt.

To keep from sliding into hopelessness, I did what I'd done as a child locked in my room: I occupied my time by composing a story in my head. The more I thought about the fauxoir, the more I realized how I could work everything around *The Tempest,* which had so many elements that paralleled *Don* Pedro's crazy story: a deserted island, a mysterious sorcerer, and an imprisoned sprite.

It even had a smart, brave, affectionate girl who was sometimes too gullible. It had deception, magic, comic relief, romance, and a satisfying conclusion. I structured the entire fauxoir in my mind, first by chapters, then scenes, then dialogue.

My imaginary world became more real to me than my surroundings. I could close my eyes and see the island, the magical herbs, the azure ocean. I could smell the tropical breezes—salt water, humid forest, coconut, and frangipani.

The men would drag me out now and then. I used those opportunities to look for escape routes, but the halls were continuously guarded by armed men in black T-shirts and olive green cargo pants tucked into black boots. They never said anything beyond "Go" and "Shut up" to me.

I thought I was hallucinating because I kept seeing the same striped cat everywhere. I'd look down one hall and there it was, licking its paw. The men would move me down another hall and the cat was sleeping in a corner.

They fed me now and then, dreadful dreck. I was grateful for the red Jell-O they sometimes included, and I craved blood. Knowing my craving was merely psychological didn't diminish its power.

In those rare moments when I stopped thinking about my fauxoir, I thought of all the selfish, stupid things I'd done in my life. It was a long list, and Ian's name appeared several times.

If Ian knew I was here, he would come to get me out . . . or to kill me, I didn't know. But sometimes I imagined him strolling in, wearing an impeccable suit, saying something insouciant to the guards while he palmed a huge tip to them, and then telling me, "Pity about Spiggott. Come along, darling."

I don't know how long I'd been there before I met the Professor. The men took me to the interrogation room and a striped cat came meowing toward me. A man said "Scram," shoved me down into a chair, and cuffed me to it before leaving.

I heard a *shsh-shsh-shsh* and a middle-aged man in corduroy pants came to stand near the desk.

"What's your name?" he asked.

"What's yours?" I said, but I noticed that he had the same gawky body as Ford and a similar face. Later I overheard the guards referring to "the Professor" and I knew this must be Ford's father.

"Do you comprehend that you are in a powerless position, Miss . . . ?"

"I'm aware that I'm being kept by people who feel exempt from the law, yes."

"It's very exasperating for me to talk to someone who is fixated on banalities."

"It's very perplexing for me to talk about untimely deaths with someone who is so curiously without affect," I said. "You seem more interested in *me* than sorrowful for the deaths of the Poindexters."

He considered this and said, "You assume that death is a permanent condition."

"You got me. I did make that assumption. Silly me."

"My associates are not particularly bright, and they're determined to use more extreme methods to extract information from you. Actually, these imbeciles use any excuse for violence. I'd rather keep your organs healthy."

"Why don't I find that reassuring?"

He ran his hands through his messy hair and said, "I've got better things to do."

"Exactly what *is* worth your valuable attention?" I asked.

He paused and then said, "I'll try to put it in simple terms. Do you see that cat there?"

"It's a clone, right?"

"The cloning's nothing. It's just a way to generate bio-identical spare parts to use in reanimating a subject."

"Frankenstein's monster," I said, chilled. "You know what happened to the monster's creator in that story?"

"That story was an allegory about the industrial age," he said dismissively. "The problem with warfare is that people get upset at the soldier deaths. I intend to provide pre-dead combatants."

"That is the sickest, most amoral idea I've ever heard in my life," I said, shrinking back in the chair.

The Professor threw up his hands. "This is why I don't bother with conversation. Any idiot could see that we'll actually save lives by using corpses as soldiers."

"But they'll still be killing living humans."

"You're a simpleton. The only thing that doesn't bore me

about you is how you heal from injury. That could be extremely useful for my project."

The Professor called to a man, someone I thought of as Average Joe, because he had the face of the guy next door, your coworker, a man in line at the bank, a face you wouldn't remember unless you saw him smile as you screamed in agony.

The Professor said, "Here's the key to my car. Keep it filled with gas and clean if I ever need to use it." He handed Average Joe a transponder key and then said, almost as an afterthought, "Also, take this subject and get her identity. No damage to her organs because I want to use them later."

"We can fill up that vat."

"Don't annoy me with trivialities."

Sometimes I have nightmares about what happened next, my fear and the pain. The water.

My life had been endangered before, but nothing had terrified me like the water filling my mouth, my nose, my lungs. The worst of it was the feeling of helplessness. The deep water rendered me voiceless, the heavy chains rendered me powerless.

The men only let up when they got bored, but then they'd come back and start again.

I didn't think they would kill me on purpose, but I thought they might do it by accident, so I held on. I held on as fiercely as I have ever since I was an embryo in my mother Regina's hostile womb.

They injected me with drugs, hoping that I would talk. I pretended to be under the influence and was able to get a cherry fruit juice box before they figured out that I wasn't Billie Jean, an unwed mother.

No further juice boxes followed despite my confessions that I was Jane, who'd spent too many years at the Lowood school for girls, or Maggie May, keeping my young lover from school, or Brandy, who worked at a waterfront bar, or sexy Sharona. I wasn't clever Lizzy, in love with a snob, or impetuous Bridget, needing a cigarette and a drink.

So who was I? What was I?

I smelled terrible. I know because the men cringed when they came to get me. I shrieked, "Attica! Attica!"

"Stop talking shit," Average Joe said, jabbing me with a baton.

"Attiga? What's that mean?" said the other guard.

"It means that you know nothing about social history or Al Pacino's best films!" I said while trying to protect myself from the blow that I knew would follow.

"Don't engage," Average Joe told his associate as he delivered a whack.

They took blood and skin samples, but the only unusual thing was my elevated white blood cell count. Even the vampire researchers didn't know why my blood didn't indicate any mutation.

In addition to the usual questions, my interrogators sometimes asked, "Who made you?"

"Mother, father, the usual. I believe they're supposed to teach this in fourth grade, but the school system is tragically underfunded, and some states aren't even teaching proper science anymore."

"Vampire mother and father? Or is 'mother' what you call the person who changed you? What were you before?"

"I was and am a normal human girl. I have the same needs and wants as any girl. A home. A family. Friends. The occasional night out. A worthwhile career. Lively conversation. Guys who aren't Satan's minions."

I don't know how long I could have gone on this way, but I remember exactly the moment I broke.

nine

Dance with the She-Devil

W e're gonna have us a little fun tonight," said Average Joe as he yanked me up from the floor of my cell. "First you got to get the stink off you."

I looked for his partner, but the guard was alone for once.

"What are you doing?"

"Shut the fuck up." He pushed me out of the room, my leg shackles clanging on the cement floor, and out into the hall. I could smell the booze on him and he swayed a little as he walked. "Not that it matters since no one will hear you, but I hear you and I'm sick of all the shit you talk."

I looked up and down the hall. It was empty except for a cat licking his privates. "Where are you taking me? Do you have your supervisor's approval?"

Average Joe bashed a giant flashlight into my ribs. "You're gonna see what happens to whores who don't shut the fuck up," he said, pushing me to the elevator.

He put his eye in front of a biometric scanner, a small light flashed green, and he pressed the call button. When the elevator came, Average Joe shoved me inside, then got in and punched the B button. The doors closed with a *ping* and we descended.

With another *ping*, the doors opened. Another hall led to another door that Average Joe opened with an eye scan.

This room was a bright and shiny state-of-the-art laboratory. There were long, black lab tables with mysterious equipment and stainless steel exam tables. There were two slanted aluminum tables with faucets and drains—autopsy tables. One wall was lined with small doors, like drawers in a morgue. The acrid smell of chemicals came from drains set into the floor.

One wall seemed to display aquariums, but when I looked closer, I saw human organs and limbs suspended in a viscous neon yellow solution that slowly bubbled.

A fuzzy striped tail hung out from a red biohazard bin.

A man in a lab coat was watching a stock market report on a small television by his computer station.

"Wassup?" the lab guy said to Average Joe, and then he stared at me and grimaced in disgust.

"Can you give me a couple of hours?" Average Joe said.

"Wouldn't you rather have a clean body? I can give you a good deal on some intact ones." He waved to a giant metal door and said, "That blonde is still in the chill room, nice and fresh."

"The Professor'd have you whacked if he knew you touched her," Average Joe said. "I'll hose this bitch down first."

His smile scared me more than all of his shouting ever had. He reached into his pocket and pulled out a small plastic bag with blue pills. "For your weekend jollies. I just had mine."

The lab guy took the bag and said, "I'll be back later. Put her out of sight when tonight's meat shipment gets delivered and don't leave a mess." He picked up a pack of cigarettes from his desk and left the room.

The doors closed, leaving me alone with Average Joe. I shuffled back against one of the steel tables.

"Scream if you want," Average Joe said with a laugh. "Hell, it's always more fun when they scream."

In that second I imagined all the victims in his past and all the victims in his future, and I knew that Ian had been right about me all along. "You're not going to hurt me and you're not going to hurt anyone else ever again."

"Whaddaya gonna do about it?" He smiled and raised the big flashlight as he came toward me, leaving his face vulnerable.

I swiftly brought my cuffed fists up against his jaw. As he staggered back, I smashed my fists as hard as I could into his belly.

He fell on the floor, and I bent over him and grabbed his head and twisted until I heard a crack, the most horrible sound that I'd ever heard.

I couldn't look at Average Joe's slack face as I reached for the ring of keys on his belt. I sorted through them quickly and found the cuff key and then the key that released my leg shackles.

His wallet was in his back pocket. I didn't want to look through it because I didn't want to know his name, or see a photo of his family, or learn his address, but I took his cash. I put the money and keys in my pocket, and my stomach cramped with hunger as I thought of the warm blood in him.

I opened the huge metal door that they'd called the meat locker, releasing a blast of frigid air. Ford and Cricket's pale, bluish bodies were lying on gurneys, hooked up to medical equipment and IVs. A striped cat was on a much smaller gurney, also attached to equipment and twitching a leg, but otherwise still.

The Professor was going to try to bring them back.

I left the chill room and closed the door. Now I noticed a set of double doors on the far wall. There was a simple steel push button to open them. This room was designed to prevent people from getting in easily, not from leaving.

I pushed the button and the doors slid open to reveal a dark parking garage. Beyond a row of black vans, I saw the entrance to the garage with a metal gate that was open wide enough for me to get through.

Don't panic, I thought.

I dragged Average Joe's body into the garage and rolled the lifeless bulk under a van. As I ran to the open gate, I saw a car with "Prophetsor" on the license plate, but if I took the car, I might attract notice.

I peered around the wall of the garage. A chain-link fence topped with viciously barbed concertina wire surrounded the lot. Cameras were mounted on posts by the gate. Beyond was a street.

When the cameras were turned away, I ran out of the garage to a pocket of dark shadow by the fence.

As I was searching for the best place to climb, and hoping that an electric jolt wouldn't knock me out, a black van turned into the drive.

I stayed hidden as the gates slid open automatically. And as the van drove in, I slipped out, and then I was out on the street, moving swiftly from one shadow to another.

When I reached the end of the block, I broke into a run, racing past desolate lots and abandoned warehouses, having no idea where I was. Speed was more important than care, and I felt broken glass on the asphalt slice my bare soles.

Average Joe's keys jangled in my pocket, and I paused to hide them in a sewer pipe beside the road.

I reached a two-lane street and followed it for several minutes. Then the briny, seaweed scent of the bay came on the wind. Another half mile led me to a narrow bridge marked with a small black-and-white sign.

I was in a barren industrial area of the City, familiar because some friends had once liberated an abandoned warehouse nearby for a party. Which proved how very, very important it is to attend every party you get invited to because they provide invaluable knowledge.

I stopped running and reached into my pocket for the money I'd taken from Average Joe. I counted out almost three hundred dollars. I was a few miles from a scuzzy urban motel, nicknamed Motel Smells Like Hell, where Mercedes housed particularly problematic bands. It was the sort of place where decent, respectable, upstanding citizens were treated with suspicion and hostility, i.e., exactly the place I needed.

Another mile took me to a seedy block where one could score drugs or visit the "Does It Itch?" free clinic. I glanced at the newsstands of weeklies. Wilcox, Ford, and Cricket had been dead for only eight days.

I gave a street person five dollars for all his coins, and he told me about a working pay phone nearby. I dialed Mercedes's office landline and left a message, saying, "Miracles can be found at places that smell like hell, no doubt; don't say a word," and hung up.

Half an hour later I reached the motel. I hid in the parking lot, which stunk of urine, rotting garbage, and pine-scented disinfectant. I contributed substantially to the stench.

An unfamiliar green car pulled up and I saw Mercedes inside. She got out and looked around. When I called out quietly, *"Hermana,"* she turned toward me.

"¡Dios mio!" Her eyes were wide behind her glasses and her mouth fell open.

"You don't have to give me an *abrazo* until I get clean. Does anyone know you're here, meeting me?"

"No one. I knew you wouldn't reference Gwen Stefani except in an emergency," she said. "You look . . ."

"I need a room and a change of clothes. Something red to drink and eat would be great." I put the money in her hands. "Keep it off the books and I'll tell you everything once we're in the room." I stepped back behind the Dumpster.

She returned ten minutes later, carrying a cardboard box, and whispered, "Where are you?"

"Here," I answered, and came out. She led me to an end unit and unlocked the door. The room had a king-sized bed covered in a shiny leopard-print polyester bedspread and mustard yellow shag carpeting.

Mercedes closed and locked the door and wedged a chair under the doorknob. She reached into the box and took out a bottle of V8, a package of Red Vines licorice, and teriyaki-flavored beef jerky. As I scarfed down my food, I saw her looking at my feet, with their mud of blood and filth, my bloodstained shirt, my jeans hanging from my hips.

I put down the empty bottle and smiled at my friend. "This is the first time that I've been here that I'm more scabrous than the room. Let me take a shower before I do anything else."

"These clothes were in the lost and found," she said, and handed me the cardboard box.

"Thanks, honey." I took the box and went into the tiny bathroom. When I saw myself in the mirror, I understood why Mercedes had been horrified. I looked like something a cat had dug up, chewed, and spit out.

As I showered, I thought about how marvelous preformed plastic shower stalls were, and how fabulous tiny bars of soap were, and how incredible lukewarm water was. Then I dried myself with a fantastic rough terry towel and picked through the amazing collection of clothes in the lost and found box.

There were several pairs of thong and bikini underwear, each far cleaner than the disgusting *chones* I'd taken off. I picked a pair that looked as if they hadn't been worn, purple glittery leggings, and a black sweatshirt with the collar ripped off.

I found a pair of pink socks, shiny black demi boots that were only a size too big, and a really fabulous pink plastic jacket with epaulets and gold buttons. I found one gold hoop earring that I put on, feeling quite piratical.

I took the plastic liner out of the trash bin and put my own clothes in it. I tied the top of the bag to contain the noxious fumes and walked out into the bedroom.

"I feel better now. How's Rosemary?"

"He's happy as the bar mascot. I've been looking all over for you." Mercedes walked back and forth in the narrow space between the bed and a fake marble counter with a cheap coffee machine. "I knew something was wrong when you didn't answer my calls."

"More wrong than abridged versions of the classics." I dropped onto the bed and stretched out. "This mattress is divine. It's like I'm floating on a cloud. Do you have some quarters for the Magic Fingers?"

Mercedes fished into her pocket, pulled out coins, and put them in the Magic Fingers slot. As the bed began jiggling, she said, "I had Los Hackeros check police and hospital reports, just in case, and nothing came up."

"I was kept off the grid."

"Anyway," she said, "I knew you weren't with Ian . . ."

"Because you knew he was in Oslo with his model-bitch-lover Ilena. He didn't tell me he'd gone. We officially broke up."

"Where *is* Wilcox?"

"Dead. Someone stabbed him and left his body at my place on the night I was supposed to meet him. I thought Ian did it," I said. "Poor, beautiful, wonderful Wil."

"Oh, Milagro," she said. "I'm so sorry."

"Me, too. I knew I was being set up, so I got out of my place as fast as I could and went to Ian's, vengeance on my mind. He wasn't there, as you know, and when I was going by the neighbors' house . . ." I took a deep breath and told her about discovering Ford with Cricket's body and how he'd hit his head and the men in the black van who took me away.

"The Poindexters' deaths were never reported to authorities," she said. "I know this dude who tracks 911 calls for alien abduction stories, and I had him scour records for anything abnormal when you vanished."

"Did your pal catch Ford's phone call about vampires?"

"No, which proves that your abductors have lots of pull. I got in touch with Gabriel to see if he knew of anything."

"And?"

"And he said everyone's gossiping about you and Wilcox, but as far as he knew, the Council was keeping out of it. You have gone out of radio contact before."

"Only when pursued by maniacs, not as a general practice," I said. "I was held in a building south of here in one of those mostly abandoned industrial neighborhoods. They had an autopsy room and they were after vampire intel." I loved throwing in new jargon. "They worked for Ford's father, because there was someone they called the Professor who was running the show."

"How do you know it was him?"

"Because he looked like an older version of Ford and because that bastard cloned Señor Pickles and didn't tell his wife. He thinks cloning is too elementary, so he's using the cat parts to try to revive the original Señor Pickles," I said. "He's trying to reanimate human bodies for use as soldiers in warfare."

Mercedes sat down on the bed beside me and hugged me tight. Then the strangest thing happened. I felt her shake and heard a choked sound. Stoic Mercedes was crying. She took off her glasses and pressed her face hard against my shoulder and bawled for a long time.

When she seemed to calm down, I reached for the carton of Barton's tissues on the fake-marble bedside table. "'It's not worth sneezing at if it isn't Barton's,'" I said, handing her a tissue.

While Mercedes blew her nose, I finally noticed the purplish circles under her eyes and the hollowness in her freckled cheeks.

"Oh, Mercedes, I'm sorry to put you through this."

She looked up at me with her big amber eyes and said, "I thought I lost you this time."

I squeezed her hand. "It takes more than mad scientists and armed guards to get rid of Milagro de Los Santos."

"What did they do to you?"

I smiled and said, "I don't want to talk about it. I *never* want to talk about it."

"How did you get away?"

"I can't . . . ," I said, and shook my head. "But they'll be coming for me when they find out I've gone."

"Then we have to decide what to do right now."

I was relieved to turn my thoughts elsewhere. "The military contractors don't know who I am, but whoever killed Wil does."

"You're assuming that Wilcox's murder was a message to you. So why Wilcox, and not you?"

"Everyone knows I'm hard to kill."

"Is there anything else?" Mercedes asked.

"Well, there is one thing," I said. "Wil's body is in my truck. At least it was when I left it there."

Mercedes put her hands to her forehead and massaged. She said, "Airports are a problem, but we can get you across the border into Mexico or Canada."

"The safest place for me is Oswald's ranch. The contractors

don't know who I am and won't look there. And if the Vampire Council is behind Wil's murder, they won't try anything while I'm with the Grants."

"Let me call Gabriel and see if he's got another safe house."

But I didn't want to go anywhere else. The ranch had been my refuge when I was first infected, and it had been my home. I wanted to go home. I said, "I just want to be there."

"What about telling Ian?"

"What if Ian had Wil killed?"

She shook her head. "I don't think he'd do that, but . . . I'm not sure."

"Ian does anything he feels like doing," I said. "That's why I could never consider him even though . . ." I stopped that thought.

Mercedes said, "Are you sure Oswald will let you stay?"

"Oswald will want to help me. That's who he is," I said with more certainty than I felt. "He's always been there for me."

"That was different. He was in love with you then." She sighed heavily. "If your truck is still near Ian's, we've got to get rid of it, get rid of your laptop and electronic trail, and get you a new ride. Pepper can help."

Ernest "Pepper" Culpepper, biker and former meth chemist, had helped us before.

"He's two hours away."

"No, he's not," Mercedes said.

It took me a second to figure things out. "You and Pepper?" It felt wonderful to laugh again. "You and Pepper! I'm amazed and intrigued. You and Pepper!" She had rejected countless musicians as not worth her time and now she was dating a biker!

"It's none of your business and, besides, did you know he plays the bagpipes brilliantly?"

"'Bagpipes' and 'brilliant' should never be uttered in the

same sentence." When I finally stopped laughing, I said, "I trust Pepper."

"He can help get you to the ranch and I'll drive up later."

"No way, Mercedes Ochoa-McPherson. I'm not going to have them come after you like they came for Wil," I said. "Promise me you'll stay away. And promise me you won't tell Ian where I've gone, if he bothers to ask. Promise you won't tell him *any* of this."

"Milagro—" she began.

"Cricket and Ford would be alive if they hadn't met Ian," I said. "Promise me."

She pressed her lips together and finally said, "Okay, I promise. Now get some rest and I'll arrange things."

I dropped back on the bed and pulled the leopard-print bedspread over me. I was dimly aware of Mercedes making phone calls and then Pepper arriving.

He shook me awake. He was a wall of a man with several tattoos (daggers, naked broads, Foghorn Leghorn) and a rusty-brown beard that sported tiny silver skull beads.

"Time to get up, babe."

"Pepper!" I threw my arms around him and he gave me a smacking kiss on my cheek. He had a comforting aroma of bourbon with faint notes of exhaust and marijuana.

"You look like you been rode hard and put away wet, Milagro."

"Now would be the time for you to lie about how I look," I said. "You don't have to do this. You're risking your life."

He laughed a big, booming laugh. "Hon, I was born risking my life. You and Mercedes are the prettiest accomplices I've had, though."

"Who knew when we met that we'd still be friends?" I said. Oswald sure hadn't; he'd never liked me going to the raucous bar where Pepper held court.

"Not me," he said. "Ain't fortune a queer bitch?"

"That she is, Pepper."

A little after four in the morning, Pepper and I said good-bye to Mercedes.

My friend said, "If you need to call me, use Oswald's office phone. The last time I talked to Gabriel, he told me he'd done a big security update on the family communications. I'll be waiting to help any way you need me to."

"Thanks. You know I love you, don't you?"

She nodded. "Back atcha, Mil."

She gave me a powerful hug and I held on tight, but not so tight that I would hurt her. "This is left over from the room charge," she said as she tucked folded bills into my pocket.

I picked up the trash bin liner with my old clothes. "This needs to be burned."

"I'll take care of it."

Pepper and I went to his Harley in the lot. The big man handed me a helmet and said, "Hoped we'd do this on a blazing day with you topless, your jugs smashed against me, and your hair flying in the wind."

"There's always the future."

Pepper looked somber for a moment. "Mil, I been to jail here and in some not-so-nice places. The first time is the hardest and you think you're never going to be okay again, but you will be. Maybe not the same as you were, but that's what life is. Change. You're going to be okay."

"Thanks, Pepper. We better go."

He took me to a spot about a mile from Ian's house and parked beneath a stand of firs.

I told him, "If I'm not back in twenty minutes, hightail it out of here and tell Mercedes." I took off the pointy half boots and tucked them inside the pink pleather jacket. I'd doubled up my socks so I could move quietly.

"Is that enough time?"

"People always said I'm a fast girl," I told him, and winked.

It was almost pitch-black on the heavily wooded hill as I set off running. Rocks and sticks poked through my socks as I cut through yards and climbed over fences, surprising wildlife.

I felt a surge of power; no one could follow me when I moved like this. Almost no one.

I approached the service lot from the hillside below. It was a steep incline, and I used my toes and fingers to grip rocks and brush. I reached the plateau of the lot and crouched as I crept toward my truck, still hidden from view behind the Dumpster, which now overflowed with construction debris.

I walked to the pickup slowly, afraid of what I'd find. But Wil's body was where I'd left it, wrapped in the cloth, under my gardening equipment. I didn't know what the weather had been like, but I hoped that it had been cool enough so that when his body was sent to his parents . . . I couldn't think about it.

My keys and phone were inside the cab, as was the big sports bag that I'd packed. I got inside and sat for a few minutes while I listened out the open window. I hoped I hadn't walked into a trap. I heard and sensed no one.

I put the pickup in reverse and released the brake. It rolled back to the middle of the lot as I turned the wheel. Then I got out and pushed the truck to the street while trying to steer.

Gravity pulls a heavy object stronger and faster than one expects. The truck picked up speed while I was running beside it. I hopped inside, pulled the door closed quietly, and steered down the hill.

I had to turn the engine on at a sharp curve that went uphill.

When I reached the meeting place, I flashed my headlights to signal Pepper and pulled over. I took my laptop and cell phone out of the truck, placed them on the asphalt, and smashed them with a large rock.

Pepper got off his bike, pulled a can of lighter fluid out of his leather jacket, and doused the electronic gear that contained all my files, those unpublished stories and novels. He scratched a wooden match across the sole of his boot and then tossed it on the debris.

The plastic melted into a toxic hot mess, just like my life.

When the flames died down, Pepper kicked away the remains and mounted his bike. I got in my truck and followed his fast but circuitous route to a lonely part of the county whose obstreperous residents had quashed attempts at gentrification.

Pepper paused at a building with metal garage doors. When they rolled up, we drove into the Dantesque scene of men with welding helmets, torches, saws, mallets, and spray paint equipment.

The noise drowned out the sound of our engines, and Pepper pulled over and waved for me to do the same. A man with a shaved head and a blue jumpsuit went to him and they talked for a minute.

I got out of my truck, the sports bag slung over my shoulder. Pepper came over and shouted in my ear, "Your ride'll be ready in a bit. Let's chow down."

"I've got something, um, incriminating there," I said, looking at the bed of the truck.

"You mean the dead dude in back?" Pepper shrugged and walked away.

I only got a few glances as Pepper led me through the garage into a walled-off kitchenette with a table and a battered leather sofa. He closed the door and shut out much of the noise.

"You knew?" I asked.

"If you killed someone, baby girl, I imagine he had it coming."

"I didn't kill *him*," I said, referring to Wil. "Someone left his body at my place to set me up."

"Hate when that happens," Pepper said as he opened a refrigerator decorated with a collage of female genitalia. "You want some eggs?"

The fried eggs doused in ketchup and slices of thick pink Canadian bacon, accompanied by cherry soda, was the best meal of my life.

Pepper smoked a joint as he watched me scrape the last bit of food off my plate. He suddenly chuckled. "I remember the first time you walked in the bar with Ian and his sister and Oswald's cousin Sam. I thought me and the boys would scare you shitless. Ironic, huh?"

"I *was* scared," I said. "Well, nervous."

"You were different then."

"I know." I wasn't a girl who drank blood and killed.

Pepper's friend came in and said, "Your ride's ready."

We went to the shop and Pepper's friend led me to a huge white truck. "Steal American," he said. "All the paperwork is in the glove compartment. Enough power to outrun someone and more than enough to roll over them. We'll piece out your pickup and get rid of anything identifying."

I looked balefully at the gas-guzzler. However, girls on the run from multiple enemies couldn't be picky. "Thank you. How do I pay you?"

"We'll handle that through Pepper. He says you're good for it."

"Thanks. I've got to move a few things."

The men politely averted their eyes as I went to my truck and unloaded the gardening gear. I carefully reached for Wil's body, not knowing what to expect after all this time.

I hefted it as gently as I could and the soft floral smell of the cloth rose to my nose. Wil's body felt as pliant as it had when I'd first hidden it. I carried him to the bed of the new truck and placed the gardening tools over him.

I got in the truck and the metal garage door rolled up. Morning had come. I drove into the light and toward Oswald's ranch, with Pepper following.

Traffic was sparse this early, and after we got past the suburban sprawl, the landscape gave way to beautiful green fields and then vineyards stretching out to the hills.

Golden poppies, banks of blue lupine, and brilliant yellow wild mustard bloomed. I wished I could have shown Wil this. His death was my fault. All the deaths were my fault.

We soon reached the town where Oswald had his office. Wine-country tourism stopped at the base of the mountain, but we drove on. And along the drive, I kept remembering my first time coming here; perhaps it was exhaustion, but I had the surreal sense of moving backward in time.

A logging truck slowed traffic and it was agonizing minutes before the road straightened enough for me to fly past it. Pepper rode in my draft. I would see Oswald soon. I'd tell him everything and he'd take me in his arms and say that he was sorry for ever breaking up with me and that he still loved me.

Pepper and I made it over the mountain, through a stretch of pines, manzanitas, and red earth, then out to open country. I turned down the road that led to Oswald's ranch. I stopped at the gate and waved good-bye to Pepper. He waved back and roared away.

I was here. I was home.

I punched in the code on the post and the big electronic gate slowly swung open. I drove down the lane shaded by English walnuts, verdant with new foliage. The two-story sandstone house was in front of me now.

Oswald's four dogs bounded down the road, barking their welcome, making me miss Daisy, my first dog. I was too anxious to drive anymore and I stopped the truck by the small vineyard of cabernet grapes. I hopped out and the dogs leapt around me.

Together we ran the rest of the way, past a new parking circle, by the garden that I'd planted, to the back entrance that led into the house, to Oswald, who would have been my husband now if I hadn't tried to please others instead of following my own wants and needs and instincts and heart.

I wouldn't make that mistake again.

ten

Is That a Stake in Your Pocket, or Are You Just Happy to See Me?

I called, "Oswald! Oswald!" as I went through the mudroom and into the bright, big kitchen.

Then I saw him.

Oswald was sitting at the long trestle table, holding open a copy of the *Journal of the American Medical Association,* with a coffee mug in front of him. It was Saturday and he was dressed in a T-shirt that said *You! Out of the Gene Pool* and old jeans.

He had been everything to me and seeing him here in this place broke my heart all over again. How could I have ever given him up?

He looked up at me with his clear eyes, as gray as river stones, and the color drained from his already pale face.

We stared at each other for long seconds. Finally he stood and said, "What are you doing here? You've got to leave."

"I need to talk to you."

"Sorry, but I can't deal with your histrionics today. Or ever again."

Oswald took my elbow and began leading me out of the kitchen. His herb-scented sunblock brought back so many memories of us together.

"Let me explain," I said.

"I see that you've finally decided to slim down, but there are healthier ways to do it than starving yourself."

"But everything's gone horribly wrong."

He grabbed a baseball hat as we went through the mudroom. "I can't do this, Milagro. It's too hard, and everyone knows you're with goddamn Ian Ducharme now, so you can go to him for whatever you want—unless you've gotten bored with him, too, and moved on to ruin some other man's life."

"Yes," I said, and that surprised Oswald. We stopped where we were, by my garden. "Yes, I destroyed a man's life in the very worst way and people are after me, including the Council, I think."

"Not likely. The Council has realized that you are their juggernaut." He let go of my elbow and then said more quietly, "Do you have any idea how miserable it makes me when I see you watching me from that café?"

"I wanted to see you."

"Why? Because it just rips open the wound again."

"I miss you, Oswald." I touched his cheek and felt the old pleasurable zizz from him. "We loved each other. We were happy. How can I pretend that never existed?"

"The same way you pretended when we were engaged and you cheated on me."

Now I was stunned. "Who told you?"

"You did just now." He closed his eyes as if he couldn't bear to look at me, and when he opened them, I saw his grief.

I thought I couldn't feel any worse, but now I wished that the earth would open up and swallow me.

"Oswald, I needed to find out if I could let someone cut me

without reacting and hurting him, and then I would be able to let you do it because I wanted you to be happy."

"*Someone?* You mean Ian. Before, during, and after me, it's always been goddamn Ian Ducharme."

"Please don't hate me, Oswald. I couldn't bear it if you hated me," I said, tears blurring my vision of him. "You're the best man I've ever known. I was wrong, so wrong, and if I could do it all over again . . ."

"But we can't turn back the clock, Milagro." He shook his head and said, "My parents told me that rumor about you and Ian and I said they were wrong, that you would never do that because you loved me, and I loved you. I want you to leave now."

"Oswald, I care for you more than you can know, but I needed to come here because no matter what's happened, I know that your goodness will always prevail." I wiped at my tears. "I'll show you why I had to come. Let me show you what they've done." I ran around the house in my stupid pointy ankle boots, down the lane, to the truck.

He came slowly after me.

I reached over to unlatch the truck's gate and that's when I saw the bare space between the gardening tools. Wil's body was gone.

"He was here. I swear, he was here!"

"What are you playing at, or have you finally found a drug that has an effect on you?"

"I'm not making this up." I jumped into the bed of the truck and began flinging out the tools even though it was clear that the body was gone. As I turned around in confusion, I saw something off to the left.

There among the grapevines was Wil with the shroud over his head like an Old Testament prophet. He raised his arm and pointed at me and his mouth gaped open. Even though no sound came out of the black hole in his green-tinged face, I knew he was saying, *"J'accuse!"*

I took two steps backward in shock. The first step was onto the truck's gate. The second step sent me off the edge.

My reactions were fast and I could have regained my balance if I had tried. But the enormity of all my guilty deeds consumed me: leading Wil to his death, killing Average Joe, cheating on Oswald, not doing anything to save the Poindexters, and cheating on Oswald with goddamn Ian Ducharme . . .

I hated who I was and what I'd done.

I thought, *If I only had another chance,* and then my head cracked against something hard, and when the darkness came, I welcomed it.

When I opened my eyes, an interesting man wearing a baseball cap was leaning over me and feeling the back of my head, and very interesting sensations were buzzing through me. The man was extremely cute, but I was feeling strangely woozy. "Excuse me," I said, and tried to scoot away from him.

"You hit your head and blacked out." His dark-lashed gray eyes peered into mine. "Your pupils look all right now."

I felt as if I'd been suddenly awakened, and I couldn't grasp exactly where I was and what I'd been doing. I looked up and saw trees and then turned my head and saw lush fields of grass and wildflowers, which was perplexing.

"Let's get you up," the man said, and took my arm.

The fun buzzy feeling returned at the contact, which made me wonder if I was high.

"Am I supposed to stand if I've had a concussion? What if all the blood rushes to my head and I die?"

"You haven't yet and a bump to the head isn't going to do it," he said as he pulled me up.

Then I glanced down at myself and screamed. I jumped away from the man. "What kind of sick freak are you to dress me like this? Did you drop a roofie on me? Because I know people—"

"Milagro, calm down."

He knew my name, but I stayed out of his reach. I glanced around at a vineyard with swaths of lupine, blue-eyed Susans, buttercups, and golden poppies growing between the rows of vines. There were California live oaks just beyond. I was in wine country.

Then I took another look at the man. He was just under six feet tall, lean and eminently boinkable, and so I tried to recall if I *had* boinked him. What *else* could I have done?

"It was a wild night, wasn't it?" I said, trying not to sound as scared and bewildered as I felt. "Alas, a girl must get home to her very concerned and proactive friends. They've probably already filed a police report that I'm missing. Do you know where my purse is?"

"You didn't bring one inside. Check your truck," he said, pointing toward a humongous white vehicle.

"Ha, ha, and ha. I don't have a truck and certainly not a gas-guzzler like this atrocity." I put my hand in my pocket and felt a few bills.

"Milagro, this isn't funny."

"I'm well aware of its unfunnyness," I said haughtily. "Very nice knowing you—not!—and I'll, um, well, it's been real and it's been fun, but it hasn't been real fun."

I turned and walked quickly down the lane toward a street beyond the fence. When I reached the gate, it automatically swung open, and I tottled forward in too-big heeled boots onto the asphalt road.

I took the bills out of my pocket and counted eighty-nine dollars, which was the most money I'd had in ages. It would have to go straight to my landlord.

I looked both ways, but couldn't see anything but road and trees. There weren't even any sidewalks.

The man was coming down the lane toward me. He stopped at the gate. "Milagro."

"If you would just point the way to the nearest bus or train station, I'll be on my way."

"You're disoriented. You hit your head."

I *was* disoriented, but other than this ookiness, I felt fine. I reached up and touched my noggin. "I don't have any bumps or soreness. Did I hit my head, or did *someone* hit me?"

"You fell off your truck and knocked your head against a rock," he said.

"My *truck* again." I laughed. "At least you committed to the joke."

He put his hands on his hips, and they were nice hips indeed. "Milagro, as much as I'd like to see you leave, I think you better let me examine you further."

"Nice try, but you had your thrills last night and I hope you don't have any communicable diseases, because the last thing I need is to catch some incurable condition from a casual encounter." I'd go to the free "Does It Itch?" clinic as soon as I got back to the City.

"What's the last thing you remember?"

The air here felt so light and warm, so clean, and the sky was the vivid blue of bachelor's buttons.

"Okay, I'll go along with this idiocy. I was going to a party for a very dear friend, Sebastian Beckett-Witherspoon, the acclaimed novelist," I said, although I hated Sebastian with the fire of a thousand suns. "I was dressed quite chicly. Obviously, I, um . . . perhaps I had too much to drink, and here I am. Where exactly *is* here?"

"The ranch."

"Thank you for your total lack of specificity," I snarked. "If you're not going to be helpful, I can manage on my own." I turned right and began walking.

He followed me, and I said, "Don't try to stop me because I'll scream."

"I won't try because you'll throw me across the road."

"You're hilarious except for the being funny part of hilarity." As I kept walking, I recalled leaving my crappy basement apartment to go to the party. I remembered waiting for the bus and worrying about seeing Sebastian, who had become successful while I was still patching together part-time jobs. What the hell had happened *after* that?

The hunky dude said, "Milagro, on the off chance that this is not a really desperate attempt to make me feel sorry for you, you need to come back with me. You can call Mercedes to come get you."

I stopped. "You know Mercedes?"

"Yes, I know Mercedes. Come back to the house."

"You won't try anything?"

"You're the one who always starts things, not me."

"Prove that you know me. What's my favorite color?"

"Trick question. Leopard print."

"Lucky guess. What's my favorite music?"

"Anything you can crank up too loud and play over and over. Your favorite clothes are too revealing. Your favorite drinks have paper parasols."

"What's my favorite book?"

"How should I know?" he said. "You quote Twain a lot."

"So I *really* know you? I mean, before last night."

"Yes, Milagro, we know each other."

I was comforted by the annoyance and exasperation on his

face, expressions not uncommon with men who knew me, and I said, "Okay, but keep your distance."

"That's what I've been trying to do." He led the way back down the lane, stopping to push a button that closed the electric gate.

Magnificent English walnut trees lined the way, and ahead I saw an impressive pale gold sandstone house. Across a field was a pretty little white cottage.

Straight ahead was a brown barn and there was a blocky building off to the side. Horses ambled in the fields that led to tree-covered hills.

We walked by the big white truck that was most definitely not my truck.

"This place is very beautiful," I said.

He led me around the house toward the back entrance. Old roses, their perfume floating on the air, clambered on a fence that enclosed a marvelous garden.

I peered over the fence and saw a slate patio beneath an ancient oak, espaliered pear trees, and all sorts of deciduous shrubs in spectacular bloom. "Your roses are gorgeous, but they should have been pruned."

"I can't do everything."

The man wasn't wearing a wedding ring, so I smiled and said, "It's still a fabulous garden. You've got many of my favorite species of rose and your viburnum are just bursting, aren't they?"

"Let's go inside."

"Okay. I'm embarrassed that I don't even remember your name."

"It's Oswald."

"I've never met anyone named Oswald before," I said as we stepped into a mudroom with an extensive display of sunhats and baseball caps.

Oswald put his cap on a hook and led me through a spacious kitchen done up in Monet shades of bright blue and yellow with high-end appliances, through a dining room, past a Mission-style living room, and into a study.

"Very manly man," I said, looking around at the leather furniture, dark paneling, and built-in bookshelves. "Whose house is this?"

"Mine."

"Yeah, right." House sitter was my guess. I flopped onto the sofa and said, "You'd think whoever owns this place could afford to buy a few novels. The *Merck Veterinary Manual* doesn't exactly sound like a dynamic read."

"You'd change your mind if you read the section on acute respiratory diseases in chickens," Oswald said, and his lips went up at one corner in a crooked smile that I found enchanting. "Let's go over any other symptoms."

"Maybe you should take me to the nearest free clinic."

Oswald went around the desk and brought out a black leather medical case with *OKG* monogrammed in gold.

"Who's OKG?" I asked.

"Oswald Kevin Grant, MD. Me, Doctor," he said, and I smiled because it was kind of funny.

"You're *really* a doctor?"

"I take care of the animals here. Do you have a headache?" he asked. "Any dizziness?"

"No to the headache, but I've always suffered from the occasional bouts of ditziness," I said as he took a stethoscope from his bag.

"Chest or neck pain? Nausea? Cold hands or tingling?" He took my hand, sending a buzz through me.

"That!" I said. "When you touch me, I get this zizz sensation, but it's nice. It doesn't itch."

"I didn't ask if it itched."

"Well, I know things aren't *supposed* to itch. It feels . . . good."

"That's not new with you."

"Of course it is. It's not normal, is it?"

"*You're* not normal." He slipped the stethoscope under the torn collar of my sweatshirt and listened, his long-fingered hands tantalizingly close to my girly parts.

I'd finally meet a fabulous man with impressive veterinary skills and I was dressed like an extra in *Flashdance*. "Oswald?"

"Yes?"

"Did we, you know . . ."

"Let's concentrate on your health now, why don't we?"

It would have been easy to lean forward and kiss him.

He asked, "How's your vision?"

I blinked and looked at the bindings on the bookshelves. I could read even the smallest print clearly. "Hard to tell with my contacts in, but it seems terrific."

"You don't wear contacts, Milagro."

I licked my finger and touched my eyeball to feel around for the lens. I poked a few more times until Oswald pulled my hand away.

"Did I get Lasik?" I asked.

Instead of answering, he went to the desk and began tapping away at a computer. "I've never dealt with memory loss."

"Can you tell when a chicken has memory loss? Regardless, I'm sure I'll remember every fascinating detail of my exciting life in a few minutes and you won't have to bother Mercedes."

Although I tried to relax and let my brain recover, I was distracted by Oswald. He had wonderful cheekbones, a clear, pale complexion, and a most intriguing, wide mouth. His chestnut brown hair was brushed back off his broad brow.

"I think you probably have transient global amnesia," he

said. "It doesn't happen often, and lasts about six hours on average."

"Six hours is a piece of cake," I said. "I once took mushrooms as research for a story about a shaman and I was hallucinating all weekend, which was altogether too long. So it's like that?"

"Except that you're not hallucinating and you might regain your lost time. If you were anyone else I'd recommend an EEG and a CT, but your body heals itself."

"No offense, but I really think you better stick to diagnosing animals. However, I'm willing to wait six hours." That meant that I could recover in time for weekend clubbing once I got back to the City. "You want to tell me how I got here?"

"I told you, you drove, but you can't drive back since you've had a period of unconsciousness. I hope Mercedes can pick you up, because you can't stay here."

I was glad I didn't kiss him. "Oswald, you're a little full of yourself, aren't you? As you may recall, I was trying to *leave* here, not stay. I have a busy social calendar filled with people far more scintillating than some random veterinary assistant."

"Yes, I know. There's always a party somewhere." He picked up his phone and made a call. In a second, he said, "Hi, Mercedes. It's Oswald. Sorry to call you this early." He paused. "She got here about an hour ago, and she can't stay under any circumstances."

He had a real attitude and I was relieved to learn that I hadn't spent the night with him.

"She fell and hit her head and may have some memory loss. Of course, there's the strong possibility that she's faking it."

"I'm not faking it," I said loudly so Mercedes could hear me.

Oswald said, "She says that the last thing she remembers is getting ready to go to that party for Sebastian Beckett-Witherspoon."

"My dear friend Sebastian!" I shouted.

Oswald shook his head and continued talking on the phone: "She's even lying about that jerk. Anyway, there are two kinds of amnesia. One is caused by a head injury and the other's more serious, caused by severe emotional distress, but disasters bounce off her like water off a duck, so—"

He stopped talking to listen to Mercedes, and I gazed out the window at a wisteria that was about to bloom. It must be wonderful to have so much space for gardening.

"What? Are you sure?" Oswald said and gave me a worried look. He listened longer, and I was sure she was telling him off for being so rude because he looked upset.

"Yes, of course," he said. "I'll do whatever is best for her."

He held the phone to me and said in a kinder tone, "Mercedes wants to talk to you."

His eyes glistened and he turned away. Mercedes could be stern, but he was a big baby.

I grabbed the phone and said, "Hey, sweetie pie, come get me!"

She said, "Are you faking this? Just say yes, and I won't tell Oswald."

"No, and I'm deeply crushed by your accusation, *mujer*. What kind of nitwit would fake amnesia? It's not as if I have a habit of crazy antics. I'm a serious and sincere woman." I glanced toward Oswald to see if he was convinced of my value as a human being and a potential girlfriend.

Mercedes said, "Milagro, I need you to stay where you are until you get better. Oswald will take care of you."

"I know you don't think that I work, but I have to go do a shift at the nursery. They're getting in a shipment of dahlia tubers and need me to do the bin display. There is, after all, the matter of paying my rent."

"I'll take care of those things. Stay there, promise me."

"You are making a big deal out of it. I feel perfectly fine. What day is it?"

"It's Saturday."

"Saturday! That means I've lost two whole days! The nursery may have fired me and that doesn't even begin to explain how or when I got Lasik."

"This is not the time to worry about those things. Now, if you really aren't faking this, Milagro—"

"Why doesn't anyone believe me?"

"Okay, I believe you. You need to stay there until you get your memory back. Oswald and his family will take care of you."

"I can call Nancy to come get me, or take the bus back to the City."

"No, you can't, Milagro. Try to listen to me for a minute. You're safe there. That's why you went to the ranch, because you needed a safe place to stay."

"You're leaving me in the hands of a veterinary tech?"

"He's a real doctor, Milagro," she said. "If you need to call me, use this line until we figure things out. Don't call any of your friends or leave the ranch."

"But—"

"Milagro, this is absolutely critical. Promise me. Either you stay where you are and do as Oswald says, or our friendship is over."

Mercedes didn't bullshit, and she was so serious that I said, "Okay. I'll wait to get my memory back. But I think you're over-reacting. Where *am* I exactly?"

She told me that I was just north of Nancy's favorite, over-priced wine country town. Well, I'd never had the opportunity to relax in the country before.

I handed the phone back to Oswald and he said good-bye to Mercedes and hung up. His expression was dolorous, I guess because he'd wanted to get rid of me.

"So I just came here this morning? You don't know where I was?"

"You were with Mercedes last night."

That was reassuring. I knew that nothing too crazy could have happened if Mercedes was with me. I yawned. "I could sleep like the dead."

"You can nap in your . . . we have a room with its own bath, if you don't mind."

"Why would I mind?"

Oswald led me to a room on a short hallway off the kitchen. It had a lumpy full-sized bed, an old wooden desk, and a bookshelf with paperbacks.

"You're sticking the Mexican girl in the maid's room," I said.

"You like this room because it faces out to the garden," he said, and, indeed, the view out the window of the garden was charming except for a dead mock-orange.

"You need to pull out that bush," I said. "This climate is far too cold for it anyway."

I peered into a white-tiled bathroom with a claw-foot tub and said, "Sweet."

Then I caught sight of someone's awful reflection in the mirror. Her cheeks were sunken, her eyes dull and hollow, her skin sallow, and her hair was several inches longer than mine. I stared until I realized the person in the mirror was me.

Oswald came close and said, "Milagro."

I turned to him and cried, "What day of the month is it? What year?"

When he told me, I turned to the wall and said, "No, no."

Oswald's arms were around me, and he pulled me to him while I said, "No, no."

"It's temporary. You'll get your memory back. I'm calling a professional to help." His lips grazed my forehead in a gentle kiss. "You'll get better soon. You always do. Come rest now."

He helped me to the bed and pulled off my stupid shoes. Then he covered me with a comforter and stayed sitting beside me. I kept saying, "No, no," and crying while he rubbed my back and said, "It will be all right, Mil."

"What happened to me?" I asked. "Why do I look this way?"

"You're stressed out. Go to sleep. You'll be well again soon, I promise."

I stared at him, waiting for recognition to come. "Oswald, how do I know you?"

He hesitated for a few seconds, and then he said, "You were the gardener here."

eleven

Countrycide

When I awoke, I looked at the clock by the bed. It was almost four o'clock in the afternoon, and I still didn't remember this place or Oswald. He'd said that this kind of amnesia lasted an *average* of six hours. I'd paid enough attention in my math course at F.U. to know that the median was more important than the average.

Something terrible had happened to me to make me look like I did. Or maybe not. Maybe it was just a wild week, or I'd finally gotten the flu or had contracted a slight case of Mad Cow. I hoped it wasn't the latter because I could hear my mother Regina's comments now.

I got up and put on the ill-fitting pointy booties. Had I lost all my fantastic fashion sense in the intervening two years? What else had happened in my life?

In the bathroom, I found a hairbrush, a new toothbrush, and toothpaste. I forced myself to look in the mirror. Oswald was quite dishy, and I looked hideous.

I tilted my head forward until it touched the cool glass of the mirror. *Don't panic,* I thought.

I went to the window and looked out. The garden had so

many of my signature touches, including Kathleen hybrid musk roses, that I should have known it was mine immediately. Oh, I'd made an herb knot just like I'd always wanted to! This was the bright side.

I walked to the kitchen and called, "Hellooo?"

There was a glass pitcher on the table with red liquid. Just looking at it made my stomach spasm with want. I got a tumbler, served myself, and took a sip. It was a tasty fruit juice, heavy on the raspberries. I gulped it down and had another glass.

I wandered through the house to the study.

Oswald was on the phone and when he saw me, he said, "I'll get back to you when I learn more. Yes. Bye."

"Hey, Oswald."

"Hello," he said, rather flirt-deficient.

"I haven't remembered anything yet. What exactly is the range of time for this kind of memory loss?"

He hesitated for worrisome seconds. "At first I thought that you had transient global amnesia, but it's possible that you have dissociative amnesia as a result of emotional trauma."

"I'm badly dressed, but not traumatized. Why have you abandoned the injury theory so quickly?" I felt the back of my head again. "I could have internal hemorrhaging, or maybe a weevil is eating its way through my brain."

"If you had taken any serious courses in college, you wouldn't be bringing up brain-eating weevil theories."

"Spoken like someone who couldn't get past the first chapter of Henry James's *The Art of the Novel*," I snipped. "What happened to your bedside manner?"

"I'm sorry, Mil. I'm under some pressure today, and I'm having a problem handling this."

"Apology accepted. So what's stressing you out?"

"Besides your condition? My grandfather is visiting. He's out sightseeing now," he said. "But don't worry about that. I got in touch with a psychiatrist through a, um, professional association. She was visiting her folks in Seattle and hopped on the first flight down. She'll be here soon."

"That's swell, but I'm sure I'll be fine before happy hour at the closest watering hole. I certainly don't need therapy. I'm an exceptionally well-balanced individual."

Oswald raised his eyebrows.

"I am *so* well-balanced," I said. "How traumatized could I be, anyway? Was I devastated by rejection letters from agents, or did I get evicted from my subterranean hovel, which wouldn't matter since I suspect that there are rats in the walls?"

"No, you didn't get evicted," Oswald said. "You own a loft."

"What!"

"You bought it with a legal settlement you got."

"That's amazing! Have I published anything?"

"Yes, you ghostwrote a memoir that became a bestseller, and Mercedes told me that you've got a commission to write the follow-up book."

"You're kidding!" I laughed with delight. "What else has happened? I expanded my gardening business this far. Do I have more clients out here?"

Oswald hesitated and then said, "Yes, you gardened here. There's something else, though. We dated for a while."

When I recalled his earlier standoffishness I said, "I gather it didn't end well."

He looked as if he was being forced to confess to an abominable crime. "We didn't just date, Milagro," he said. "We were engaged and you lived here."

I stared at the stranger, waiting for memories to come back to me. "I don't think so."

Oswald opened one of the desk drawers and rummaged

beneath notepads and folders. He lifted out a framed photo and said, "Look."

I took the frame from him and saw a picture of Oswald and me. His arm was around me and I was leaning in toward him. We were standing under a grape-covered pergola by a white stucco building. My left hand was on his chest and I was wearing a shiny ring. We were laughing.

A strange feeling rose in me and I shoved it back down.

Oswald said, "That's the winery where we were going to have our wedding."

"What happened to us?" I asked, as incurious as I would be if someone was telling me about a movie he'd seen.

Oswald pressed his lips together and then said quietly, "We just couldn't manage to work things out. There's another thing. You got a *condition* from me. It's a rare family thing. It makes you crave red foods and that's why your eyesight is good."

"The buzz I feel when I touch someone's skin? Did you give that to me?"

"Not me, but it's an ancilliary trait. You're stronger, too, and you have faster reactions. You heal easily from cuts and injuries, but you're not a carrier of the condition."

"So I'm like a superhero?" I said with excitement.

He laughed a little, a nice, warm laugh. "No, you're not a superhero."

I thought he had a narrow definition of superhero. "It sounds as if my life is fabulous. I certainly haven't suffered any trauma except that I look as if I've been really sick or starving myself."

Oswald's brow wrinkled and he came close to me. "You *have* suffered trauma. Your latest boyfriend, Wilcox Spiggott—"

"How cool to date someone called Wilcox!" I said. "Wil-cox."

"Someone murdered him and left his body at your loft."

A shiver went down my spine. "Did I . . . was it me . . . was I the one?"

"You told Mercedes you didn't and she believes you, which is good enough for me."

"What happened then?"

"You took his body and got out of there. That was about nine days ago. You showed up last night back in the City."

"Was I in love with Wilcox?" I asked. "I'm sorry. That was a thoughtless question."

"It's okay." Oswald ran his hand through his thick brown hair. "Mercedes said you liked him a lot. That he sounded . . . fun. A fun guy interested in progressive politics."

A fun guy named Wilcox Spiggott had been left dead in my loft. "It seems wrong, to have someone die and not remember him," I said. "That's the least we can do for those we care for, those we love, to keep them alive in our thoughts."

"I'm sorry about your friend, Milagro."

"Thank you, Oswald. Did you know him?"

He shook his head.

"What did I do with his body?"

"You told Mercedes you had it, but I didn't see it. You just showed up here out of the blue looking crazier than usual."

"Where was I during the time *after* I found his body and *before* I got here?"

A buzzer sounded, and Oswald said, "We can talk about that later. That must be the psychiatrist."

"I don't need a psychiatrist. We need to go to the police."

"We *can't* go to the police because of complications," he said. "Who's seen the body? You and the killer. Whoever set you up is probably looking for you and is willing to murder your friends. That's why Mercedes made you promise to stay here."

"I don't understand any of this—secret enemies, misplaced

corpses, superhero powers." So I started shouting, "Wake up, wake up, wake up!" and then I slapped myself in the face.

"Stop that. You're already awake," Oswald said. "You'll understand when your memory comes back and then we'll figure out things. Now I've got to get the gate."

He stood up and I followed him to the hallway, where he grabbed a hat. He said, "My family is sun-sensitive, but you're not."

"I've always tanned beautifully," I said. "I'm not paying for a psychiatric visit that I didn't request."

"It's taken care of. The most important thing is for you to get well."

I went with him outside. "Why are you doing this for me, Oswald? Did we stay friends after we broke up?"

He stopped and gazed into my eyes. "It was too hard to stay friends, but I've never stopped caring for you, Milagro. I've never stopped worrying about you." Then he continued walking to the gate.

I couldn't help but notice Oswald's nice butt in his faded jeans. I'd seen that butt without jeans, and yet, alas, it was to me as a stranger's butt. Oswald was what I'd always dreamed about in a man, wasn't he? Someone serious and accomplished and sexy, and I wouldn't have gotten engaged to him unless I loved him. Shouldn't I feel *something* besides lust?

I walked in my stupid pointy booties to the stupid truckasaurus. Looking through the window, I saw a bulky sports bag. I opened the truck door and pulled at the strap of the large bag, lifting it effortlessly.

At the end of the lane, Oswald opened the gate and a new white Prius drove in and stopped. The driver was talking to him.

I took the sports bag inside to the maid's room and unzipped it, curious to find clues about my life. I unpacked jeans, T-shirts, sweaters, and tennis shoes. Beneath these were lacy and silky things—sexy bras and panties more expensive than anything I'd ever owned. A black and turquoise polka-dot vinyl bag contained high-end cosmetics and toiletries. I'd awoken in a much improved economic bracket.

Several composition books were bound by a large rubber band. I opened the top one and a slip of paper fell out. The upper- and lowercase alphabet was written on it, along with basic words.

The first pages of the notebook contained an outline for a metaphysical story based upon Shakespeare's plays, all done in the same handwriting, but with a different pen. I must have been using my talent for forgery on the ghostwriting project.

I spotted a red velvet cloth covering something. When I unwrapped it, I saw three pressboard books. The volumes were the first edition of *Jane Eyre*. It seemed incredible that I could have something this rare and valuable. I opened the pages and inhaled the scent of the paper.

The next finds were even more puzzling: a tangle of black velvet ropes with padded straps and an incomplete knitting project, a blue-gray scarf.

The last item was a leather case. I opened it, expecting to see my costume jewelry, and saw instead *real* jewelry, mostly exquisite antique gold pieces with rubies and garnets. There were also elegant enamel fountain pens, a delicate engraved gold pocketknife, pretty old postcards, tiny carved stone animals, and amusing plastic mirror ball earrings.

Had Oswald or Wilcox given them to me? I took the books, the velvet ropes, and the jewelry, and hid them in the corner of the closet, behind a box of old shoes.

As I changed into the clothes in the sports bag, I examined my body. I was gaunt, but otherwise healthy enough. The only thing I didn't recognize was a pale pink scar on the inside of my arm. Perhaps it was from a gardening accident.

The cups of the periwinkle satin bra were loose, as were the jeans, but the slip-on flats and T-shirt fit okay. I spackled concealer to hide the dark circles under my eyes and blush to make me less corpse-like.

I found Oswald in the study with a pretty woman wearing a leaf green cotton dress and a bold necklace of purple glass beads. She had a wonderful tumble of black curls, contrasting with her ivory skin, and she managed to be both slim and voluptuous, which seemed unfair to the rest of womanhood.

She smiled when she saw me and said, "You must be Milagro." When she stood to shake my hand in both of hers, she was a few inches taller than me. Her eyes were green-hazel and angled up at the corners, making her look as if she was smiling even when she wasn't.

"I'm Dr. Lily Harrison, but you can call me Lily. It's such a pleasure to meet you, Milagro. I've heard so much about you."

No one had heard about me, but I said, "Very nice of you to come, but I'm sure I'll regain my memory toot sweet. My gray matter is usually quite reliable."

Lily looked at Oswald and said, "If Milagro and I could talk alone, please."

He left us, closing the door behind him.

"Let's sit, Milagro." When I joined her on the leather sofa, she said, "People don't recover quickly from disassociative amnesia, DA, and you're an unusual case anyway."

"I'm really just a normal *chica*," I said. "I feel fine."

"DA is your brain's way of protecting you from painful memories."

"Not to state the obvious, but someone died," I said. "Also, I conked my head hard enough to knock myself out. Oswald, while decidedly fab, is being very dismissive of my physical injury."

So was she. "Incidents of DA are extremely rare, Milagro, but people who get it usually share one thing, an abused childhood."

"That's not me. I wasn't abused."

"What about your mother?"

"My mother Regina never even raised her voice to me."

"I had conversations with Mercedes, Oswald, and his family on my drive from the airport. Everyone's on the same page about your mother. They say that her neglect was criminal, and your father did nothing to intervene. You could have died on many occasions."

"But I *didn't*," I said. "It wasn't as if my mother Regina ran after me with a butcher knife screaming."

"She left you in a shopping mall."

"My mother Regina was very busy that day."

"She gave you spoiled meat."

"My mother Regina wasn't interested in food, so she didn't pay attention to those things."

"She let you play alone in a pool when you were a toddler who couldn't swim."

"I didn't drown, did I? The water, the water . . ." There was something about water that I didn't want to think about.

"You were having so many 'accidents' that your grandmother took custody of you before you were three. When she died and your mother had to take you back, she locked you in your room after school and on weekends."

"It was a treat to have time alone with my books. It's one of the reasons I excelled academically. So you see, it all worked out for the best."

"You can't even call her 'my mother' or 'mom.' Can't you see that you were as abused, if not more so, than a child who is beaten?"

I smiled patiently and said, "No one has a perfect childhood, but I'm absolutely fine. I went on to a fabulous university. I own property, a loft in fact."

"You were on the verge of being kicked out of your apartment before you met Oswald."

"I have fabulous friends and date fabulous men."

"Your friend Nancy didn't invite you to be part of her wedding because you couldn't get along with her husband. As for men, you use your sexuality to get the attention you needed as a child, but you can't sustain a relationship with any man. The last one was murdered."

"I realize that looks bad, but it was an individual incident. I have a fabulous career as a ghostwriter."

"I did some research, Milagro. You haven't published anything of your own. The only recognition you've ever gotten was winning a regional contest for a horror story about a llama."

"It wasn't a llama; it was *La Llorona*, the terrifying weeping woman of Latin American folklore," I said. One stupid typo—hitting the "replace" button on a spell-check program—had defined my entire literary career. "Lily, I appreciate your eagerness to help, but your profession always assumes that everyone is damaged in some way. I prefer to assume the best about life and people, including myself."

"Milagro, you're in complete denial about your current situation and your life. You don't realize it, but you're screaming in pain, and I'm here to help you heal and become whole. Won't you please work with me?"

Lily looked so earnest, and I had nothing better to do until my memory returned, so I said, "If it would make you happy, of course I'll work with you."

twelve

Headshrinkers, Blood Drinkers, Mental Blinkers

As a general rule, when you can't remember where you left a corpse, you have to accept that maybe you could have done some things a little better.

So I really tried to listen when Lily yammered about integrating my inner child with something or other. I nodded my head a lot while admiring her necklace and noticing that my fingernails looked terrible even for a gardener.

When Lily called Oswald back to the study, she looked as happy as a kleptomaniac who's found an unsupervised perfume counter. She said, "We're in agreement now about the need for therapy."

I wanted to be proactive so I said, "Give me a quick synopsis of everything that's happened in the last two years and then we can go after the dirty bastard who killed Wilcox."

"That's Milagro all over," Oswald said to Lily. "She rushes into situations."

Lily looked sympathetic to my goals. "Milagro, your mind

is fragile now. You're going to go through a process of evolving like—"

"Like a butterfly from a chrysalis?"

She tipped her head. "I was thinking more of a frog from a tadpole."

"Not as appealing," I said.

"Use whatever image you like," she said with a patient smile. "Oswald and Mercedes have agreed not to overwhelm you with information when you don't have your own perspective on your recent history."

"Okay."

Oswald looked concerned and said to Lily, "Usually she's *much* too curious."

Lily smiled at me but spoke to Oswald. "Milagro's lack of curiosity is a symptom of her illness. Her inquisitiveness will return when she's feeling more secure."

Oswald nodded and said to me, "Mercedes and I have talked to my cousin, Gabriel, who's a security specialist. He'll investigate Wilcox's murder. You should sleep now. It can be the best short-term restorative and, who knows, you might wake up with your memory."

I felt the need for comfort so I reached out to take his hand, but Lily shook her head. "No skin-on-skin contact, Milagro. It will just be more confusing until you're better. Let me walk you to your room."

We went to the maid's room, and I sat down on the bed and said, "Lily, what is this *condition* that Oswald told me I have?"

"It's a genetic autosomal recessive anomaly. You're the only person I've ever met who didn't inherit it. It's extremely rare and not in the books."

"*Everything* is in some book."

"I have the condition, too. It's specific to people descended from a few villages in Eastern Europe." She sighed. "It makes life complicated."

"Life is always complicated. So I was engaged to Oswald? I have a friend named Nancy who's sure I'd get married in a night-club to someone without a legitimate job who spends all his time partying. I can't wait to tell her 'I told you so.'"

"But you and Oswald broke up. We can discuss your relation-ships later," she said. "Now try to rest."

Sleep knocked me out like an anvil on the head of an unsus-pecting coyote. I woke up on my back, with my mouth open and dry. I sat up quickly, listening to see if anyone was near.

The room was dark, but I could see everything perfectly, which was extremely weird and yet fantastic. The red numbers of the clock radio glowed 4:47 a.m. and the house was quiet.

I was hungry in an unusual, painful way. I went through the dark to the kitchen, hoping the refrigerator wasn't as bare as that of most bachelors. I opened the door and saw high-end food-stuffs: gourmet pasta and grain salads, imported cheeses, roast turkey, exotic condiments, juices and wines, perfect fruits and vegetables . . .

And steaks. There were six New York strips in the meat bin, brazen in their tight plastic wrapping, enticing me with bright ruby juices. So this is what Oswald meant when he said I craved red foods.

Since I'd missed dinner I didn't think he'd mind if I grilled one up. I took a skillet from the pot rack and put it on the six-burner range. My cooking skills were limited, but even I should be able to cook a steak.

I was about to drop a New York strip in the hot skillet when I got the urge to smell it to see if it was fresh. It smelled delish. Then I thought that giving it a lick would be no worse than eat-ing steak tartar, and then I thought that cooking the excellent beef would compromise it, so I began gnawing and sucking on the raw flesh.

The salty, rich juices were so delicious that I moved on to the next steak. It was only after I'd finished my invigorating snack that I realized that Oswald might not appreciate me raiding his fridge. As I was hiding the chewed-up gray steaks in the trash, I heard footsteps behind me. Without thinking, I grabbed a knife from the sink and turned around.

A silver-haired man in striped cotton pajamas and a white terry robe clicked on the overhead light and looked startled. "Good evening, or rather, good morning." He looked like an older, slightly shorter version of Oswald, but with blue eyes and features sharpened by age.

I dropped the knife in the sink and said, "Hi." I resisted the urge to glance down and see if I had any spots of blood on my clothes. "I'm sorry, but I can't recall if we've met."

"I'm Oswald's grandfather, Allan George Grant, AG. You must be Milagro."

"I am. Hi, Mr. Grant."

He went to a cupboard and pulled out a bottle of scotch. "I can't sleep. Would you like a drink?"

"Sure, thanks." I spotted a shelf of glasses and took two tumblers down.

"Let's go to the lounge." He began leading the way and said, "We haven't met, but I've heard about you. My grandson says you have amnesia and don't remember the last few years."

"I thought it was simple amnesia and I'd be over it by now, but everyone thinks I'm traumatized." The blood snack had filled me with warmth and I felt the very opposite of traumatized. "I'm sorry to impose on your family."

"No imposition for me," Mr. Grant said as we went to the living room I'd seen earlier. He searched for a light switch; I saw one and turned on a lamp with a mica shade, which cast an amber glow on the cream walls and Mission-style furniture. "I wish it was under more providential circumstances."

"My policy is always to make the best of a situation." I placed the glasses on a cocktail table and Mr. Grant poured the scotch.

He lifted his glass and said, "To our friendship," and we toasted, then sat down in comfy club chairs.

I ran my hand on the butter-soft leather of the chair. The room was attractive, but nothing seemed familiar and there were no traces of me in the room. I asked, "Are you and Oswald close?"

"Not yet, but I hope we will be. I got here a few days ago. This is my first visit to his ranch," he said, and smiled as he shook his head. "Does that seem odd?"

"No, but I haven't seen my parents in . . . I really don't know, but I think it's years now."

"Every family has its problems. Oswald's grandmother and I divorced long ago, and I moved away. Unfortunately, that means I only see my grandsons on their rare visits."

"Exes can be a problem," I said, thinking, *Especially when you find them dead in your loft.* "Did you remarry?"

He raised his eyebrow. "Once bitten, twice shy."

"That's where we're different. I don't mind being bitten, as long as I get to bite back."

He laughed and said, "Maybe it has to do with who does the biting. I think that there are some people who are so extraordinary that they overwhelm you. If you lose them, you can go on to other relationships, but you'll never fully recover and you'll always regret not doing absolutely everything and anything to keep them."

Was Oswald one of those people to me? I asked, "Where do you live now?"

"A place called Peggys Cove, no apostrophe, near Halifax. It's foggy, but I like that."

"I adore fog. Where did the name come from?"

We'd finished our scotch, but I didn't feel the slightest effect.

Mr. Grant picked up the bottle and poured another glass for each of us. "There are lots of different stories, but all agree that Peggy was the only survivor of a wreck at sea during a ferocious sleet storm. When she was found, she didn't know who she was, and the family who took her in named her Peggy."

"That's a wonderful story," I said. "I wonder what the chances are of having a place named after me. Milagroville. Milagroberg. Milagrocita. None of those sounds quite right."

He chuckled in that charming way that silver foxes do, as if you've said something terribly clever. "With you, I'd say they're much better than average. My grandson wasn't expecting you, but I'm glad you're here. I was quite curious about you."

"Did you hear good things about me, or bad things?"

"Interesting things. I did hear that you were very pretty, and you are."

"That's sweet, but you don't have to lie. It's not as if I'm a vampire and can't see my own reflection in a mirror. I've never looked more hideous."

"But you *are* pretty. Very pretty. Of course you'd have to be for Oswald, because beauty is his business."

"I thought he was a doctor."

"Yes, and he went on to become a plastic surgeon. Didn't he tell you?"

"There was a lot of material to cover." I never imagined myself with a plastic surgeon. I bobbed in my seat to see if everything jiggled the way it was supposed to. When Mr. Grant stared at me, I kept bobbing up and down and began humming. "Ever get a song stuck in your head?" I said. "What inspired you to visit here?"

Mr. Grant considered for a moment before saying, "Since you and Oswald broke up, he's wanted more grandfatherly guidance. I could understand what he was going through since I lost the only woman I ever loved, the woman who gave me wonderful children and carried on the family line."

"That's so romantic and tragic," I said. "A love that dare not bite again."

Someone behind me cleared her throat. "Well, AG, I see you've made friends with the Young Lady."

In the doorway was a petite older woman dressed in elegant sea blue satin lounging pajamas with a matching robe and sleek brown leather slippers. Her shining silver hair was cut close to her elegant noggin, and she turned her luminous, exotic green eyes toward me.

"Hello, Milagro. My grandson tells me that you claimed to be transporting a dead body in a pickup, on the run from unknown assailants, and that you've conveniently acquired amnesia."

She was the sort of woman who enjoyed intimidating others, so I looked sincere and said, "That story does sound implausible, but I'll work on a few subplots to fill it out so that there's sufficient foreshadowing and a reasonable justification."

"That's the spirit, Young Lady." And then her bravado was gone and she turned away.

AG stood and said, "Edna, are you all right?"

"I just need a moment."

I jumped up and went to her. "Can I do anything?"

She produced a handkerchief from her pocket and dabbed at her eyes. "Yes, give me a hug."

"But Lily said I was to avoid flesh-on-flesh contact."

"Good God, you always make everything sound sordid," the woman said, giving me a look that would have seared a T-bone in seconds. "Are you going to listen to her or me?"

I put my arms around the woman and felt her soft cheek against mine. She smelled marvelous, like the scent released by lemon verbena in a spring shower, and I got a comforting zizz from her. She drew in a ragged breath and I patted her on the back and said, "I wish I wasn't making everybody miserable."

"That's always been your way, Young Lady, leaving a wake of destruction in your rush to the next party or attractive man," she said, and then we both started laughing.

"That sounds like someone I know," said Mr. Grant dryly. "I think I'll go back to bed. Good night, Edna, Milagro."

When he left the room, the woman stepped back and looked at me, and I looked at her.

I said, "You do know me, right?"

"Much to my eternal regret. I'm Edna Grant, Oswald's grandmother. Your new friend, AG, is my ex-husband. They told me you were in bad shape."

"I am. I've wasted away." I held my arms out. "Can't you see how emaciated I am?"

"Your emaciated is another woman's normal. You look fine."

"Perhaps we have different standards," I said. "I don't hold to the unrealistic, airbrushed consumer-media ideals. I think feminine curves are delightful."

"Traumatized or not, you are as full of nonsense as ever. Let's go for a walk."

I looked to the window and could see dawn edging in past the espresso brown velvet drapes. "What if someone attacks me outside?"

"Fight him off."

"Because I'm like a superhero now, right?"

"No," she said. "There are private security guards stationed outside the gate, and you're also protected by our family."

"Family like family, or family like the mob?"

"The mob? I'm sure that would appeal to your absurd fantasies."

"I don't have absurd fantasies, but I don't expect those who are more prosaic to comprehend my vibrant inner life." I followed her through the kitchen to the mudroom, where Mrs. Grant plucked a wide-brimmed straw hat from a hook and put it on.

"The sun's not even out," I said.

"I'm sun-sensitive and you should protect your skin, too, so you won't grow to look like a worn-out easy chair."

"Your concern is deeply moving."

The sky was lightening along the edges of the mountains in the distance, and the air carried the heady perfume of all the antique roses, strongest in the morning dew.

A pair of red-handled Felco pruners had been left on the ground. I picked them up and wiped them clean on my jeans. I walked to a fragrant climbing rose, Madame Alfred Carriere in spectacular bloom, the snowy imbricated petals almost glowing in the predawn shadows.

I said, "It was quite astonishing to find out that I was engaged to Oswald."

"I know I was astonished when it happened."

"Did you object to my engagement to your grandson?"

"You managed to wreck that all on your own. I'm having a very difficult time believing that you actually have amnesia."

I snipped dead flowers off the rosebush. "I didn't believe it either until I saw myself in a mirror. My hair hasn't been this long since I lived with my grandmother," I said. "My mother Regina didn't like dealing with it so she'd take me to have it hacked off every four months. I looked like a boy."

"And you've been compensating for your gender confusion ever since," Edna snarked.

I cut off a flower and stuck it in my hair. "Do you think so?"

"Consult your psychiatrist."

"Let's walk around and see what's here. I want to test my superpowers, too. Tell me if you see a fly so I can try to snatch it out of the air."

"You don't have any superpowers." We walked across the field toward the white cottage.

"Who lives there? It's darling."

"I do for now. It's the guesthouse." Then she said, "You and Oswald lived in it for a while. You called it the Love Shack."

It hit me then, what I had lost: happiness with a fabulous man, a home, family. I shook off these thoughts and pointed to two structures down the drive from the house. "What are they?"

"One's the swimming pool compound and the other is the barn. Even with memory loss, you should know what a barn looks like. Heaven knows, you bored me enough nattering on about Faulkner and 'Barn Burning.'"

"Mrs. Grant, treat me any way you wish, but I will not hear you disparage William Faulkner. In fact, I think we should discuss his short stories as we traipse around the fields."

"Please God, no," she said, but the corners of her mouth lifted slightly.

"I wish I was from the South so that I could write Southern Gothic stories. You really can't do California Gothic. What would that be?" I mused. "Depravity and criminality in the desert set to an Eagles soundtrack? It's nothing that would work in this day and age. It would become some inane comedy with movie stars and margaritas and alien abductions."

I waited for Mrs. Grant's retort, but she didn't say anything. A fly buzzed by and I reached out and grabbed it. "See, I did it!"

"Add that skill to your résumé."

I opened my hand and released the insect. "I wonder if I have telekinetic powers."

"Why don't you try lifting your feet off the ground so we can continue our walk?" She turned down a path through newly planted crepe myrtles toward the closer building. It was lined with a new grove of crepe myrtle. "We like to come here at night, especially when it's hot in the summer."

She stood expectantly at the doors to the redwood structure, and so I opened them for her. As she walked inside, I saw a large swimming pool surrounded by an expansive patio and outdoor furniture. The surface of the water was as smooth as ice.

My heart thudded and I stepped back, feeling something pressing down on me like an incubus, sucking the breath out of my lungs.

Mrs. Grant said, "If you want to take a dip, the swimsuits are still in the . . ." Then she looked around to see me standing back at the door. "What is it?"

"I don't know. I just . . . I'm feeling claustrophobic." I rushed outside and bent over, my hands on my thighs. I tried to stop from shaking, and the breeze chilled the sweat on my forehead.

Mrs. Grant came out and watched me as I thought, *It's something about the water*, but I didn't want to know. When I stood up, she put her arm through mine and said, "Let's keep walking."

We went by the barn and she pointed out the porch on one side. "Ernesto has an apartment there. He's the ranch hand and our friend. Your friend, too, and we explained what happened to you," she said. "Mercedes used to like coming here to ride and swim."

I grinned. "So I was able to help give her some time off from work! That's great."

"As shocking as it seems, Young Lady, Mercedes thrives on work, just as my grandson does."

Mrs. Grant took me on a loop through the property, pointing out a shallow creek with gray stones, which I could look at without reacting, and the corrals for the horses, which she called turnouts.

We walked to the far side of the fields and she said, "By that fence is a pond where you planted native wetland grasses, but we don't have to go there."

I noticed a mound of soil that was marked with a boulder and a green oval of rosemary. "This looks like a grave."

"Your dog is buried there. Her name was Daisy. You have another dog now, Rosemary. Mercedes has him at her club, and your chicken, Petunia, is living in the coop by the barn."

"I finally get pets and I can't remember them. I can't remember Wilcox either." I bent to pull weeds from the grave. "Faulkner said, 'The past is never dead. It's not even past,' but I don't think he took amnesia into the equation. How can I feel sorrow for those I can't recall?"

"You will, Young Lady. Now let's go make breakfast."

I walked with Mrs. Grant back to the white cottage, the Love Shack, so she could change out of her pajamas. The interior was a surprisingly modern white and blue scheme. I thought it was sad that she had a framed photo of Thomas Cook, the gorgeous movie star, on a sideboard. I'd had a major crush on him when I was a teenager, but I got over it.

Once we were back at Oswald's house and in the kitchen, Mrs. Grant said, "I'll whip up a cold berry soup with crème fraîche, and we can have omelets with red peppers and wild mushrooms."

"Sounds yummy. What can I do?"

"Why don't you make your lemon-almond pancakes?"

I looked around the shelves until I found flour, sugar, lemons, almonds, eggs, and a bowl. I grabbed baking powder and baking soda, too. I figured two cups of flour per person should be sufficient, so I measured this into the bowl.

Mrs. Grant glanced over and said, "You have no idea what you're doing, do you?"

"No, but maybe if I go through the motions, it will come back. Sense memory. I'm guessing that I must have learned how to cook."

"You did, but maybe you should just make the coffee this morning."

"No problem!" I looked on the counter and spotted an intimidating chrome espresso maker. I approached it and began waggling the handles.

Mrs. Grant sighed. "There's a drip coffee machine in the cupboard to the right of the sink. You can grind beans, can't you?"

"Yes, I can grind coffee beans on my own," I said, and I had an odd sense of almost remembering something. And then it was gone.

Oswald came for breakfast, looking extremely man-pretty in faded jeans and a navy T-shirt under an old cotton flannel shirt. He gave Mrs. Grant a kiss on her pale cheek. "Morning, Grandmama."

"Hello, dear."

"Morning, Milagro," he said. "How's your memory?"

"Happily vacationing elsewhere," I said. "Perhaps it will send a postcard saying 'Wish you were here.'"

"I'll keep checking the mailbox." His crooked smile was more charming every time I saw it. He said, "How do you feel otherwise?"

"Fine, although I still have a sense of unreality. I'm sure the French would have a term for it, because they're so good at phrases for elusive feelings. *Esprit d'*ookiness, or in Spanish, *espíritu de* ookiness."

Lily came into the kitchen, wearing a cornflower blue linen

dress and carrying a huge shopping bag. "Morning!" she said cheerily.

Oswald grinned. "Hi, Lily. Did you sleep well?"

"Yes, my room is as comfortable as a luxury hotel." She looked at me and said, "How's our patient?"

"Incapable of making pancakes," I said, "but able to grab insects out of the air."

She looked a little confused, but smiled and held out the shopping bag, showing a jangle of gold bracelets on her wrist and gold and amethyst rings on her slim fingers. "I picked up some things for you at the spa in town."

"How sweet!" I took the bag, then glanced down and saw dun-colored material.

"They're your new outfits," Lily said. "It's part of your therapy. Let's go to your room and you can change."

As we went together to the maid's room, Lily said, "Oswald explained that you find dressing appropriately challenging, so I thought we could eliminate that one area of worry and discomfort for you."

I placed the bag on the bed, already worried and discomforted about what I would find. My dread was justified. There were four identical pairs of beige drawstring pants and four shapeless beige, round-necked smocks. "These are . . ."

"Organic undyed cotton and hemp," Lily said. "You'll feel so relaxed in them."

At the bottom of the bag were several pairs of beige granny panties, baggy beige socks, beige stretch bras, and thin beige gloves. The *pièce de* repugnance was a collection of beige scrunchies.

"Those are yoga bras, so they're not constricting," Lily said. "We need to break down your artifice, so you'll be more in harmony with the natural world around you."

"I'm a gardener. I'm always in harmony with the natural world."

"Milagro, since drug therapies would have no effect on you, I thought we would go this route."

"How do you know? You haven't even tried giving me drugs!" But I remembered how I hadn't felt the scotch.

"It's part of your particular condition," she said. "No makeup, no jewelry, and I'd like you to wear gloves around others, so you don't revert to your pattern of presenting your sexuality to divert from meaningful interactions. If you pull your hair back, you won't be prone to some of your flirtatious gestures."

I stared at her in astonishment. "You're wearing mascara and lip gloss and a pretty dress and you've got a darling 'do!"

"I'd like you to stop and think before automatically comparing yourself to other women."

I regretted telling Lily that I'd go along with her therapy. "Sure, fine, whatever."

Lily smiled brightly and said, "Change your clothes, and I'll see you at breakfast."

It was with a heavy heart that I put on the dismal clothes. The bra smooshed my bozooms like overly ripe fruit, and the granny panties left significant, visible lines. But when I went to the mirror to see the totality of the horror, I was stunned.

My eyes shone and my complexion was bright. My hair was shiny and healthy. How had this happened when yesterday I'd looked like a cadaver?

I French-braided my hair and put on a heinous scrunchie. I dabbed on clear lip gloss and a little mascara and brushed on a hint of blush, since it would be a crime to waste my newly stunning cheekbones.

When I went back to the kitchen, Mr. Grant had come downstairs. Everyone turned to look at me.

"Oh, good grief," Mrs. Grant said with a roll of her eyes that was so extravagant that I knew I had to practice eye-rolling later.

I smiled serenely and said, "I find this clothing very liberating, very freeing, very evolved. Thank you, Lily, for this thoughtful gift."

We sat at the long trestle table. The delicious food and vase of bright flowers were in striking contrast to the ramen and tortilla-based meals I subsisted on in my crappy basement apartment.

AG smiled at his ex-wife. "This is delicious, Edna. I wish you cooked when we were married." He looked at the rest of us and said, "All she could do was mix Manhattans and set out bowls of cashews."

Mrs. Grant narrowed her green eyes at him. "That was a long time ago. I *did* raise children, AG."

Oswald looked at his grandparents, shook his head, then turned to me. "Milagro, we've got a call scheduled with Mercedes and my cousin, Gabriel, in half an hour."

Lily said, "And after that we'll have a session. It will be a real treat getting into your mind."

Mrs. Grant *hmmph*ed and said to Lily, "Your optimism is sadly misplaced. Milagro's mind is like quicksand: the harder you struggle to escape, the deeper she'll drag you in."

"Grandmama," Oswald said at the same time that AG said "Edna."

Lily looked surprised and turned to the older woman. "Let's not discourage the recovery process. Milagro is in a very vulnerable place right now."

"The Young Lady is about as vulnerable as a crocodile in a bunny hutch," said Mrs. Grant. "I warn people, but they keep hopping within range of her jaws." She got up and put her dishes in the dishwasher.

AG said, "Edna, I thought we could drive over the mountain and do a little sightseeing."

She gave him a look that wasn't encouraging, but it wasn't discouraging either. "All right, AG," she said, and they left the kitchen to head toward her cottage.

When Oswald ran down to the barn to talk to his ranch hand, Lily and I cleared the dishes. She said, "I hope you won't let Mrs. Grant's attitude bother you."

I thought Mrs. Grant's pointed remarks were as delightful as the stunning red barbs of the Wingthorn rose, but I tried to look wounded. "I'll try not to, Lily. Thank you for your support and sympathy."

When Oswald returned from the barn, his jeans were a little dusty and he had a strand of hay stuck to his shirt. The golden filament against the dark navy fabric disturbed me, and I was going to dust it off, but Lily was watching, so I just followed him to the study for our phone call.

"Come sit close," he said as he made the call.

I took the chair near the desk and, after a few clicks, I heard Mercedes say, "I'm here with Gabriel."

"Hey, girlfriend," I said.

"This is Gabriel," said a man's voice. "Milagro, how are you doing?"

I reached over and brushed the hay strand from Oswald's shirt. "I'm absolutely fine."

Oswald glanced at me. "She looks much healthier today, but she still can't remember anything. Lily Harrison is having a session with her later. We'll see how that goes."

The man, Gabriel, said, "Mercedes has updated me on everything she knows and I've contacted the Council."

"What's that? Or who—if it's *counsel*?" I asked.

"What," Oswald said. "The Council is our extended family's governing body."

"You sound very organized," I said. Families were all a mystery to me, since I didn't have one to speak of.

Gabriel said, "Wilcox's assistant, Matthews, reported his employer's disappearance two days after they flew into the country. In fact, Matthews is near the ranch now. Until things are cleared up, Matthews will be visiting his daughter, Nettie, in town. She's Granddad's new assistant."

"Wow, that's a coincidence," I said.

"Not really," Oswald said. "His family has a longtime working relationship with our network of families.

"What does Matthews know?" I asked.

Gabriel said, "Only that he was on the flight after Wilcox's and they were supposed to meet up. He knew that Wilcox was having a surfing vacation and visiting you. Wilcox was supposed to call him that night, but never did."

"So we've still got nothing," I said.

"Milagro, Matthews told the Council that you might be connected to his employer's disappearance. He and his daughter are very upset. You met Nettie in London."

"I can't believe I forgot a trip to London."

Mercedes said, "Gabriel would like permission to visit your loft with a forensics expert and see if they can find any fingerprints or trace evidence."

I imagined a crime scene light illuminating body fluids everywhere. "Um, so long as you understand that I'm a single girl entitled to some privacy."

"Thanks," Gabriel said. "We'll keep out of your lingerie drawer. I'd also like to go into your bank records and track the days leading up to and after Wilcox's arrival."

"Sure. I'd like to know where I was, too."

Mercedes said, "We'll tell you whatever we find out."

"What about my missing time? I mean, in addition to the two years I've lost."

There was a pause on the line and then Mercedes spoke, "Lily advises, and we all agree, that you need to recover your memory 'organically' to prevent the possibility of false memories."

She was keeping something from me, but I didn't seem to care.

Mercedes said, "Okay, I've got all your account info from the last time I upgraded your laptop, and I'll give Gabriel the key to your place."

"Sure, whatever," I said. "Where's my laptop?"

"Don't you have a therapy session?" Mercedes said. "The faster you recover, the better chance of us finding Wilcox's killer."

I said good-bye to my friend, and Oswald put the call on hold and told me that Lily was waiting for me in a small parlor down the hall.

I went past the staircase and saw an expansive family room through one doorway.

The parlor, on the other side of the hall, was a cozy room lined with bookshelves with a plum-colored velvet sofa. I'd look wonderfully melancholic reclining on this sofa while I mused about the intricate workings of my psyche.

Lily was sitting at a delicate writing table, working at her laptop. She looked up as I came in. "Hi, Milagro. Please take a seat." She reached for a notepad and a ballpoint pen.

When I sat across from her, she said, "Let's start off with a few word associations."

"Fantastic. I'm all about the words. I like them whether they're mono- or multisyllabic. I like onomatopoeia and foreign words and expressions. I like funny words like 'bric-a-brac' and 'noodle' and 'persnickety.'"

"Good. Just say the first thing that comes into your mind without thinking," she said. "Hot."

"Chocolate."

"Cold."

"Hands, warm heart."

"Cat."

"Pickles."

She paused before writing down my answer and then said, "Tree."

"Prune. The verb, not the fruit."

"Just one word is fine, Milagro. Black."

"Bra."

"Red," she said.

"Wine."

"Blood."

I wondered if she knew that I snacked on the steaks and said, "Blue."

"Blue?"

"Blue-bloods. Fancy-pants, hoity-toity."

"Oh." Lily wrote for a few seconds. "Knife."

An image flashed through my mind of a knife slipping through flesh, crimson fluid welling in the cut, a man's hot mouth hungry for my flesh, but I answered, "Spork."

Lily looked confused, so I said, "It's the combination of a fork and a spoon, a spork. Ah, the elusive charm of the spork!"

We went on in this fashion for a few more minutes. I must have done well, because Lily looked utterly captivated by my answers. I said, "I'd be thrilled to do some inkblot tests, or we can go outside and I can tell you the shapes of clouds."

"That's all right. I need a little more of your personal history, so I'd like you to tell me your earliest memories."

It was refreshing to talk nonstop about myself. While I gabbed,

I also tried to use my brainpower to lift a book off the shelves. It was a slim volume called *Spiritual Transformations: Adventures of a Shapeshifter* by someone called *Don* Pedro. I scrunched my face in my effort to make it move.

Lily put down her pad and said, "I know this is a painful process."

"It's arduous work, but I'm happy to soldier on." The damn book hadn't budged a smidgen.

"I'd like you to process what we've discussed and we'll have a session this afternoon."

"Okay, thanks," I said, and when Lily glanced down at her notes, I grabbed the book and took it back to the maid's room.

It had an intriguing cover with a man morphing into different shapes, including a platypus. The memoir used the same flowery language I'd seen in the composition books I'd brought, and I recognized several of my favorite words and expressions.

This must be the memoir I'd ghostwritten, and I knew I was commissioned for a follow-up. I went back and forth from the book to my outline and somehow I knew the story I wanted to write. When I put my pen to paper, the words flowed easily.

Lily and I had a quick lunch of strawberry yogurt and then she said we should return to the small parlor.

"The day is too nice to be stuck inside. Let's go outside." She pursed her lips as she thought, so I added, "It's wrong to waste such fresh air."

"All right. Let me get my notepad."

She left the kitchen, I spotted a half bottle of zinfandel on the counter and took several glugs to quench my red-thirst. I was wiping my mouth when she came back with her notepad and a jaunty cotton hat.

We went into the garden, where there was a table and chairs in the shade of the old oak. I noticed that the truckasaurus had been moved to the covered carport. I grabbed the red-handled pruners from where I had left them.

"You don't need those," Lily said. "I want you to focus on our session."

"Gardening puts me in the zone. Otherwise I'll just be distracted by all that needs to be done here."

"All right. I may as well weed while you whack."

"Do you know anything about gardening?"

"My parents garden," she said. "I had my own flower plot and worm bin growing up, but I don't know much about roses. Are these heirloom varieties?"

I grinned and said, "Let me get my gloves so you won't get snagged by thorns."

I dashed to the ugly truck, grabbed my goatskin gloves and a plastic bin for green waste, and ran back. I handed Lily the gloves and led her to a large shrub growing over an arch. "She's called Reve D'Or, or Dream of Gold. The flowers get more goldy-pink if the plant is in partial shade."

"It's gorgeous," she said.

"The best thing is the fragrance." I plucked off one of the creamy flowers and held it to her nose.

"Heavenly." She crouched down, and I saw her pinch a weed at the base and pull it up by the roots. Pleased that she knew what she was doing, I began to snip at the roses.

Soon we were working harmoniously, moving from one shady area to the next as the sun moved across the sky. The novelty of giving a self-centered monologue wore off. I preferred the interactive drama wherein I nattered as inanely as possible and Mercedes tried to talk sense into me, or Nancy said something even more outlandish.

"Lily, where do you live?"

"Lately in Boston, but I've been all over for college, med

school, and training," she said. I'd given her the pruners and she was holding them toward a shrub. "My folks are north of Seattle. What about this branch?"

"Leave it, because we can train it over the top of the fence. What do you do for fun?"

"I like to sketch and do watercolors."

"What about guys? Do you have any patients doing transference and falling madly in love with you, or hot docs who want to do in-depth consultations?"

She laughed. "It's completely unethical to get involved with patients, and my situation is complicated by the family condition."

"You and Oswald keep using that word: 'complicated.'" I reached over and plucked a leaf out of her hair. "I look at Oswald and I can't imagine what our life was like together, and the sex . . ."

"Mmm?"

"He must have been incredible, or why would I get engaged to him? I look at those long fingers and think of what they could do to a woman's body, and that mouth, oh, my. The way he smiles crookedly is sexy, don't you think?"

"Well . . . ," she said uncomfortably. "He does have a nice smile."

"'Nice'? There's such a thing as taking understatement too far, Lily," I returned to waxing poetic about our host. "I'm enraptured by the way his jeans lovingly embrace his ass, and those eyes, like the color of storm clouds, portending something thunderous to come, and by 'come' I mean—"

Lily said, "Milagro?"

"Hm?" I glanced up from the damp soil and saw Lily staring at something behind me. I turned and saw Oswald. "Oh, hi, Oswald."

His storm-cloud gray eyes portended nothing at the moment.

He raised his eyebrows and said to Lily, "Is this part of your therapy?"

"I, uh," she began.

"It *is* part of the therapy, Oswald, taking me on the same emotional journey in order to build a framework for my memories, right, Lily?"

"Yes," she said. "I read about it in the *Nordic Journal of Psychiatry.*"

"Oh," Oswald said, taken aback. "I'm sorry for interrupting then. I thought we could have cocktails in about a half hour on the terrace. My grandmother is trying out new recipes."

Lily said, "Wonderful. We'll see you then."

When he nodded and went inside, I laughed and Lily said, "I can't believe you said that."

"I can't believe you went along with it."

"Only because I'm open to any theory right now. If you can connect with the feelings you had for Oswald, you might trigger memories. But think about him, the whole person, not just his body."

"I'll try, but that body is utterly captivating, don't you think so?"

She smiled a little slyly. "It's not my role to disagree with your opinions, Milagro."

I changed into a clean set of the boring clothes and was putting my hair into a scrunchie from hell when there was a knock on my door.

"Enter."

The door opened and I saw an adorable man with red-gold hair, black slacks, an ecru button-down shirt, and eyes the same pellucid pond-green as Mrs. Grant's.

"Hi," I said, lowering my voice for maximum flirt effect.

"Hi, honey," he said. "It's me, Gabriel. We spoke on the phone this morning. You look as if you're leading a revolt against good taste."

"It's part of my therapy, like no skin contact."

"Good luck with that." He dropped into the old green armchair beside the desk. "We checked your apartment and found a million fingerprints and more body fluids than I want to think about."

"I probably had parties," I said. "You know how people get."

"Actually, I do," he said, and grinned. "We've tracked your activities on the day Wilcox arrived. You left a debit card trail all the way into the late evening. We also found Wilcox's rented car in the visitors' parking area of your garage. There was blood in the trunk."

"Does that clear me or implicate me further?"

"The timeline seems to clear you, but it's not conclusive. I've given a report to the Council and there's not much they can do without a body."

"Mrs. Grant scoffed at me when I asked if 'family' means mob. What kind of family hires forensics experts?"

Gabriel smiled, showing delightful dimples. "We've found it useful to support each other's businesses and careers. We're more like a cultural group."

"Except that 'cultural group' sounds more like potlucks and clog dancing than sexy Titian-haired security managers," I said. "I suppose I know all about this."

"Yes, you met with the Council when you were going to marry Oswald," he said. "Now, if you don't regain your memory . . ."

"But I will. I'm not going to toss away two years of my life because, ooh, I can't face reality. I'm willing to do the hard work of wearing my big-girl granny panties."

"You in big granny panties, how hot!"

"You'd know if you gave me a full-body search." When he stopped laughing I said, "I'm also not supposed to flirt even though I'm guessing you don't swing my way."

"If I swung your way, I'd swing your way," he said, and winked.

"Hey, that's something I say!"

"Who do you think I got it from? All right, no flirting, but I'll pass along a pointer I learned from a waitress. The higher the ponytail, the bigger the tip."

"You have earned my respect forever." I pulled out my scrunchie and gathered my hair into a high ponytail. "Now let's have a drink."

The sun was low in the sky, just edging behind the mountains, and the sky was deepening to indigo. Lily sat in one of the teak chairs beside AG. Mrs. Grant was mixing a shaker of cocktails, and Oswald set a platter of antipasto on a table.

"Sit by me, Young Lady," Gabriel said, as he took a chair on one side.

I looked at him and said, "Why does everyone call me that?"

The others looked at Mrs. Grant, who said, "Because I've always hoped you'd act like one."

"Ha, ha, and ha," I said. "What are we drinking?"

"Pink cellos from my homemade limoncello, vodka, and cranberry juice." Mrs. Grant poured out the drinks in martini glasses.

I took a sip of the tangy, fruity drink, and AG turned to Gabriel. "How is Charlie's hotel search going?"

"He's still looking in foggy towns for a place he can remodel into a boutique hotel for family members."

"Do you want the responsibility of a hotel?" Oswald asked. He leaned back against a pillar facing us and I admired his shoulder-to-hip proportions.

"It's Charlie's dream," the redheaded man said. "I can't complain about him taking a time-consuming project when I'm gone so much."

I was thinking that the vista was so beautiful and that it was such a treat to enjoy the evening with companions, to share this relaxed time, this spirit of camaraderie, when Oswald said to his cousin, "You're lucky that you've got a partner who has his own interests to pursue instead of someone so bored that she . . . I mean, um, you're lucky he's got a career."

In the silence that followed, I deduced that Oswald's comment was a reference to me. I put down my drink and said, "Excuse me, but I'm feeling worn out. I think I'll go rest."

I felt their eyes on me as I left, and Gabriel whispered, "Oswald!"

Even though I didn't know Oswald, I was hurt and very confused. How could I have been bored, when I'd always had so many things to do? I'd reached the door to the maid's room when my ex-fiancé caught up to me. He took my arm and turned me to face him.

His eyes were the same hue as the scarf I'd been making. I must have been making it for him even though we'd broken up.

"Milagro, I'm sorry."

"It's all right. I have a history of screwing up relationships and clearly something went wrong between us. You didn't ask for me to come here, didn't want me to stay, and it's good of you to take me in now when you don't have to."

"That doesn't excuse my behavior." He touched my exposed wrist, sending a zizz through me. "I was the one who brought you into my life and my problematic family. I gave you the condition. I'm responsible for you."

I looked up into Oswald's clear gray eyes. "Did you love me, Oswald?"

He hesitated and then said, "Yes, even though you drove me crazy. You still drive me crazy."

"So why did we break up?"

"We took missteps and every time we tried to fix them, others interfered." He ran his fingers up my sleeve and along my arm, making me want to lean into his touch. "Both of us made mistakes, but if we had just gone ahead and gotten married, this never would have happened to you."

"And how was it when we made love?"

"Amazing," he said. "I remember the last time. We were in the City and we'd registered for wedding gifts. Then I'd done some consults. I came back to our hotel suite and you were wearing a white plastic miniskirt," he said, and smiled.

I smiled, too. "That sounds very glamorous."

"We were going to go out, but we stayed in and spent the night making love. If I had known it would be the last time . . . ," he said. "Oh, Milagro, I've missed you so much."

He was serious and sincere, an irresistible combination in a fabulous man, so I didn't even try to resist. I put my arms around him and his lips went to mine. Delicious sensations rippled through my body, and I thought of the magical kiss that awakens a sleeping princess and the magical kiss that transforms a frog.

Oswald pushed me through the doorway into the room and kicked the door shut behind us.

Each taste of his tongue sent all sorts of happy signals along my synapses. Maybe my memory could be recovered by a different magical act. I pressed myself against him, wrapping my leg around his, and then someone rapped on the door.

Oswald took his mouth from mine.

"In a minute," he called out. To me, he whispered, "You always do this to me." He went to face the window, blowing out his breath and adjusting himself in his jeans.

Through the door, Lily said, "Please don't do anything detrimental to the healing process."

Oswald said, "We'll be out in a minute."

After a few seconds, we heard her walk away.

He said, "I'm sorry. I shouldn't have done that when you're not well."

"I liked it, Oswald. I like you."

"When you get your memory back, you may not feel the same way about me."

I thought of the scarf I had found in my bag and I thought of how I'd come here when I was in trouble. "Can't we start over? If we loved each other once . . . unless you're involved with someone else."

He gazed out the window for a long time and said, "There's been no one else for me since you left."

"So maybe . . ."

"Maybe. Let's go back out." He came to me and stroked his finger along my throat. "I think you came back to me for a reason."

"I think so, too."

When we returned to the terrace, everyone acted as if nothing had happened, but Oswald sat by my side and I kept glancing at him.

I had amnesia, but I also had a second chance with exactly the sort of man I'd always wanted—someone worthwhile, a human version of a substantial, hardback book, instead of the guys I usually dated, paperback beach reads that could be left on the bus for the next bored and aimless girl.

thirteen

Once Bitten, Twice Snide

After dinner, AG and Mrs. Grant went to watch a movie in her cottage, and Oswald and Gabriel went to the study to talk.

Lily said to me, "I've got to make phone calls. Will you be all right on your own?"

"I'm fine. I can work on my project."

"The memoir?"

"From what I can tell from my notes, it's entirely fabricated. I'm thinking that it's more of a fakeoir, or maybe a fabrimento. I'll see you tomorrow."

After I'd zipped out a chapter, I felt the need to stretch my muscles. I changed into sneakers and a T-shirt and went outside.

I looked up, astonished at the canopy of bright stars. I'd never seen so many in my life. I began moving slowly, testing myself, but after I'd reached the edge of the field, I broke into a jog, and soon I began to run.

I avoided the area where Mrs. Grant had pointed out a pond and circled the property. With my improved vision, I saw a luminescent outline on small critters and insects. A coyote yipped in the distance.

The air was crisp and fresh in my lungs, and I felt so strong that I went around two more times.

As I faced the house, I saw the lights on upstairs, and a light glowed from the downstairs study. I walked quietly and stood to one side of the window where I could peer in.

Oswald and Gabriel listened as a man's voice came over the speakerphone. The man said, "Wilcox's parents are demanding an immediate Council investigation and you know what that means."

Gabriel said, "Sam, she doesn't remember anything, and we *know* Milagro. She didn't kill Wilcox, or anyone."

The caller said, "Don't you wonder, Gabe? She's definitely capable of violence, and she's not always in control of her emotions."

Oswald said, "She's not the only one capable of violence."

I was so preoccupied with these aspersions on my character that I didn't notice the fuzzy young possum ambling toward me until it was on my foot.

"Shoo!" I hissed, trying to get it to move away. "Go!"

Oswald said, "Sam, you didn't see her when she came here. She looked worse than when she was fighting the first infection, and that almost killed her. Do everything you can to buy time so she has a chance to recover."

The possum snuffled at my ankle, and I caught only a few words of what Gabriel said, something about "as a Council director, he has the responsibility and right to interview her no matter what you think of him."

I waved my hands in front of the stupid possum's face and it fell over and feigned death on my other foot. By the time I'd edged my shoe out from under the creature, Oswald was saying angrily, "Fine, but the only way I'll have him here is if he agrees to my conditions. It's still my house and she's still . . . what *is* that smell? Skunk?"

I ducked into the bushes as Oswald came to the window, shut it, and closed the drapes.

The next day, Monday, I got up early and found Oswald in the kitchen pouring a cup of coffee. He was dressed in a dark blue suit and a pale blue shirt, and his hair was brushed back.

No one was around so I went to his and leaned against him. After a moment he kissed me softly, his mouth tasting of tooth-paste.

"Mmm, minty. What does the rest of you taste like?"

He laughed and pushed me away. "Not now, Mil. I've got to go to work."

I took his coffee cup and took a sip. "So you're a plastic sur-geon. Why did you decide to do that?"

"You always had a problem with my career because of your mother's plastic surgery. I always had a problem with your lack of a career."

"I'm a writer *and* a gardener. That's *two* careers. Back to my question."

"Okay, I'm fascinated by the structure of the human body. Muscles, tissue, skin, bone, blood vessels. I'm not going to go into this when you could get your memory back and recall all of our previous discussions."

"Fair enough," I said. "Maybe later tonight we can have an in-depth talk." I smiled and tipped my head to make my ponytail swing.

"Morning!"

I turned to see Lily. She looked younger and sexier in a pair of jeans and a stretchy teal T-shirt.

I handed back Oswald's coffee cup and we both said good morning to her. "Lily, if you're all part of an extended non-Mafia family, how come you haven't met Oswald before?"

They looked at each other quizzically. She said, "Good question. I was signed up on the dating registry, but they matched me with one of the Van Burens. I went out with him for six months and decided I'd rather die a spinster, so I pulled my name off."

I tried to puzzle this through. "Your family has a dating service? I think I'm a little squicked out."

"It's the equivalent of dating someone from a neighboring town," Lily said, "but we can meet people who share our condition and values."

Oswald smiled. "Actually, Lily, I think we met at one of the Council's career retreats when we were in sixth grade. I remember a very intense, pretty, curly-haired girl who spent a lot of time disputing Freudian theory."

She laughed and said, "That was me! Who were you?"

"I was the skinny little kid trying to impress you by talking about the endocrine system. You told me that you thought I had narcissistic personality disorder."

"You were that pest! I noticed you at that big millennium party in Quebec."

Oswald's nice brows knit together as he stared at Lily. "I would have remembered you."

She shrugged. "I'd cut off all my hair because I wanted to be taken seriously. You were running with the fast crowd, that fashionista Cornelia . . . um, a different crowd."

"I've settled down since then."

"So I've noticed," Lily said.

After Oswald left to go to his office, and Gabriel joined us for coffee.

When Lily wasn't looking, he flipped my ponytail, then said,

"Lily, we're trying to stall the Council before they question Milagro . . . or take further action, but they're under pressure from Wilcox's family. I don't know how many days we have."

"What? You can't put a deadline on a recovery." Lily's forehead furrowing in irritation. "I've got a week of vacation left, and I planned to help transition Milagro to another therapist."

"Maybe we could just figure it all out ourselves," I said. "I can help. I can go undercover in a blond wig."

"No," Gabriel and Lily said together.

So after breakfast, I had another session with Lily. She wanted to talk about my grandmother, and I found myself happily reminiscing about my small *abuelita* and her affectionate embraces, her sweet smile.

"I still miss her, and I wonder what she'd think of the person I am now," I said. "She wanted me to be happy."

"What do you think would make you happy, Milagro?"

"Not *what*, but *who*. I saw a photo of Oswald and me and we were happy."

Lily scribbled on her notepad, then said, "You can't look to others for emotional fulfillment, Milagro."

"Lily, if others can make you unhappy, it seems to reason that the opposite should also be true."

After lunch, when I suggested having our session outside again, Lily agreed, but once we were working, she asked me to talk about my father.

"There's not much to tell. He started with one pickup and some old tools and built up a good landscaping business doing corporate campuses," I said. "His name is Ray and his slogan, 'Let Ray D-light you with a perfect new lawn,' was on all the trucks."

"Would he be proud of this garden?"

"Oh, no. He likes manicured lawns and uniform borders of

shrubs. He always made sure that he imposed order and symmetry on nature."

"Why did your mother marry your father?"

"He's handsome and a hard worker," I said. "He devoted himself to providing for her."

"So he's a hardworking man who likes order and strict aesthetic standards, and lives with a dominant female," Lily said. "Are you making any connections?"

"You're the professional. You tell me."

"Milagro, you're supposed to work toward your own mental health."

"If I go to a mechanic, he doesn't charge me by the hour and make me guess what's wrong with my car. He just fixes it."

She glared at me for a moment. "We return to patterns that are familiar, our comfort zones."

"This is the very opposite of my life with my family, so your theory is completely loony." Her mouth set in a line, so I changed the subject. "Let me show you how to fan out rose canes to encourage bloom."

I took off my cotton gloves to grip the branches as I demonstrated, and a large thorn caught on the back of my hand. It ripped my skin, and the jagged cut welled with glossy ruby blood.

"I'm so careless," I said, and licked away the blood, revealing skin that suddenly mended over. It was as smooth as if it had never been damaged. "Holy cow." I held out my hand for Lily to see.

She stared in amazement. "I heard you healed fast, but I've never seen anyone heal *that* fast."

"It's because I'm a superhero, right?"

"No."

* * *

After Oswald returned we had cocktails on the terrace. AG and Mrs. Grant seemed much cozier than they had when I'd first met them. She handed him the first limoncello martini and he raised it to her before taking a taste and looking out to the horizon.

"Perfect," he said. "Is this what I've been missing all these years?"

"It was your decision," she said.

He smiled a crooked smile like Oswald's. "Grant men are helplessly drawn to impossible women."

Gabriel said, "That's why I didn't even bother with women. Although if I did, the Young Lady would be at the top of my list."

"Thanks, Gabriel. If I was a gay guy, you'd be at the top of my list, too."

Mr. Grant looked at his ex-wife and said, "Sometimes the world is too modern for me."

"AG, you were old-fashioned when you were twenty," she said. "I think your body finally caught up with your mental age."

"You always called me a fuddy-duddy."

"Did I?"

"I could tell some stories . . . ," he began, and Mrs. Grant glanced in my direction and said, "This is not the time."

The conversation turned to other topics, and I shared my weird experience about healing from the cut. "The question is, how can I use my super powers for good?"

Edna started laughing and Oswald said, "You don't actually have any powers," and Lily said, "That shouldn't be a concern right now," all of which I found very discouraging.

After dinner, Oswald asked if anyone wanted to go for a swim. I wanted to be with him, but I panicked just thinking about the pool. Why did the pool's clear water hold such darkness for me?

"I'm going to write tonight. Don't worry about me."

"I'd love a swim," Lily said.

I went to the maid's room and wrote feverishly, filling up page after page, until my fingers cramped. I put the pen down and it rolled off the desk. When I bent down to retrieve it, I saw my initials scratched into the underside of the desk. Beside them was DAISY, RIP.

The ooky factor rose in me again, so I decided to run off my tension. When I went into the night, I made a game of seeing how fast I could dart around rocks. "I'm a superhero!" I said to myself as I leaped over a boulder.

After several laps, I stopped to tend the grave on the far side of the property. I pulled weeds and found rocks to add to the mound. "Daisy," I said, trying out the name. "My dog, Daisy."

A flash of memory came, an image of a furry dog with golden eyes peering over the edge of a bed at me. Then it was gone, leaving me with a pang, a yearning.

I practiced saying "Daisy" again, but nothing happened. When I turned back toward the house, I noticed the open door of the barn. Maybe seeing other animals would help jar my memory.

I hadn't visited the barn before, but I'd heard the Grant family talk about Ernesto, the ranch hand who had an apartment at the front of the barn. As I walked into the structure, the rich animal smells came to me.

Stalls ran on both sides and cats prowled atop bales of hay and on rafters. Cats everywhere . . . and they reminded me of something.

A bay horse swung his huge head over a stall door, startling me. "Hey, horsey," I said softly.

Just then I heard a woman's laugh. It came from farther down the barn. I listened and heard the murmur of voices. I crept to a stall with light eeking out from beneath the door.

I swung it open and saw the Grant family in armchairs in a comfortable room. A beautiful Oriental carpet was on the hardwood floor and sconces cast warm, diffused light.

At a sideboard, a compact, muscled Latino dude was pouring drinks into wineglasses.

"Aha!" I cried.

Mrs. Grant looked at Oswald. "I told you she'd show up. You owe me a quart of Madagascar vanilla."

"Hi, Milagro," Gabriel said.

"I can't believe that you'd leave me out of . . . what is this?"

A delicious coppery tang scented the air and I saw the dark red color of my companions' drinks.

"It's blood. You're drinking blood." Some things that we do in private, such as snacking on raw steaks, seem much more freaky in group settings. My craving for the drink conquered any ambivalence.

Oswald, his hair still wet from swimming, said, "Let me explain."

I gave him a haughty look. "I'm not some unsophisticated rube. In fact, I've eaten fried brains at an Italian restaurant and I loved my grandmother's *menudo,* which is a soup made with tripe."

"Hey, *mamacita,*" the Latino guy said. "I heard you forgot everything. I'm Ernie. Want a drink? It's the usual, lamb, raised on new grass."

"Nice to meet you again, Ernesto. That sounds very intriguing. I think I will try it."

The others were exchanging looks as Ernesto poured viscous red liquid from a green wine bottle into a glass and added carbonated bottled water and a twist of lemon.

"Thank you," I said, and took the glass. As they all watched me, I took a sip of the salty, mineral-tasting drink and swished it in my mouth. "Yes, I get the grass notes and also something like chamomile. Delish." Then I gulped down the rest of the drink. It hummed through me, making me feel alive and sexy.

I pulled off my scrunchie and shook out my hair. Then I sat on the arm of Oswald's chair, very casually, as if I was merely resting.

Lily pivoted in her chair toward me. "Do you think it's normal to drink blood, Milagro?"

"The Masai subsist on blood, milk, and bark. Are you saying they're abnormal? Excuse me if I find that culturally insensitive of you."

Lily looked pleased and said to the others, "Her level of denial is amazing. It's a pity I can't write a case study on her."

"Lily, don't you ever go off the clock?" I said, moving my leg closer to Oswald's and admiring his jean-clad thigh.

The others began talking about investment property, but I put my mind to a more serious topic: maybe my superhero talent was *receiving* brain waves. I attempted to read Oswald's mind and find out if he was sending any lustful messages to me. I wasn't sure, but I thought he probably was.

The hour grew late and we all said good night to Ernie. AG walked Edna to her cottage, and Gabriel took Lily's arm and guided her down the drive toward the house.

When I bent over to retie my shoe, Oswald politely waited for me. I retied the other shoe and said, "I don't like it when they're not equally tight."

"I know."

"It's strange having you know all about me when I don't know anything about you." The breeze blew his chestnut hair forward and I reached over and brushed it back. The zizz from him melded with the buzz from the cocktail in a most remarkable way.

He said, "I don't know much about what you've been doing lately. Everyone avoided talking about you because they thought it would upset me."

"Ozzy, how did we meet?"

"It was at that book party for your ex. You were the sexiest thing in the room, and when I asked if you wanted to leave, you came right along. You've always been ready for a good time."

"Is there anything wrong with that?"

"I was definitely in need of a good time, then," he said. "Later, though, you got bored here. Or you got bored with me."

"How could I be bored in a place like this? It's fantastic. And you're fantastic, Oswald."

He took my hand, and I felt the urge to lean into him and extend the wonderful zizzy feeling over my body. But something in the distance caught my attention.

Far across the field I saw something that looked like a man, greenish in hue, dressed in a shirt covered in dried blood, with a white shroud draped over his head. He pointed a long, bony finger at me and his mouth opened like an abyss, like hell.

I gasped and closed my eyes.

"Milagro!" Oswald put his hands on my shoulders. "Babe, what is it! What's the matter?"

"I thought I saw . . ." My heart was racing.

"There's nothing here. It's just me. No one can get past the guards at the gate, and I won't let anyone hurt you. You're safe with me."

I opened my eyes and saw nothing but the dark field.

"See, Mil, nobody's there."

I already knew there was no *body*. It was the vengeful spirit of my boyfriend, Wilcox Spiggott.

fourteen

You're No Body Until Somebody Bloods You

Despite my stories about supernatural creatures, I wasn't a superstitious *chica*. I understood that the ghost was actually a manifestation of my own guilt.

"It was a rat," I said.

"What is it about you and rats?" Oswald said. "It's the country. There are lots of animals here. Which reminds me, you should watch out for skunks at night. One was near the house yesterday."

"Maybe I should go inside."

As we walked back to the house, I kept glancing to the field, but my hallucination was over for now.

Oswald kissed my cheek and said, "Sleep well." When I was alone in the bedroom, I locked the windows and the door. Better safe than scary.

Gabriel came to my room soon after I got up the next morning and told me, "I've got to make a run to the City, but I'll be back tomorrow." He took my gloved hand in his. "Do you like your therapy?"

I twined my fingers with his. "Do you see any improvement in me . . . in who I am?"

"Honey, I always thought you were fabulous."

"Thank you, Gabriel. It would be wonderful if Oswald thought I was fabulous, too. I'm so lucky to spend this time with him, to have another chance at our relationship."

Gabriel kissed my hand. "Yes, well, take care of yourself."

My disappointment at seeing him leave was alleviated when I went to the parlor and Lily told me she was going to try to put me in a relaxed, focused state.

"You're going to try to mesmerize me, aren't you? Mesmer coming from Franz Mesmer, who had a whole school of spiritualism based on animal magnetism. These days we use "magnetism" to describe sexual attractiveness, but Mesmer thought our bodies contained magnetic fluid. Wacky."

"How do you know about Mesmer?" Lily asked while I arranged myself on the purple velvet sofa.

"I wrote a story in college about a man who was so charismatic that he could convince people at a glance to do his bidding. Of course, no one is *that* charismatic. Charismatic is derived from an ancient Greek word, 'kharisma,' meaning gift. Hmm . . ."

"What?"

"Some words and phrases raise my ookiness level. You should ask me about that when I'm under." I crossed my hands over my chest and said, "Okay, mesmerize away."

"Why don't you come sit here?" She indicated the chairs.

"This is more dramatic."

She didn't look convinced, but said, "If you're more relaxed there, you can stay."

"Totally relaxed. Yet focused. Keenly focused."

"Good." Lily dimmed the lights and moved a chair next to the sofa. She had a small penlight that she clicked on and held it in front of my face. "I want you to focus on the light and imagine yourself in a wonderful safe place. Where are you?"

"I'm lying on the ratty old sofa in my friend's nightclub. A wonderful band is practicing a new song."

"Good," Lily said somewhat skeptically.

"It's a great club. What music do you like?"

"Hmm? Classical and soft jazz. Relax and start counting backward from one hundred."

"One hundred, ninety-nine. . . . ," I began, and when I was in the eighties, I got bored so I switched over to Spanish. By the time I got to *quince,* I went to French, because I could count up to *quatorze* in French.

"Now, Milagro, are you comfortable?"

"Very."

"You're safe here and warm. Let's go back to the night you were supposed to meet Wilcox. You were excited and happy to see him again."

"I'm always happy to see cute guys. He's cute, right?"

"So I was told. You go to the restaurant to meet him. You're wearing a pretty dress."

"Which one?"

"Whatever you want to imagine. You walk into the restaurant—"

"Hold on. If he's a surfer, maybe I would have gone with jeans."

"You wore a dress."

"Are you sure?"

Lily clicked the light off. "I don't think you're in a relaxed, focused state."

"*Quelle* bummer. I thought things had changed." I told her how I used to earn money at F.U. by being a psychology test subject. "I didn't score well for hypnotic susceptibility."

"Why didn't you tell me that first?" she asked, and I heard a note of irritation in her voice.

I sat up and looked at her. "Because I wanted it to be like a Hitchcock movie, where the beautiful and brilliant psychiatrist uses hypnosis to draw out the memories from the fascinating amnesiac."

Lily blinked for a few seconds and twirled one curl around her finger, so I said, "Wouldn't that be fun?"

"This is supposed to be healing, not fun."

I shook my head. "I think it could be both, like a spork is both a spoon and a fork. Let's go outside."

She narrowed her hazel-green eyes at me, which I didn't think was in the shrink handbook, and said, "I'll go outside if you'll do something for me."

"What is it?"

"I'll tell you outside."

"Okay." When we were in the garden, I said, "Okay, what is it?"

"Let's work awhile."

I soon became engrossed in replanting a conifer that had outgrown its container.

When I stood back to admire my work, Lily said, "Who is your favorite humorous writer?"

I was glad she was going to talk about books. "I have lots, but Mark Twain would be one of my top three."

"What's his style? What's his voice?"

"It depends on his topic, but he often wrote in first-person, past tense, and his narrators are frequently ironic or terrifically deluded," I said. "I can recommend a few books, if you like."

"What's a 'serious' literary voice?"

I shrugged. "I was taught to write in present tense, third person, stripped-down emotionally detached prose."

Lily raked leaves from under a bush. "Tell me about the time your mother left you at the mall, but this time describe it in present tense, third person."

"But I *already* told you what happened."

"You said you'd do what I asked if we could come outside. This time don't call her 'my mother Regina.' Say 'her mother.'" Lily did the eye squint thing again, and I realized that she had an edge under the smooth professional surface.

"Fine," I said, and I wondered why I felt so annoyed. "The girl is ten years old and her mother takes her to the big indoor mall. At first she's excited because her mother never takes her anywhere and she thinks her mother wants to be with her," I said in an affectless voice. "Her mother is very thin, perfectly groomed, and perfectly coordinated in new clothes."

"How did the girl feel?"

"She's proud of her mother," I said, surprised to remember how I'd felt at seeing her looking as striking as a crane in a flock of frumpish pigeons. "Her mother tells her to sit on the bench by the fountain and wait."

"What happens then?"

"The girl does as she's told because she wants her mother to be pleased with her. Her mother is never pleased with her. The girl waits and the hours pass. The girl watches other people buying and eating food, and she's hungry because it's lunchtime. She thinks of going to look for her mother, but that would make her angry and the girl will be locked in her room again."

My mood, the happiness of being in the garden, was gone.

"Go on, Milagro."

I took a breath and then said, "Her classmates walk by, but they ignore the girl because she's new to the school and she isn't allowed to visit anyone or have anyone over. Her mother doesn't like the mess and noise of children."

"Does the girl just sit?" Lily asks. "Or does she do anything else?"

"The girl has books in her backpack that the librarian gave her. Laura Ingalls Wilder's Little House books. So the girl begins to read. Soon she forgets that she's hungry and she forgets that she's waiting and she forgets everything but the world between the covers. She's in that world with Laura and her family."

"What is she feeling?"

"She's feeling what they're feeling: the bone-chilling prairie winters, the sweetness of an orange at Christmas, the terror of scarlet fever, the happiness of a family who loves one another."

My throat constricted and I turned my face away from Lily.

"What happened to the girl then?" Lily said quietly.

"She wants to be one of them, living within the pages of a book. Night comes and the mall empties. A cleaning lady sees the girl and speaks to her in Spanish. She takes the girl by the hand. The lady's hand is warm and firm and the girl misses being touched so much and no one has touched her or loved her since her *abuelita* died. She is so small and alone and her grief is so enormous. All she wants is human touch and she cries and begs the woman, 'Please can I live with you?'"

And then I couldn't speak anymore. Something inside me felt broken.

Lily was there with a tissue, and I wiped at my eyes and tried to calm my breaths.

"What are you thinking, Milagro?"

I glared at her. "I'm thinking that this isn't my story. My story isn't a tragedy or a drama. My story is full of laughs and has a happy ending. Everyone says I'm a happy-ending sort of girl!"

"Who says that?"

"I don't remember!" I shouted. "And this stupid exercise won't help me remember." I walked into the house and to my room, slammed the door shut, and picked up my pen. I wrote in first person, past tense, and let myself get lost in *my* story, a happy, magical story. When I heard the dogs barking and a car coming down the drive, I closed my composition book and went to investigate.

AG was ahead of me, opening the front door and saying, "Come in, come in."

A pretty young woman with long red curls entered the house and handed him a folder. "Here's the prospectus you wanted, Sir," she said with an English accent. She was wearing a blue cotton dress the same color as her eyes, and I felt self-conscious about my sack-of-potatoes outfit.

When she saw me, she looked stunned. "Hello."

"Hi."

"Milagro, this is my assistant, Nettie Matthews," AG said. "She was acquainted with your friend, Wilcox Spiggott."

"You knew Wilcox?" I asked. "Gosh, I've been wanting to talk to someone who could tell me about him."

AG said, "You girls go and chat while I look this over."

I said, "Let's have lemonade on the terrace."

Nettie followed me into the kitchen and stood silent as I poured two glasses of pink lemonade. I led her onto the terrace and we sat down.

After she took a few sips of her drink, she said, "Mr. Grant told me that you have amnesia. You really don't remember me?"

"I'm sorry."

She gazed at me and smiled sadly. "I wanted to come see you earlier, but the Grants said I should wait. We met when you were on holiday in London."

"Did we? Honestly, it's awful that I forgot that trip."

"You and I wrestled in bikinis in a nightclub."

"You're kidding! That's great. In mud, or Jell-O?"

Her smile widened. "In a vat of red liquid."

I laughed and said, "I can't wait to remember that."

"When we first met, I wasn't aware that you were Milagro de Los Santos."

"It's not like I'm anyone important. I'm so sorry about Wilcox. How did you know him?"

"My family has been employed by the Spiggott family for generations. Wil and I always knew each other and . . . he was a lovely lad," she said. "I was shocked when my father told me he'd disappeared and then the Grants reported that he had been . . ." She shook her head, distraught.

"I wish I could tell you something about what happened to him. I don't even remember him. All I know is that I liked him and that he surfed."

"That was one of his passions," Nettie said. "His other was passion. He loved to party and laugh and shag and talk. I thought he would always be in my life." Her eyes glistened with tears.

I put down my lemonade and wrapped my arms around her.

After a few minutes, Nettie pulled away and wiped at her tears. "I'm not supposed to upset you in your condition."

"Nettie, I'm supposed to stay here until I remember things. You're welcome to come and visit whenever you want."

She gave me a tight smile. "Thank you, but my father, who worked for Wil, is visiting and I want to spend time with him. Mr. Grant has leased me a sweet house in town with a purple gate and big yellow and pink roses. I hate leaving my father there, worrying about Wil. Besides, my father's not fond of employees and employers consorting."

"Consorting sounds like we're sex partners or criminals. We'll just be cocktailing."

"I'll try," she said, but I could tell she was being polite.

Late in the afternoon, I went out to dig up the dead mock-orange shrub. Lily came into the garden and said, "Are you okay?"

I regretted letting her get to me so I spoke normally. "I will be when I remove this. It has a heavenly scent that always reminds me of being in love, but I don't know what I was thinking planting it here. This climate is far too cold for this species."

"Maybe you were thinking of being in love."

"Perhaps," I said as I dug around the trunk. "I might have forced it to survive, but it never would have thrived."

"Oswald just called and he'd like me to visit his office to do a psych evaluation on one of his partner Vidalia's charity cases. Will you be all right by yourself?"

"Vidalia, like the onion?" I hauled out the shrub and said, "Sure, I'm fine. Go have a little fun. You've been trapped here with me and missing out on all the wonderful sights. You and Oswald should go out to dinner, too."

"You wouldn't mind?"

"Lily, my policy is, when a fun chick suggests a good time, say yes."

She laughed and I think we both felt better.

Lily must have taken my advice about dinner, because she and Oswald weren't back by the time I went to bed. I wished I could be out and about, having fun with Oswald, too.

I didn't sleep well that night. I had disturbing dreams that made even less sense than most dreams: I was in a car that lost control on a mountain road; I was dressed in a white robe watching a creepy ceremony in a strange ugly language; my ex-boyfriend Sebastian was kidnapping me.

The worst was a dream of myself as a small child. It was a hot day and my mother Regina had filled an aboveground pool with water. She set a ladder beside it, and then she turned and went into the house and locked the door.

I didn't know how to swim yet, but the water excited me. I

climbed the ladder, jumped in, and sank. Suddenly I wasn't a child anymore but a woman, and my wrists and legs were bound by heavy chains, and mans' hands held me down as I struggled to reach the surface.

I awoke fighting the blankets, in a cold sweat, ready to kill anyone who would hurt me. But I was alone in the dark.

Oswald came to see me in the morning before he went to work. He looked fresh and handsome in a navy suit and ivory shirt.

I felt proud of him and said, "It's wonderful that you donate time to care for those in need. I really admire you for making a difference."

"Maybe when this situation is over you can pursue a career that helps others, like teaching. You can always write about zombies and monsters in your free time."

"But my political horror stories do help others," I said, surprised that he didn't understand.

He frowned a little. "Yes, of course."

"I'm so glad you took Lily out last night. It's a pity she has to spend her vacation stuck here with me."

"She doesn't feel that way at all. She loves her profession, and she thinks you're a very intriguing case."

"If I'm the most exciting thing on her plate, I find that a little sad. I hope you took her out somewhere nice for dinner."

He paused and said, "There's a hillside winery with a tram."

"Oh, but I would have loved to go on a funicular!" I said. "It's got 'fun' right in the name."

He got an odd expression and seemed about to say something when the dogs started barking to announce someone arriving. "I'll see who that is."

I went outside with him and was thrilled to see that Gabriel had returned. Oswald wanted to talk alone to his cousin, so I ran across the field to Mrs. Grant's cottage. I knocked on her open door and she said, "Come in."

She was drinking coffee and relaxing on the sofa with a pile of celebrity magazines. Her legs were curled beneath her and her silver hair was charmingly mussed.

"Are you busy?" I asked as I sat across from her, feeling very sack-of-potatoish by comparison.

She put down a glossy weekly. "Would it matter if I was?"

"No. I was just being polite. Were you ever in the movie biz?"

"On the periphery, Young Lady. I knew people, but my family didn't approve of being in the limelight."

"That's too bad." I picked up a magazine, opened a dog-eared page, and saw a fashion spread of gorgeous, copper-skinned Thomas Cook in designer clothes. "Mrs. Grant," I began.

She rolled her eyes. "Lily said I should let you establish our relationships, but would you please stop calling me that? You always call me Edna."

"Edna," I said, feeling pleased with myself. "It's very peaceful here, isn't it?"

"If you mean boring, say so."

"Oh, no, far be it from me to find fault with this bucolic wonderland. Your grandson and I are getting along swimmingly. So don't give up hope that you may yet have the opportunity to buy a grandmother-of-the-groom dress. I'm thinking something in puce."

"Why puce?"

"It's a nice purply color, even though puce originally meant flea-colored."

She ignored my fascinating information.

"Young Lady, do you really want to reconcile with Oswald?"

"It's not reconciliation if I don't recall breaking up. How could I do any better than Oswald?"

227

"It didn't work out before, Milagro."

"But I'm different now, careful and thoughtful, serious and sincere. There should be a way for people who've loved each other to correct past mistakes. Isn't that what you and Mr. Grant are trying to do?"

She thought before answering. "I don't know if that's what I want. How much should one compromise in order to be accepted by another?" She sighed and suddenly looked much older. "My family would be overjoyed if AG and I remarried."

I flipped open the magazine to the photos of her obsession, Thomas Cook, and held it toward her. "Better a real relationship with a real person who's stable and reliable and still foxy, than a fantasy about someone who probably looks like a toad in real life."

"Do you think so?" she said, a smile playing on her lips.

"Oh, yes, these photos are airbrushed and Photoshopped. They can make anyone look like Adonis. He's not real."

"You may be right, Young Lady."

"I am, Edna. Now, if you need to talk again, I'll be in my room."

I wasn't sure, but after I left I thought I heard her laughing.

By the time I returned to the house, the mood had changed drastically. Oswald, Gabriel, and Lily were in the kitchen with a fresh pot of coffee. Oswald had taken off his jacket, and Gabriel was pacing.

"¿Que pasa?" I said, and gave Gabriel a non-skin-contact hug.

"Hey, baby," Gabriel said. "I was just telling everyone that we're having a visit from our Council director tonight."

"He's no one special," Oswald said, his mouth turning down at the corners. "We told the Council you still don't recall anything."

"He's going to interview you," Gabriel said. "He'll ask the same questions we have."

"This is unreasonable," Lily said. "Milagro's not in any condition to be pressured by the Council."

Gabriel ran his hand through his pretty red-gold hair. "We've done everything we can to buy time. But someone is dead, or at least we *think* someone is dead, and that takes precedence."

Oswald came to me and put his hand on my shoulder. "I've canceled my appointments so I can be here for you. Lily will give the Council director her evaluation and our cousin, Sam, an attorney, has set up guidelines that he must follow so that you're protected from any difficulties."

"Oswald, don't worry. I'm very good at answering questions. Just ask Lily."

I glanced at my shrink, who was suddenly fascinated by the coffee in her mug.

Oswald said to me, "Can we talk?"

I nodded and he led me upstairs to his bedroom. I looked around at an airy room with luxurious white linens on the bed and a beamed ceiling. It looked like the room at a luxury hotel, a room out of a magazine.

Oswald closed the bedroom door and then went to a bed table and searched around in a drawer.

I glanced at the bare surface of the dresser and an image flashed in my mind: the same dresser with a clutter of books and jewelry and colognes by a vase of flowers.

The image had vanished when Oswald came to face me. He looked more nervous than I'd seen him yet and said, "How's your fauxoir going?"

"Fauxoir? That's the perfect term for it. Why didn't I think of that?"

He smiled briefly and took my hands in his. "I had a good talk with Lily last night. She explained how your parents' neglect affected your behavior. I should have realized it before, but you always made it seem like a joke. Will you forgive me?"

He smelled wonderful, of the herby lotion he used, and his clear gray eyes looked into mine.

"Of course I will, Oswald." I tucked my head against his shoulder. I could feel his chest rise and fall.

"Mil, now I understand why you need so much attention. I should have tried to help. I *want* to help."

I thought he could help me right now by taking off his clothes. "You've been very helpful, Oswald."

He kissed my forehead at the temple, making me nuzzle closer to him. "Milagro, I want to make you happy."

I hoped he would drop his trousers, but instead he dropped down on one knee and then reached into his pocket. He held out a ring with a huge, glittering yellow diamond in a classic setting. "Will you marry me, Milagro de Los Santos?"

I stared from the ringasaurus to Oswald.

Smiling, he said, "It's your engagement ring. Before you hit your head, you told me you still loved me."

"But it's so soon, Oswald!" I was just as thrilled by the offer as I was shocked by the suddenness.

"I know, but we don't have to set a date. We can wait until you remember your love for me, or until it develops again," he said, still holding out the ring. "I brought you into my life, my world, Milagro, and I will always do my duty by you."

"Don't offer because it's your responsibility."

"I wanted to wait, but it's important for your own protection to be engaged now. It will prove to the Council that we trust that you didn't kill Wilcox, that we fully support you." He shifted to his other knee. "I'll be a good husband, Milagro, and I'd like to be the father of your children. Please tell me that you'll marry me when you're well again . . . if you love me again."

My policy was always to say yes when a successful, sexy, fabulous man asked for a romantic commitment. Besides, I could always change my mind later. "Yes, Oswald, yes!"

I pulled him up and kissed him, laughing as he took off my ugly glove and slipped the ring on my finger. I looked at it there for a few seconds. It seemed like a ring for a rich woman with demanding taste, the sort of ring my friend Nancy would love.

I was more interested in the man. I yanked his T-shirt up and ran my hands over his back, zinging wonderfully before my hands traversed the denim over his marvelous butt.

His hands were under my smock, but stopped around my waist. He pinched the flesh and said, "You want to be careful not to gain too much back."

"But the clothes I brought fit perfectly now. This is my normal size."

A smile flitted across his face. "Yes, but I thought that you'd like to stay the weight you were when you came, except healthy, of course."

I drew away from him. "If people didn't have unrealistic ideals, they wouldn't submit themselves to being cut up."

"It's not me, Milagro. *You* were concerned about your puppy fat when your wedding dress wouldn't fit."

His lips went to my throat, and I was thinking, *Puppy fat?* when there was a knock on the door.

"Hello?" I called out.

"Milagro," Lily said. "Can I have a minute?"

I looked at Oswald and he nodded. "Just a sec," I said. My fiancé, fiancé! and I went to open the door.

Lily waited with her hands clasped in front of her like a girl in etiquette class. "Would you like a session before the Council director gets here?"

I glanced at Oswald and he smiled nervously. "Oswald and I just got engaged again!" I held out my hand so she could see the ring.

fifteen

Shrinks, Kinks, and Drinks

I expected Lily to do what any normal girl would: grab my hand, squeal, and shriek "Oh, my God!" Well, she did say "Oh, my God!" but it came out with a gasp.

"Isn't it great?" I asked.

"But you don't even remember Oswald! He's a stranger to you!" She was so surprised that everything she said was an exclamation. She glared at Oswald. "You're taking advantage of her condition!"

"Lily, I may have amnesia, but I'm well aware of what a fantastic couple Oswald and I are. We're educated professionals with similar values and . . ." I tried to think of other things we had in common, besides a hypothetical history of amazing sex.

Lily had a bit of a fit, so I let her sputter on about professional ethics as I stared at my marvelous fiancé, who looked both guilty and resentful, like a kid in the principal's office.

Finally, Lily said to me, "What about our agreement that you wouldn't use your sexuality to avoid facing your problems?"

"Lily, this isn't sexuality. It's mutual respect and admiration." I respected and admired Oswald's body like crazy.

Lily glared at my fiancé, fiancé! and said, "Oswald, I don't think this is right, and I question your motivation and timing." She turned and stormed off.

I shook my head. "I know Lily cares, but I tried it her way. Now let's try it our way." I clutched Oswald's shirt and pulled him with me back into the room.

I maneuvered him into an armchair and said, "I intend to lick you all over." I started with his excellent jaw and moved down to his warm throat. I pressed my tongue against the pulse there and then I nipped gently, making him groan and grab my hips.

I moved my lips to his ear and whispered, "Tell me something we liked to do."

When I looked in his face, his eyes focused on mine.

"Milagro, you know how you like our savory cocktails? We liked to taste each other's blood. Small cuts," he said. "I dream of the way your blood tastes."

It was complimentary, yet disturbing, and I leaned away from him. "If you or anyone tried to cut me, I'd slap the bloodlust right out of your mouth."

"You asked what we liked. I would never do anything you didn't want to do."

I relaxed somewhat. "I'm sure you adore me for other reasons, Oswald, including my seriousness and sincerity."

"Sure," he said, while his clever fingers slipped under my wretched smock and ran up and down my back, sending ripples of pleasure through my body. "This time we won't let anyone interfere with our wedding."

I closed my eyes and rocked against him, saying, "We'll do what I've always wanted, a wedding with friends and a kick-ass band in Mercedes's club. Lots of fizzy drinks with tiny parasols and dancing, and I want to wear a slinky retro dress."

"Or we could have a quiet formal event." He moved me off his lap and stood up. "Your friend Nancy can arrange it. She's a ditz, but she has good taste."

"Nancy's not actually ditzy, and her taste is excellent, but too ritzy. Ritzy as in booking the Ritz."

"Don't worry about the cost."

"I'm worried about the glitz." I had the ooky feeling that we'd had this conversation before. "I think we should avoid anything ending in *itz*."

"Would you please be serious, Mil?"

"I *am* being serious." We'd left the bedroom door open, and we heard footsteps coming up the stairs. A few seconds later, AG, Edna, and Gabriel appeared, talking over one another and asking if it was true, were we engaged, what was going on?

Distracted from my disagreement with Oswald, I showed them the giant, glittering ring. They reacted with varying degrees of enthusiasm.

AG seemed the happiest about our news and looked at my hips and said, "Those are child-bearing hips. I'll finally get some grandsons who can go out in the sun."

"We haven't discussed children," I said.

Gabriel said, "I guess congratulations are in order," and Edna just frowned.

Nevertheless, we went to the living room and Oswald opened a bottle of champagne. The conversation was awkward because we were all aware of Lily's absence and disapproval.

AG sat beside me and asked, "Have you set a date?"

"We're not deciding anything until Milagro recovers," Oswald said.

AG looked meaningfully at his ex. "It could be a double ceremony."

Edna stood up and said, "Not so fast, AG. And, Oswald, I can't believe you asked the Young Lady when she doesn't even remember why you broke up."

"It's all right, Edna," I said. "He apologized."

"You're incapable of accepting reality," she said. "We're vampires."

The others froze at the word, but I laughed. "There's no such thing as vampires. Please. You have a recessive genetic autosomal condition. A *medical* condition."

Edna raised one eyebrow so high that I thought it would float away from her forehead like a helium balloon. "We drink blood and can't tolerate the sun. The transmission of our blood into a normal person's system is usually fatal, you being the exception to the rule. AG is hoping you'll bear children who will have our genetic advantages, without the disadvantages we vampires suffer."

I smiled and explained patiently, "Your so-called vampirism is a condition. Photosensitivity is part of it, as is a craving for high-protein foods and drinks."

"I give up," Edna said. "I'm going to my cottage."

"I'll come with you, dear," AG said.

"No, you won't." Edna walked off, her heels clicking on the floor.

I watched her tidy figure leave and felt a little deflated. I said, "It's been very exciting and I haven't even had my breakfast yet." I headed toward the kitchen.

Oswald began to follow me, but Gabriel said, "Cuz, I'd like a word with you."

"Not now, Gabe."

The smaller man put his arm on Oswald's. "Goddamn it, Oz—"

"That's enough, Gabriel!" AG snapped.

"This is between Oswald and me, Granddad."

"Don't you talk back to me, young man. I'm trying to be tolerant of your lifestyle as it is."

Gabriel's face went cold. "Not as much as I'm trying to be tolerant of yours, old man. Don't think I don't know how you've kept from being lonesome all these years."

I didn't know what was going on between them and I didn't really care. "It's okay, Oswald. I'm feeling a little overwhelmed."

I could already see what Oswald meant about people interfering. I also remembered his comment about puppy fat, so my breakfast consisted of a glass of tomato juice.

The thought of Lily being upset bothered me, so I took off the ring, pulled the glove back on, and went to find her.

She was in the small parlor, tapping away on her laptop. She barely glanced at me as I came in and sat on the plum-colored sofa.

"Hey, Doc, I thought you wanted a session before the Council director arrived."

She stopped working and said, "You shouldn't even be here. You should be in a professional treatment center. Our family has a place in Geneva where you could get the best care to resolve not only your amnesia but your long-term behavioral disorders."

"Lily, I'm sure if I did some digging around your psyche, I'd find some unpleasant little corpses. Why can't we just accept each other as we are?"

She looked annoyed and said, "You have *amnesia*, Milagro. Now if you don't mind, I have to get this report done. I'm leaving as soon as my meeting is over."

"Don't go away mad, Lily! People come from all over the world to vacation here."

"I was brought here to help you. You're fighting your treatment, and Oswald has put his own interests ahead of your well-being."

I moved to the chair next to hers, took off my gloves, and took her hands in mine. "Oswald *is* looking after my well-being by offering marriage. The engagement will prove to the Council director that Oswald believes in my innocence. Even though I don't intend to marry him until I fall in love with him, or when I remember my love, I appreciate how gallant and noble he is to make this offer."

She was taken aback "That's the reason he asked you to marry him?"

"Yes, I think so. That's the kind of man he is. How could any woman resist a man like that? Especially one as sexy as Oswald."

She dropped her head and looked down at our hands. "I don't know. He's wonderful, isn't he?"

"He's certifiably fabulous."

She raised her hazel green eyes to mine. "And you promise me that you won't marry him until you're better and only if you both love each other?"

"I promise." I had a feeling that the falling-in-love process could be expedited with some hot sex, but I didn't need to share that with Lily.

My psychiatrist said, "All right. I'll work with you through the rest of my vacation and try to find someone to take over your treatment."

It was an odd day. Oswald and Gabriel made phone calls in the study, and AG took off to meet with his assistant, Nettie, at the rental house in town.

While Lily was finishing her report, I went to visit Edna in her cottage.

She didn't answer the door at first, so I knocked again. After another five minutes, I shouted, "I hope you haven't fallen and can't get up!"

The door opened wide and she gave me a look so derisive it was practically exfoliating. "Young Lady, what do you want?"

"Edna, I was concerned about you. I thought you might have developed agoraphobia, in which case I would offer to escort you across to the Big House."

"Isn't 'Big House' a colloquial term for a prison?"

"Lily's staying for the rest of her vacation. She reconciled herself to my engagement when I explained that I won't be running off to Vegas with Oswald until I am better and/or in love with him."

"You seem very confident that your feelings for him will develop into love."

"As Wil Shakes says, 'What's past is prologue.' I don't doubt that my personal feelings will follow the same path as before."

"Yes, I had that thought as well, Young Lady," she said. "How is your fauxoir going? Don't you have a deadline?"

"Yes, but I don't know what it is. I'm tearing through the pages like, what is that called, spirit writing? Yes, channeling thoughts from somewhere else. I think it's the best thing I've ever written."

"Better than your llama story?"

"Ha, ha, and ha. That is so funny, not," I said. I noticed that the studio photo of Thomas Cook had been replaced by a photo of AG. "Edna?"

"Yes?"

"Do you think I'll be happy with Oswald?"

"Young Lady, if I knew the secret to a happy marriage, you're the first person I would tell."

"Do you love Mr. Grant? He seems infatuated with you."

"AG is infatuated with carrying on traditions, but there are good traditions and bad traditions. Now go back to the Big House, Young Lady, and stop prying into my life."

* * *

I was in my bedroom when Oswald came in to check on me just before the Council director was supposed to arrive.

My fiancé, fiancé! gave me a long, warm kiss and said, "Everything will be better once this is over."

"Should I change into something nicer for the interview?"

"No, stay exactly as you are. We want him to see that you're, well, sincere and serious."

"I am. I'm überserious. I'm megaserious. I'm somber to the nth degree."

"I know you are, babe. How did you convince Lily to stay?"

Smiling, I said, "I had a reasonable and serious conversation with her, although she does seem a little cranky today. I think she's worried about me."

"Milagro, I'm so happy that we're engaged." Oswald reached into his pocket and took out a gold chain. "I borrowed this from my grandmother so you can wear your ring as a necklace."

"I can take off these gloves and wear it on my finger."

"I think it's best if you don't have physical sensations confusing you tonight."

"I guess you're right."

He smiled and said, "Come to the study in an hour. You can meet my cousin Sam again, and then you'll be interviewed by the Council director. He's brought his longtime girlfriend, who'll visit with my grandmother. They'll stay for dinner and once they leave, we can relax."

"I'm looking forward to that, the relaxing part," I said. "Maybe we can have some serious and sincere naked relaxation time."

"We will when you're well." He reached into his pocket again and took out something silver. "This was yours."

He'd given me such wonderful things that I didn't know why I hesitated before taking the object. It was a small sterling penknife engraved with "To MDLS with Love. OKG."

Suddenly I saw a hotel room, all creams and browns, and the windows outside showed the city skyline. I felt my love for Oswald, and I saw my hand holding the knife that I now held. And now I *knew* that I had truly loved him, but I hadn't liked the knife.

"Milagro?"

"What? Thank you." I didn't want this gift. "It's lovely."

"I hope you'll want to use it . . . eventually."

I smiled, which seemed enough for him, and he said, "You're going to do great."

When Oswald left, I put the knife in the desk drawer. Then I took a look in the bathroom mirror. My *chi-chis* were tragically flattened in the yoga bra, so I changed into a red lace number that had amazing perking properties.

The ostentatious engagement ring needed to be dressed down. I looped a length of green gardening twine through it and wore it around my neck.

Still, I felt plain. I remembered the disco ball earrings. No one could object to such inexpensive trinkets. I put them on and when I moved my head, they swung amusingly.

I used such infinitesimal smidges of makeup that they were practically theoretical.

I knew the guests had arrived when I heard cars, dogs barking, and then faint voices.

I walked to the study, where Oswald was waiting with another man, who was wearing a brown suit and a pink shirt. He resembled Oswald, but with lighter brown hair and gentler features, like a kind accountant who calculates your taxes from a collection of crumpled receipts.

"Young Lady." He held out his hands and took mine. He

glanced down at my gloves and then back at my face. He smiled so warmly that I grinned, too, and said, "Hi."

Oswald said, "Milagro, this is Sam Grant, our cousin and our legal counsel."

"We're old friends," Sam said in a slow, moderated voice. "I wish I could have come earlier, but Dr. Harrison thought that too much activity would interfere with your recovery. You really don't remember me?"

"If I'd remember anyone, it would be you, Sam," I said, and winked.

Oswald said, "Milagro, the Council director is with Gabriel and Lily now."

"Will you be with me for the interview, Ozzy?"

"No, it's a private interview, and the goddamn director better not stray from the guidelines."

Sam blinked his large brown eyes and said, "Milagro, just tell him what you remember or don't. If you feel uncomfortable at any time, ask for a break and come see us."

Oswald took a breath and said, "Ready?"

"Absolutely, I can't wait to be done with this."

Oswald and I went to the living room, where Gabriel and Lily were sitting on a sofa, a bottle of red wine and glasses on the cocktail table in front of them.

Across from them in a leather club chair was a man with dark curly hair, wearing a flawless black suit and an immaculate white shirt. His dark eyes had hooded lids, his nose was aquiline, and he had a full, sensual mouth.

I thought he was the most beautiful man I'd ever seen.

Oswald's expression grew tight and he said, "Let me introduce you. Milagro, this is the director from our family's organization, the Council, Ian Ducharme."

The man stood up and gave me a languid look, as intimate as

a caress, that made all my girl parts clench and throb in a flight-or-flirt instinct.

He smiled slightly when he saw my earrings. As he came close to shake hands, I smelled his fragrance . . . like leather, spice, old books, a wood fire.

He said "Hello, Milagro" in a low, rich voice that made me think *sex, sex, sex.*

Then Oswald glared at him and said, "Ian, you're just in time to hear the good news. Milagro and I are engaged."

sixteen

Zombies and Vamps, Oh, Please

Even though Ian Ducharme didn't react to Oswald's announcement, the room seemed to grow cold and I felt a shiver run down my spine.

Ian smiled, showing white teeth, teeth that made me think about biting into flesh, and said, "Congratulations, Oswald. Now, if you don't mind, I'd like to begin." He spoke English like someone who had learned it from his British tutor.

Gabriel said, "We'll be in the study." He gave his cousin a sharp look, and Oswald said, "Yes, in the study. Come on, Lily."

After they left, Ian went to the sofa and said, "Come sit close to me so I can see you."

"Said the wolf to Little Red Riding Hood."

His laugh was a seductive rumble, and I sat at the other end of the sofa. He poured red wine into glasses and when he handed one to me, I saw something that looked like sorrow in his deep brown eyes.

We clinked glasses and he said, *"Sanatate."*

"Back atcha."

"Dr. Harrison's given me a quite disturbing report of your condition."

"Don't quote me, but Lily's a bit of a drama queen. She takes things too seriously. I keep trying to emphasize the importance of fun to her."

"That's a noble endeavor," he said, and a smile flashed across his face, making me feel as if I'd dedicated myself to curing a putrifying disease.

"It's the least I can do for her."

"I'm sure she's appreciative. She believes that your childhood history has made you susceptible to memory suppression."

"Lily has shared that opinion with me, but I disagree that I'm damaged goods. I'm more like those books on the discount table. Perhaps there's a smudge on the cover, or someone has dog-eared a page, but otherwise the book is perfectly fine, Mr. Ducharme."

"Do call me Ian."

"Ian," I said, and looked into his eyes. It made me feel more exposed than one of those dreams when you're caught naked in public, so I acted as if it was normal. "Ian."

"I've talked to Mercedes and Gabriel, too, as well as Pepper, and Gabriel's given me the forensic investigator's report from your loft."

"Who's Pepper?"

"Ernest Culpepper, a trusted friend," he said. "Wilcox was involved in an activist movement, but no one took his dabbling seriously, so we doubt that was a motive. We thought it more likely that a jealous ex-lover had killed him, since he was a popular fellow, but Wilcox had a talent for staying on good terms with most."

"What about me? Did I have any enemies or jealous ex-lovers?"

Ian hesitated and said, "Yes, but they've been cleared."

"It's so strange to think that anyone would care that passionately about me anyway."

"You're alone in that opinion."

I laughed. "You make me sound like a notorious femme fatale."

He smiled and gazed at me. "We'll continue to investigate Wilcox's disappearance."

"I wish I could help, but I can't remember what happened," I said. "That's not everything, though, is it? No one will tell me about the time between Wilcox's death and my arrival here."

"They thought it would impede your recovery."

"It suddenly strikes me as quite bizarre that I didn't want to know before. Tell me what happened."

"I'll tell you what you told Mercedes. An acquaintance of yours was dabbling in blood play. She accidentally cut an artery and bled to death. You stumbled upon the scene and witnessed her husband slipping, striking his head, and dying."

It sounded incredible, but I believed him. "How could something like that have happened? This was unrelated to Wilcox's death?"

"It's the world we live in, and things happen around you."

"As if I'm a catalyst?"

"Yes, you could put it that way. You were discovered at the scene and taken in for questioning by a private security group." Ian paused and again I saw sadness in his eyes. "You wouldn't tell Mercedes what happened."

"They hurt me, didn't they?"

"She believes so. They held you for over a week before you were able to escape."

"Why didn't I simply tell these people what had happened, when the evidence would have backed me up?"

"You thought it would implicate your friends. You suffered in order to protect them." He reached out and then pulled his hand back. "I'm so sorry."

"That's why I won't remember," I said. "Did Lily tell you that I'm terrified of water?"

Ian nodded.

"I can't even think about filling a tub for a bath. What are the police doing about these accidental deaths?"

"Your acquaintance who died, Ford Poindexter, was the son of a scientist who works for a military contractor. They're influential enough to keep the deaths off police records."

"Will these contractors come after me?"

"They didn't discover your identity, but that doesn't mean you're entirely safe. I believe Mercedes knows more about their location, but she won't disclose anything else." He took out a phone and said, "Will you call her and give your permission to tell me anything she knows about where you were held?"

I nodded and he pressed a few buttons on the phone and then said, "Mercedes, I'm here with Milagro. She'd like to speak with you."

I took the phone and said, "Hi, sweetness."

"Hey, Mil. So you're with Ian?"

"Yes, he's interviewing me about what I know. What did I tell you about where I was held?"

"You weren't sure of the location. I've tried to narrow down the possible neighborhoods from your description."

"Okay, I give my permission for you to tell whatever you know to Ian."

"Are you absolutely sure?"

I looked at the dark-haired man. "Yes, I'm absolutely sure. Oh, and guess what? I got engaged to Oswald again!"

"Oh," she said. "Let's talk tomorrow, okay?"

"Hokay, love ya." I returned the phone to Ian who said, "Thank you, darling."

The term seemed so personal that I was startled and then I

realized that Ian was one of those continental smoothies who probably called every coat-check girl "darling."

"If Mercedes hadn't seemed so concerned, I wouldn't have believed any of this," I said. "I thought I was supposed to be answering your questions."

"You are. Did you kill Wilcox Spiggott?"

"I frequently say that I *want* to kill someone, but I hope I would never do anything so unforgivable. I couldn't stand myself if I took another life."

"I don't believe you killed Spiggott. You were fond of him," Ian said. "Lily's quite concerned about your answers to word associations and your refusal to accept that we're vampires."

"That's Lily in a nutshell: a pretty and serious girl who has a shared delusion that she's a vampire," I said. "Now, you as a vampire, that's far more plausible. Are you mad with the desire to bite my neck and drink my blood, Ian?"

His lips parted and he let out a soft breath as he stared at me. I felt like a deer who'd run into the road on a dare and was now paralyzed by the oncoming headlights of an eighteen-wheeler. Finally Ian said, "The Grants fully anticipated that when they established the conditions for our interview."

I felt myself grow hot, and I looked away. He had charisma, and that made me mistrust myself around him. I said, "Back to Lily, I'm very fond of her, especially since I think she's a natural gardener. I wish she would focus more on horticulture and less on headshrinking."

Ian reached out and put his hand over mine, making me want to rip off my glove so I could feel his skin.

"She told me about this therapy," he said, and moved his hand to the rough fabric of my sleeve, making the smooth pink scar on my arm throb hotly in response. "Is she protecting you from your sensuality, or others from its effects?"

My voice came out as a whisper as I said, "What do you think, Ian?"

His lips turned up in a dangerously sexy grin, and just then I heard heels clicking on the floor. I turned to see a stunning, tall, thin woman in the doorway, and Ian moved his hand off my sleeve.

The woman's straight, waist-length hair had a gold-over-silver luster. She wore skinny white pants, spiky electric blue sandals, and an ice blue silk camisole that matched her ice blue eyes.

"I am tired of the waiting for you, Ian," she said with some sort of European accent. She gazed at me and made a *tcha!* sound. "How ugly the clothes."

"Milagro, this is my friend Ilena," Ian said. "Ilena, that was a very thoughtless comment."

"It is indisputable of the fact," she said with a moue.

I plucked at the fabric of my shapeless pants. "It's okay. These clothes *are* hideous."

Ilena puffed out her lips and said, "Why is the chubby little pickle always in need of your attention, Ian?"

I looked at Ian to see if he understood what she meant.

He said, "I have a passion for gherkins."

I thought it would be rude to say that no one had a passion for pickles. "I'll mention it to Edna and maybe she can serve some at dinner," I said. "Do you know Edna?"

"Yes, I'm well acquainted with all of the Grant family," Ian said. "I think we're done here for now. It was a pleasure spending time with you, Milagro."

Ian Ducharme seemed like a man who knew a lot about pleasure, and his eyes searched mine for a moment before he stood and went to the beautiful blond girl. He took Ilena's arm as they went to the study, and I followed frumpily behind.

Oswald jumped up and came to me, putting his arm around me. "How did it go?"

"We're finished," Ian said.

Oswald smiled and said, "Excellent."

Edna had made dinner, extremely rare lamb, dripping in juices, new potatoes, and tomatoes roasted in balsamic vinegar. It was warm enough to eat outside on the slate patio, and Oswald turned on the tiny fairy lights that outlined the impressive old oak.

Sam opened bottles of a California pinot noir that was as soft and fragrant as the night air. Oswald sat across the table, beside Lily, facing me, and he seemed in an especially lively mood.

Ilena sat beside Gabriel and sipped a glass of water.

"You're a lucky woman, Ilena, to have such an incredible figure," Oswald said. "My clients work so hard to get what's natural to you."

Lily's smile seemed stiff. "Is it accurate to say that they work hard, Oswald, when you're the one performing the surgery?"

He grinned. "They work hard to pay for the surgery."

"Don't you like lamb?" Gabriel asked her.

She made a *pfft* sound and waved her hand. "It is easier not to eat than to be the bulimic with the bad teeth, or to be the sweaty sports girl in the tracksuit."

"Yes, Ilena," Ian said, "but dining like this is one of life's delights."

He could have said anything, like "What a lovely bowl of bananas," and I would have found it wildly erotic. Every now and then I caught him watching me, and my body went right into its flight-or-flirt response.

"Ian's right," Sam said. "Grandmama and Gabriel, it's all delicious. So, Ilena, what have you been doing since we last saw you?"

Ilena brought up trips she had taken and said, "I went with Ian to Lviv, to shop for a chalet. Oswald, you must come for the ski parties. So many potential clients are on holidays there, and I only want to see the pretty faces."

I said, "Lviv is the new Warsaw."

Ian tilted his head and stared at me. "What was that, Milagro?"

"What? I don't know. I don't even know where Lviv is."

"It's in the Carpathians," Oswald said. "Thanks, Ilena. I don't have much opportunity to get out of the country, though."

AG filled Edna's glass and said, "Would you like to go with me there sometime?"

"Do you travel now?" she asked. "You used to hate it."

"Like Oswald, I was working and had a hard time getting away from my responsibilities."

She said, "I know you were doing it all for us, but the children and I would have loved for you to be part of our vacations."

"There are always the grandchildren and their children. Just Sam's daughter for now, but there will be others soon, I hope." AG smiled at me as if I was a prize heifer, and I suddenly realized that I didn't like him at all.

As the evening wore on, the wine had its effect, and conversation grew more animated as my companions talked over one another and across the table. A bottle of port was brought out, and AG put his jacket over Edna's shoulders.

I'd been happy before here, but now I felt such disquiet, as if something was terribly wrong, but I wouldn't know it until it was too late, like driving on a mountain road and discovering my brakes didn't work. *Espíritu* de Wyle E. Coyote. So when Sam said he'd like coffee, I stood up. "I'll make it."

As I went toward the house, the entrance gate opened and a red BMW turned into the property. I decided to see who it was, so I walked to the drive.

The car stopped in front of me. The door opened and a golden-skinned man wearing a black T-shirt and charcoal gray slacks got out. His jet-black hair was cut short, showing off the dramatic angles of his face.

He took one look at me and tossed his keys. I grabbed them automatically as he said, "Park that for me, Milagro, and faking amnesia is no excuse to dress like a depressed slug."

"You're Thomas Cook!" I gasped, thinking that he looked even better than his photographs. He was tall and beautifully proportioned and as yummy as a freshly baked cookie.

"Where's my lady?"

"Who?"

"You're a terrible actress. You should stick to being an assistant, but you're bad at that, too. But I'll go along with your improv. Where's Edna?"

"Around back on the patio."

He strode off around the house.

I got in the warm leather driver's seat of his car, thinking, *My bottom is sitting where Thomas Cook's bottom sat!*

After parking his car, I returned to the others. Edna was standing beside the gorgeous actor, who glared at AG and said, "When are you leaving?"

AG ignored the question and said to Edna, "You can't be serious about this boy."

"AG, behave yourself," Edna said. "Thomas, I thought you were away for two more weeks."

"I have to go back. I couldn't stand being away from you when I knew *he* would be here."

"How very chivalrous of you to save me from my children's father, Thomas," she said with a sly smile.

In a fabulously cheesetastic moment, the actor turned adoring eyes on Edna and said, "I'd cross the oceans for you, my queen. I'd slay dragons for you."

AG shook his head in disgust, and Gabriel said loudly,

"Thomas, I'm sure Ilena and Milagro would love to hear about your experience as an underwear model. We *all* want to hear it again," and everyone fell silent for a moment.

Thomas said, "If you insist."

And Gabriel responded, "Oh, I do."

AG said, "I don't have to waste my time listening to this idiocy," and went into the house.

Thomas led Edna to the table, pulled out her chair, and took the seat beside hers. He smiled his dazzling toothpaste commercial smile and said to her, "You are always sexier than I remember."

Just as she had looked suddenly weary in the cottage earlier, now she looked vivacious. She narrowed her exotic green eyes and said, "Tell your story."

Oswald handed Thomas a glass of wine and he took a sip, then said, "I had only been in Hollywood for a week when I heard about the audition . . ."

Although Thomas's monologue was one of the most enthralling tales I'd ever heard, my ookiness level increased until I could barely listen to the conversation.

When everyone moved inside, I lagged behind and walked out into the inky night across the field. The grasses brushed against my legs and crickets chirped.

As I reached the boulder by Daisy's grave, I was startled to see Ian right behind me. "I didn't hear you," I said, and sat down. "You're too quiet."

"Weren't you enjoying the company?" He sat on the stone beside me.

"Something feels different tonight," I said. "This is my dog's grave. I planted it with rosemary, for remembrance, but I don't remember her, just as I don't remember Wilcox. Rosemary shouldn't remind us to remember; it should represent how essential the *act* of remembering is to our humanity. It's an important distinction."

We were only a few inches apart and now I looked into the night sky and pointed with my gloved hand. "Those stars are Pollux and Castor, the twins raised by wolves," I said, but I didn't know who had taught me that. "I wonder if anyone out there is looking at us here on Earth."

"I should think so, when the view is so captivating."

Ian was like me, reflexively flirtatious, but he had no idea how powerfully I was drawn to him. My strong reaction must be engagement jitters.

"Your girlfriend is stunning."

"I think she's the most dazzling creature in the world." His dark eyes shone in the darker night. "I love her more than I thought possible."

"She's fortunate to have you."

"Not in the least. I've only brought her pain and misery."

"She seems happy enough."

"Her happy nature is one of the countless reasons I love her," he said. "I love her intelligence, the mad mischief in her eyes, the way she makes me laugh, and the way she challenges me. I love her tremendous joie de vivre, her passion, her deeply affectionate nature, her belief in goodness and kindness. When I'm with her, I feel so alive and the world seems full of wonder and possibility."

I desperately wanted to be the woman he described. "Whatever you've done to hurt her, can't you make it up to her? Won't she forgive you?"

"I shall never forgive myself," he said. "If I could do it yet again, I would have tried harder to let her go instead of allowing my desire to rule my actions."

"She's an adult. She can make her own decisions about her life. It's rather patronizing of you to determine what's best for her."

"Perhaps it is."

I wanted to do things to Ian Ducharme that made a lickathon look like a chaste date with your spinster aunt. I wanted to rip his clothes off and suck the very air out of his lungs like a succubus. I wanted to fall at his feet and submit entirely to his most perverse desires like a minion. I wanted to pin him down and tear into his flesh like a wolf. I wanted to drink his blood and possess him like a vampire.

However, a sincere and serious young amnesiac in therapy does not attack a stranger in a field, no matter how gorgeous and in need of comfort he is, especially when her fiancé and his most-beautiful-in-the-world girlfriend were nearby.

"Perhaps you shouldn't listen to me," I said. "I'm not qualified to give advice about your love life."

"What disqualifies you?"

"The usual—a dead boyfriend and his misplaced corpse, amnesia, an engagement held together by duct tape, ghostly visions, a tendency to walk into crime scenes, and unknown enemies."

Ian laughed and said, "Besides that," making me laugh, too. "Tell me about your ghostly visions."

"I think they're over. I must be getting better, or worse. You can ask Lily for her opinion, although I'm sure it will be dire."

"Milagro, do you want to stay here, to be with Oswald?"

"It's very beautiful here and Oswald's been wonderful. He took me back when I needed help. And I know he loves me, because he's given me gifts that only someone who truly understood me could give me, like a first edition of *Jane Eyre*."

"He gave you the ring around your neck," Ian said.

"It's more traditional than my usual style, but I think these earrings are from Oswald, too, because I kept them with my special things." I turned my head from side to side to make the disco balls swing. "See how fun they are?"

"They're tremendously fun. And do you love him?"

"I must, or why would I have come back? He's serious and sincere and successful. He's noble and he does good deeds." I paused, wondering why I didn't feel more enthusiastic. "I'm sure I'll find that we're perfectly compatible in every way."

"You mean you haven't—"

"That's none of your business, and no doubt when we did before, it was amazing," I said, but I thought uneasily of the silver penknife.

As if he could read my mind, Ian said, "Even though he's a vampire and will want to drink your blood? You would let him cut you and taste you?"

"Oswald's a good man, an admirable man, and I'll do what's necessary to make the relationship work," I said. "I'll do better this time. I won't make the same mistakes. I won't take risks and be silly and needy and let people interfere with my relationship."

"Milagro, you need not explain."

"I don't know why I'm telling you this," I said, and pivoted to face Ian. "Even though I can't remember, I know my behavior has caused others to be hurt. To die. So I'll marry Oswald and be happy here, instead of rushing into situations and getting diverted by parties, and by any random fabulous man who comes my way, a man who makes my pulse race and my temperature rise, a man like you . . ."

"Milagro," Ian began, and I knew that if I stayed with him one more second, I would do something unforgivable. Then I heard Oswald's voice calling across the field, "Milagro!"

I quickly stood. "I have to go."

Ian put his hand on my arm and said, "Wait," and I stopped to face him.

"We're staying at the hotel in town and we'll be leaving tomorrow morning," he said. "I wanted to say good-bye. Good-bye and I wish with all my heart that you'll have the happiness you deserve."

"Do you have a heart, Ian?"

"Yes, damaged and in anguish, but beating still."

As I stared into Ian's brown eyes, I panicked because I felt as if I was losing something essential and precious. Nameless feelings rose in me, like a drowning swimmer fighting toward light and the surface. "Won't we meet again, Ian?"

"It's best if we don't. Good-bye, my own girl."

My eyes welled and I swiped them away clumsily with my horrible gloves. "Good-bye, Ian," I said, and then I ran across the field.

Oswald was in the lane and when I saw him, he came to me and said, "Where were you?"

I blinked away my tears. "Visiting Daisy's grave. It made me sad. I'm going in now."

"Sure, babe," he said, and I hurried into the house and the maid's room, feeling lost and stupid and confused and consumed with nameless grief.

I sat in the worn armchair in the dark, staring at nothing and trying to remember something, *anything*, even the ugly things that scared me.

Some time later, I heard cars leaving, and after that there was a knock on my door.

"Milagro, it's Oswald. May I come in?"

I got up and opened the door, keeping the light off. "Sorry, I'm tired."

He stood in the hallway and smiled a little drunkenly. "Sam's gone home and goddamn Ian Ducharme's finally left. Looks like we won't have any trouble from the Council."

"That's good news. Can you come in for a minute?"

"Sure," he said, and swayed forward.

I took him by the arm and brought him into the room, closing the door, and then I led him to the bed. "Sit with me."

He sat and immediately pulled me to him. His kiss was like a stranger's kiss: pleasing and interesting, but unfamiliar. His fingers went to the pulse point on my throat.

I pulled away from him. "Oswald, do you love me?"

He reached for the ring around my neck. "I wouldn't have given you this if I didn't. Do you like it?"

"It's beautiful," I said. "But what exactly do you love about me?"

"You're sexy and pretty. You're smart. You're, uh, tasty. My family likes you."

"When do I meet your parents again? Does your mother adore me?"

"You'll meet them eventually. There's no rush." He removed one of my gloves and lifted my hand to his mouth. "I want to taste you again so bad. I know how to do it so there's no pain."

His kinky lust quelled any desires I had. "It's late."

"You're right. We've got the rest of our lives." He kissed me again and then stood. "I think I'll go for a swim."

"Be careful. You've been drinking."

"I won't dive in. I'll just float on one of the mattresses and kick back. Why don't you come? You don't have to get in the water if it's too weird for you."

I shook my head. "I'm not ready yet."

"Sweet dreams, babe."

"Night, Oswald."

I washed up and went to bed. When I closed my eyes, I kept imagining Ian Ducharme's face, his voice, and I kept turning his words in my mind like a puzzle, searching for other meanings.

A long time later, when I hadn't heard Oswald return, I worried that he might have hit his head diving in the pool, and then we'd both have amnesia. I got up and dressed in jeans and a T-shirt.

I had stepped into the kitchen when I heard someone moving about in the front hall. Thinking it might be Oswald, I went there and saw AG by the open door with a suitcase.

"Hi," I said. "Are you leaving?"

"Nettie is picking me up," he said, his mouth twisted in a frown. "I can't be expected to stay here while Edna's got her gigolo here. She never could be trusted around other men."

Without thinking, I grabbed AG's shoulders and gripped hard enough to make him wince. "That is a very disrespectful way to talk about the mother of your children. If you ever say another unkind word about Edna, I'll . . ."

"You'll what? Kill me, like you did Spiggott?"

I dropped my hands and took a step away from him.

He rubbed his shoulders. "You *would* defend her. You're two of a kind. Maybe you didn't kill Spiggott, but I know how you betrayed my grandson."

"I never betrayed Oswald," I said, but I had a strange queasy sensation.

"*Everyone* knows but you," AG said with an ugly laugh. "Ask Oswald how you broke up his *first* engagement."

I knew what the sick feeling was: bitter, indigestible truth. "I thought you liked me."

"What I think about you personally is irrelevant so long as you are capable of having healthy children."

A gray Honda came down the drive and AG said, "If you say anything to Oswald about this, I'll tell him you're lying. It's only his sense of responsibility that keeps him from throwing you out in the gutter where you belong."

AG went to the car, put his suitcase in the backseat, and got in. As the car turned around in the drive, I saw Nettie, who smiled apologetically as she passed.

My curiosity, quiescent for so long, now replayed AG's comments and I tried to make sense of them. I'd broken up Oswald's *first* engagement. I'd betrayed him. He had asked me to marry him because he felt responsible for me.

As I walked out to the pool compound, I broke into a cold sweat. Perhaps I could just peek in somewhere to make sure Oswald was okay. I was circling the redwood structure when I spotted a knot in one of the boards.

I thought I'd have to pry the knot out, but it slid out smoothly. I was relieved to hear Oswald's voice faintly, and then I put my eye to the opening.

My fiancé, wearing swim trunks, sat at the edge of the pool, his feet dangling in the water. He took a drink from a half-empty bottle of vodka and passed it to Lily, who sat beside him wearing a modest one-piece suit.

My psychiatrist said, "You're not really going to marry her, are you?" She was sozzled and said "reeely."

"I have to, don't I? It's my fault she got infected in the first place." He was drunk, too, and he said "firsht plashe."

"Even if you never love her again?"

He shrugged and took another long drink. "What else has she got? Doesn't have a job, can't pay condo fees, her latest boy toy is dead, lost her mind."

"Her memory, not her mind." Lily said. "At least she's hot for you."

Oswald laughed so hard that he choked and Lily slapped him on the back. Then he said, "Yeah, but she won't let me cut her like a wife is supposed to. She looks freaked every time I mention it and doesn't want to taste me, either. That's okay. It's my duty to care for her."

"Oh, poor Oswald, *poor, poor* Oswald." She took a drink and handed the bottle back to him.

"It all started because of a stupid, stupid mistake. I met her at a party—that's the kind of girl she is, always at some party— and she was pretty and fun and how was I to know she'd get infected?"

"You're so good," she said as she leaned against him. "So beautiful and good and brilliant. You're fabulous."

"You are, too. Why did we meet again like this, Lily? Why weren't we matched up by the dating service? Because I think you're the perfect woman."

"Oswald, let's have one night together, one night we can remember forever of what should have been."

I didn't wait to hear more. I ran from the awful scene.

But I was trapped here, the fence corralling me like an animal, and I ran from the field toward the vineyard, because I needed to get away, and I could climb the side fence and escape without the guards seeing me.

As I crossed a row of grapevines, the horrible specter of my dead boyfriend, Wilcox Spiggott, rose up, arms spread wide, his beyond-the-grave voice rasping, "Milagro!"

seventeen

This Is Your Brain Unplugged

I'd had a very emotionally taxing day, more so than any sensible girl could be expected to handle with grace. So I shouted, "Come on, you evil dead imaginary bastard, just try to eat my brain!"

"Chillax, cutie."

"You're a figment of my sick, damaged mind! You're not real."

"Ouch. Maybe someone needs a spanking, but give me a kiss first."

I would face my own hallucination and prove to myself that it was only air. But the phantasm wrapped his coldish arms around me and kissed me on the mouth with his cool, greenish lips and his breath that smelled of . . . of flowers and tropical rain.

It was the magic kiss from a zombie.

The protective shell of amnesia cracked open like an egg on the edge of a cast-iron skillet, memory spilling out and sizzling on the scorching surface.

My knees buckled and Wil grabbed hold of me and said, "You okay?"

I started laughing and clutched him to me. "You're alive!

You're really alive!" I kissed his cheeks, his forehead, his eyes, but I was remembering the man I had killed, Average Joe. Thoughts and images rushed at me, but nothing was as important as Wil. "I'm so happy that you're alive!"

"I'm not sure I'm technically alive. I was stabbed."

"Who did it?"

"My houseman. That old bastard followed me to California to keep me from his daughter. I had an awesome day riding the waves, was on my way to meet you when he caught up with me at a rest stop. The next thing I knew I woke up bloody dead in the back of your pickup."

"Matthews claimed that you had asked him to join you."

"Pure bollocks. I told you how I felt about him."

"Yes, but you neglected to tell me that Nettie was his daughter. Besides, recalling things has been a problem. I fell and hit my head and got amnesia. Your kiss brought back my memory."

"A shock to the system."

"Here's another one. Nettie's in town and Matthews is, too."

"What's she doing here, and where are we?"

"She's my fiancé's grandfather's thrall and we're at my fiancé's ranch. My *ex*-fiancé, Oswald Grant. We were engaged again until about ten minutes ago," I said, and tried to integrate Oswald's recent behavior with our past together. "He's busy having sex with my psychiatrist by the swimming pool right now."

"You don't seem upset."

I grinned. "It's just sex, Wilcox."

He laughed hoarsely. "I'm starving. Do you have anything to offer besides brains? I've been living off old walnuts and greens. Most of the time I've been sleeping. Sometimes the dogs come and kip by my side."

"Wil-*cox*," I said, and took his thin hand. I kissed it. "You smell like spring."

"I think I'm a vegetarian now. Odd."

We walked to the house and he said, "I've had to learn to move again, but I'm improving every day."

I took him to the kitchen and he slowly bent to sit in a chair. I laid my hand on his chest and felt a faint, slow beat. "You're alive."

"I feel alive. But different."

I thought of Average Joe and asked, "What was it like being dead?"

He considered and said, "It's as if I was a cup of water poured into the ocean and gathered up in a different vessel—not quite the same and yet essentially myself."

I had hated Average Joe, but I felt relieved of my guilt for having permanently ended his existence.

I quickly assembled a plate of food for Wil: olives, arugula dressed with lemon and oil, a slice of fresh asiago, smoked almonds, and raspberries. I took a bottle of zin out and he said, "White wine would be nice," so I found a bottle of crisp French white.

I had a glass and watched him while he ate. When he leaned back from the table, I said, "We've both been in limbo. I'm so sorry, Wil, for what happened to you."

He looked more serious than I had ever seen him. "Milagro, I can go out in the sun now without any protection. It's fucking amazing. I think I don't mind being dead."

I remembered *Don* Pedro's words and said, "You're in the realm of the middle place, 'life after life and before deathly death.' I wrapped you in that cloth, which was woven with herbal remedies, and you came back."

"I'm a zombie, then?"

"It's more positive to think of you as life-impaired. Or pre-dead."

He laughed. "Whatever turns your engine, Mil. I'll tell you

what happened with me, and then you tell me what happened with you."

"Deal. Let's start with Matthews."

"He just said 'Useless bastard,' and he stabbed me. If I knew he felt that way, I would have fired him earlier."

"You fired him?"

"Yes, he took me to the airport and I said, 'Now see here, Matthews, I can't have you about because my new lady says that it perpetuates class divisions, et cetera."

"I never said you should fire him!"

"Didn't you? Oh, well."

"He must have taken my house key when he came by your flat to get your laundry. He left you, your body, at my loft on my bed," I said. "You're in love with Nettie, aren't you? You came to see her, not me."

Wil shrugged his bony shoulders. "Sorry, Mil, but Nettie knows how to put a lad like me in my place. I hoped to convince her to come back home with me."

"Wil, the bad news is that you're a zombie. The good news is that I think Nettie loves you, too."

My friend Nancy had been quoting a lot of Sun Tzu to me recently, so I followed his advice to appear in places the enemy doesn't expect, i.e., Nettie's house at three in the morning.

Wil asked, "Why not let the Council handle it?"

"I'd like to truss up Matthews and deliver him to the Council personally to clear my name."

"You really are a hot, sexy bitch. If not for Nettie . . ."

I gave Wil a pair of jeans and a T-shirt that were in the maid's closet. As he changed clothes, he said, "Look, none of my body parts fell off and all are in perfect working order. Allow me to demonstrate."

Laughing, I said, "Not now. Go wash your face." When he went into the bathroom, I took the velvet ropes from the closet and put them in the sports bag.

He came out of the bathroom with my makeup case. "You'll have to teach me to use this. I can't go looking like shit to Nettie."

"Just use the cover stick for under your eyes and a little blush on your cheeks, like this," I said, and touched him up, lining his eyes, too. I smoothed clear gloss on his lips to counteract the dryness and he bit my finger and sucked it. "You're incorrigible, Wil."

"It's been yonks," he said. "How do I look?"

Oswald's old jeans were falling off Wil's thin hips, but a good meal and cosmetics had done wonders. "You look sizzling for a cold body. *Vámonos.*"

Wilcox picked up the white woven cloth. "I've become attached to it."

I took the sports bag when we went outside to the big ugly white truck. Once I was sitting high in the cab and revving the engine, I had to admit that it seemed like the right kind of ride for a confrontation. "Strap in and hang on."

We drove to the gate, which swung open and I waved to the guards in the black cars. I could have talked to them, but that would have slowed me down and I felt a need for speed. One car door opened and a man in a navy suit jumped out, but I was already racing to Nettie's house.

The sky was still dark, and the road was all ours; it was too early for the meth dealers to head home, or the commuters to go to work. The guards were tailing me and one tried to speed up, but I put the pedal to the metal and lost them at a turnoff onto the highway into town.

When I'd lived at the ranch, I spent many hours going through the small town looking for potential gardening clients. There was one house with a purple gate and exuberant Climbing Peace roses. I stopped a few houses down from the single-story stucco bungalow. A light was on inside, showing through the curtains at the edges.

"I can't wait to see Nettie again," Wil said. "What are you going to do?"

"Grab her father and turn him over to Gabriel Grant, Oswald's cousin who handles security and has a sense of compassion."

"Perhaps Nettie will try to defend him and you can have a wild catfight, clothes being ripped off, nipples twisted, bottoms spanked, that sort of thing."

I reached behind me, unzipped the sports bag, and grabbed the black velvet ropes.

Wil opened his mouth, and I said, "Not now, Wil. I don't anticipate any problems, but I want you to stay outside until I've subdued Matthews."

As we approached the house, I pointed to a purple smoke bush and whispered, "Wait there."

I went to the front door and was about to bust it down when it occurred to me that I could just try the doorknob.

It turned, and I walked in to see Nettie wincing as she sat on an old tweed couch beside AG Grant. AG was sucking on her arm while one of his hands was groping under her T-shirt.

I shrieked in disgust and Nettie shrieked in surprise.

"You horrible man!" I said to AG. "So this is how you keep from being bit twice."

He licked his bloody lips. "It's my right as her master."

"It's no one's right to exploit another human being."

"I knew you were faking amnesia," he said. "I'm going to file a complaint with the Council and have you locked up until you're as old as you are crazy." He reached for the phone on the end table.

"Pick up that phone and I'll beat you with it like you're a

snare drum at Mardi Gras," I said. "Nettie, move away from that creep."

She slid to the other side of the couch and said, "Milagro, you're having a relapse. You don't know what you're doing. You need to get back to the ranch and have a session with Dr. Lily. I can take you back."

"Tell me where your father is."

"Why?"

"Because he murdered Wilcox Spiggott."

Her shock looked real. "My father didn't murder anyone!"

"That's not what Wil says," I answered.

I heard a noise behind me and turned to see Matthews.

He held a long, sharp knife. He gripped it like a man who knows how to efficiently French-trim a rib roast.

"You again, you troublesome woman."

"Daddy, what are you doing?" Nettie said. "You promised me that you didn't hurt Wil."

"Natalie, I didn't. Not that he's of any consequence. He was nothing but a disgrace to his noble people."

"Daddy!" Nettie said, and stood up. "Wil was wonderful. He loved me." She stepped forward until she was beside me. "I loved him, too. I wanted to be his thrall."

"You're too good for the likes of him," Matthews said to Nettie, but his eyes didn't waver from mine. "You deserve a respectable master, like Mr. Grant here."

I said, "Wilcox was trying to make a positive difference in this world!"

"We don't need a 'positive difference,' you disgusting half-thing," Matthews sneered, "with your graphs and charts, your timelines and your American ideas about equality and progress! You would have destroyed our whole world."

"Then you should have come for me, not Wil."

"That I would have, but I couldn't very well kill Lord Ducharme's favorite whore, could I?" Matthews set his feet and adjusted his grip on the knife. "But now that that's done with, he won't care if you have an accident, or disappear."

Time slowed in the moment that Matthews lunged for me. I waited so that I could move away from the knife and grab his wrist.

But Nettie jumped in front of me, and the sharp blade slid into her flesh.

We were silent as we took in the horror of what had happened. Matthews's face froze. AG stood and then stumbled back to the couch.

Nettie looked down at the knife in her chest and the blood leaking out over the handle, and then at her father.

I held my hand in front of Matthews and said, "Don't pull it out—you'll cause more bleeding. We'll call nine-one-one!"

Nettie's knees buckled. I caught her before she fell, and I remembered catching Ford as he fell. Her eyes were fixed on her father's and she said, "I love you, Daddy."

He screamed "Nettie!" and grabbed her hand.

Wilcox came running into the house then and saw the dying girl. "Nettie!"

He reached for her and I handed her into his thin arms. "Nettie," he said. "I love you."

She smiled as she looked at him and then I saw the light fade in her eyes, as it had faded in Ford's, in Daisy's, and in Average Joe's. I knew she was dead before I checked for a pulse, but I was saying, "No, Nettie, no!"

Matthews wailed, "My beautiful girl! My beautiful baby!" He fell to his knees and began keening, a sound that tore through me, the sound of a father's anguish, while AG sat and stared in shock.

I said, "It's not her time," and then I ran outside, down the street to the truck. I flung open the passenger door and grabbed the woven shroud. I was already back in the house when Wil, still weak, staggered with the girl's body.

I spread the cloth on the floor and said, "Set her down on it."

When Wil did this, I told Matthews, "I'm going to take the knife out now and she'll bleed. Then we'll wrap her and she'll come back, like Wil came back. All right?"

Matthews finally noticed his former employer. "You're alive?"

"Alive enough. Say yes."

"Yes, do it!" Matthews said. "Please do it."

I braced myself and pulled the knife out of Nettie's chest. Blood gushed from the wound, and I tried to be swift and gentle as I wrapped Nettie in the soft, fragrant while cloth.

Her blood soaked through it, as bright red as an Iceland poppy. I was terrified that the magic had been used up, but suddenly the blood stopped spreading on the fabric. Then it seemed to be absorbed back into the cloth as the scent of spring grasses and flowers filled the air.

The Grant family's security guards barged into the room, and I was glad to see them because they were able to divert the cops, who arrived a few minutes later.

eighteen

Dead Reckoning

AG remained at the rented house, and the rest of us returned to Casa Dracula. The guards drove Matthews, Wilcox, and Nettie. I took my truckasaurus and was the first one through the gate.

I remembered why I'd come to hide out at the ranch, desperately wishing that I could turn back the clock to the time before I had blood on my hands.

The day was dawning, as it had been then. The dogs bounded forth to greet me, as they had then. I remembered my new dog, Rosemary, now, and deadlines and bills and all the big and little things that I'd been able to ignore as an amnesiac. I remembered why Oswald and I had broken up.

And I remembered what had happened to me when I was at the military contractor's compound.

I parked the truckasaurus and went into the house through the back door. Gabriel's guards must have called the Grants, because everyone was in the kitchen waiting.

"Babe," Oswald said, but I walked right past him into Edna's arms.

"The bitch is back, Edna," I told her.

"I've been expecting you, Young Lady," she said, and kissed my cheek. Then I gazed around the room. Oswald stood looking dignified, while his accomplice in the horizontal hokey-pokey was wide-eyed and nervous.

That's when Wil came in, struggling as he carried Nettie's shrouded body. Matthews stayed outside with the guards.

I said to Wil, "Take her to the living room. Once I leave, she can have the maid's room. She'll be able to smell the flowers coming in on the breeze."

Things quickly became chaotic. Everyone was asking questions about the green-tinged man and the body. I told them about Wil's murder and reanimation, and how Matthews had accidentally killed Nettie and the magic of the gift from *Don Pedro*.

"That's impossible," Oswald said.

"I'm sure there's a rational scientific explanation, but I'd rather think it's magic," I said. "Oswald, I'd like Nettie to stay here until she recovers. Lily, if you decide to extend your vacation here, I think you can help her cope with the transition."

"But *you* still have underlying emotional problems," Lily said.

"I've got important business to take care of now. I'll deal with my personal life later."

Oswald said, "You're leaving? To do what? Milagro, haven't you learned anything? You're not actually going to rush off and do something foolish and dangerous, are you? I'm trying to take care of you!"

"Actually, I *have* learned something, Oswald. I can't run away from things, or run back to the past. Maybe I haven't figured out what my purpose is yet, but I know it's bigger than my little life, and you can't protect me from it, because I'm a catalyst—things happen wherever I am."

Oswald and Lily glanced at each other, and then he said, "Milagro, I'm willing to honor my promise to marry you."

I stared into his storm gray eyes. "That's very good of you, considering what you and Lily were up to last night."

"We didn't do anything," he said. "Lily and I have a purely professional relationship."

I looked at my psychiatrist and said, "What do you think about that, Lily?"

That's when she lifted her hand and slapped Oswald across his face.

Oswald clapped his hand to his cheek and said, "What the hell!" and Lily said, "Oh, my God, I can't believe I did that!" and I said, "If you didn't, I would have," and Edna said, "I tried to warn her about the quicksand."

Edna caught up with me as I was putting my packed sports bag into the truck. She said, "Lily hasn't confessed to anything yet, but I foresee cheap melodrama by nightfall."

"Guilt and anger will do her a world of good. Being perfect must be exhausting."

"You'll never have to bear that burden."

"We can start a club," I said. "I'm thrilled that you made the irrational decision to keep your addled young paramour over your cranky ex, and not just because Thomas is prettier, but because he adores you."

"You *did* say addled," she answered with a slow smile.

"I may have contributed to AG's departure by requesting that he be more respectful of you."

"Oh, is that what you call assaulting and threatening him?"

"I thought that's what I said." I tried raising one eyebrow, but both went up. "What is it about Grant men?"

"Do you mean Oswald and Lily? I wondered when you'd notice."

I shrugged. "It was Marx who said things happen twice, first as tragedy, then as farce."

"I didn't know you studied political theory, Young Lady."

"I didn't. I studied farce. I'd love to chat, but now I've got to kick serious military contractor ass."

"I could ask you to be careful."

"Careful is for other people, Edna, not for superheroes."

"I give up," she said. "Go on and be a superhero."

I drove back to the City, and the scenes out the window were like a slideshow of my life with the vampires: here was where Edna had taken me to buy clothes, here was where Oswald worked, and here was where my sabotaged car had plunged off the mountainside.

It was too early for Mercedes to be up, so I went to my loft, anxious about what I would find. I unlocked the door and pushed it all the way open so I could see inside. The place smelled stale and a layer of dust covered the surfaces.

I set down my sports bag and walked in slowly, listening and peering around. Things were moved fractionally and drawers weren't completely shut. Even though Wil's murderer had been apprehended, I was still uneasy being here. After searching the apartment, I locked the front door and used the bolt lock.

I had to act fast while Ian was still with Ilena. How could one *chica,* albeit one who had recovered her fabulous style, defeat a building filled with men who were trained in battle?

I came up with ten plans in half an hour, each more convoluted than the last. It occurred to me that I hadn't slept last night, what with the excitement of reanimated corpses and catching killers. I wrapped myself in a comforter, lay down on the pink sofa, set my alarm for noon, and passed out.

When I opened my eyes, the first thing I saw was the overcast sky outside my windows. The Grants had sent me home with a care package, so I drank a calf's-blood spritzer while I fried fresh eggs and topped them with salsa.

As I was washing the dishes, the buzzer sounded from the front entrance.

"Yello?" I said.

"It's me," Mercedes said.

"Come up." I pressed the button to open the building's entrance and waited in the hallway. In a few minutes, my friend came from the elevator, holding a paper bag. My brown dog, Rosemary, trotted at her side.

Mercedes smiled broadly and said, "You should have called me. Gabriel phoned as soon as he got the news from his family." She hugged me, and I kissed her cheeks and mussed her dreads until she pushed me away and said, "Cut that out."

I scratched Rosemary's back and he wagged his tail and licked my hand, but he didn't seem as elated as I thought he should be.

Once we were inside my place, I locked the door and said, "I've missed you like crazy."

"I'm glad to see you looking healthy again." She went to the kitchen table and put down the paper bag. "I've got to go to the club in an hour. Can you tell me what happened in that time?"

"I can edit for brevity, I suppose, but you'll miss out on my insights." When I'd finished telling my story, Mercedes sat open-mouthed.

"So?" I asked.

"You seem very blasé for having resurrected Wilcox."

"Once you've seen a wolf shapeshift, you get a little jaded."

Mercedes paused and I could see that she was deliberating. After a minute, she said, "Are you still going to marry Oswald?"

"He's a fabulous man, the sort of man any sincere and serious young woman would want to marry. The top item on my to-do list, however, is stopping a mad scientist from creating an army of zombie slaves."

"Let it go, Milagro. Ian called late last night and I told him everything you told me."

"Does he know the location of the facility? Did he say he was going to do anything?"

"He was still with Ilena when we spoke. You never gave me much to go on. I hope he *does* find those bastards." She bent over and rubbed Rosemary between his ears, and he gazed up at her with devotion.

I watched my friend's expression and said, "Rosemary's as crazy about you as I am. Take him home."

"Milagro, you already lost a dog."

"Rosemary and I have given it a good try, and we could keep trying to be right for each other. But the thing about dogs, Mercedes, is that you know when you've met the right one. And the dog knows, too."

"Are you still talking about dogs?"

"And more, perhaps," I said. "What's in the bag?"

"A laptop and a phone. You've got a new number, and it's set up to relay your calls through overseas hubs, so it's hard to trace. For the computer, I uploaded your data from the last time you brought it to the club."

"How do you know I don't regularly back up all my data?" I recalled the flash drive I'd taken from Mercedes's trash bin—the flash drive with a worm so poisonous that Mercedes wouldn't even look at it.

"Please, *mujer*," Mercedes said, "the day you start being tech-savvy is the day I'll start flirting outrageously with every pretty boy I see." She was grinning, though, and so was I.

After Mercedes and Rosemary left, I put the composition

books with my second fauxoir on my desk and turned back to my cogitating.

As I was musing, I noticed that one of my first dog's toys, a chewed-up squeaky bear, was on my windowsill. Ford's mother must've been suffering from the loss of her son and her cat, and I knew she was the only one who could influence Professor Poindexter.

I made a phone call to *Don* Pedro. He said, "My sweet little bat, I have been sending my spirit guide to help you. I am very worried!"

"*Don* Pedro, I definitely needed a spirit guide, but the blanket you gave me was very useful. What are my chances of getting more?"

"*Chula,* I will answer a question with a question. Have you finished transcribing the riveting story of my adventures among those who are in the twilight world before death?"

"I'll finish it in two weeks," I said. "I composed the story in my head while I was being held captive by a mad scientist, and I somehow was able to access that part of my mind while I recently had amnesia. I recovered from the amnesia when a zombie kissed me."

"Your adventures are almost as exciting as my own, little bat! What will you give in exchange for the weavings?"

"What about the second installment of my payment?"

"The weavings are so especial and valuable, are they not?" he said. "What price is life?"

"Real life is priceless, but zombified life should be on the clearance rack."

"Or is it even *more* precious for having almost been lost?"

"*Don* Pedro, you are a shifty little bastard. Yes, you can keep the second installment in exchange for two cloths. I need them as soon as possible. Where are you?"

"The second and *final* installment of your payment," he said.

"I came to the City because I knew you would need me. Let us meet in thirty minutes at the same restaurant as the last time."

Last time, we'd met at a waterfront bistro. "Somewhere else?" I asked.

"It must be there, little bat, or not at all. Bring what you have written so far."

I said good-bye to the crafty little fellow and took a quick glance at the notebooks. I would have liked to clean up the story, add interesting metaphors, delete redundancy, and develop the imagery, but perhaps I could do that if *Don* Pedro gave me a chance at the copyedited manuscript.

I put the composition books in my backpack and walked quickly toward the restaurant.

Because it was the middle of a chilly gray afternoon, the restaurant's deck was empty except for *Don* Pedro. He was sitting at the table nearest the bay, dark green water lapping only a few yards away.

I glanced around and saw one of his bodyguards/followers, leaning against the wall of the building. I took a deep breath and walked toward the table. I kept my eyes on the gray wood planks beneath my feet and took a seat that faced away from the water.

"Good afternoon, *Don* Pedro."

He had a pot of tea in front of him, and he poured a cup for me. "*Mijita,* I am quite delighted to see you well again."

"I'm glad to be well." I took a sip of tea and then reached into my backpack and took out the notebooks. "I'm about halfway through. The weavings?"

His old brown leather shoulder bag hung from the chair. He placed it on his lap and withdrew a package wrapped in plastic. "Use them wisely, Milagro de Los Santos."

"I will," I said. "Also, I'm available to line edit for a reasonable fee."

He was about to say something, but he stopped and squinted his big brown bug eyes behind the glasses and said, "We shall meet again on your island, Isla Milagro, with your friends back from death."

"It sounds like a plan," I said. "I'll be in touch when I've finished your fauxoir."

He stood up and I thought he was going to try to hug me, but the little man took off his huge black-rimmed glasses, set them on the table, and slipped off his soft brown moccasins.

He smiled at me and took a few steps to the edge of the deck. I didn't want to look at him standing so close to the water, but I couldn't help myself.

Then he stepped over the edge and splashed into the water.

I waited for him to bob up again, and I squeezed my fists so tight that my nails dug into my palms. When he didn't come up, I turned to his bodyguard/follower and shouted, "*Don* Pedro fell in! Get him."

The stolid man looked at me impassively.

"He'll drown," I shouted. "Save him."

The guard said, "He will transform into a fish. Or maybe a frog."

"Goddamn!" I pulled off my shoes and went to the edge of the deck. I couldn't see *Don* Pedro, and I was cold, cold from the wind blowing across my nervous sweat. Superheroes couldn't be afraid of water. I closed my eyes and jumped.

For a moment all I felt was fear. Then came the shock of cold and consuming panic. I thrashed in the water, turned about, and saw the lighter surface above me. *Don't panic,* I told myself.

I looked around until I saw *Don* Pedro's white shirt billowing in the water. I swam to him, and he reached out his small hand to me. When I took it and pulled him upward, he was as light as a rubber duck.

He clutched the edge of the deck and I pushed his butt up to help him scramble out of the water. Then I pulled myself out.

Don Pedro was shaking the water off like a dog and he beamed.

"You crazy little—" Then I realized that I'd faced the water and survived.

"I thought I was a platypus again." *Don* Pedro winked at me. "Until we next meet, my miracle girl."

I started laughing and said, "Yes, until next time, *Don* Pedro."

I trudged in my wet clothes to the grocery store. The clerk stared at me as I bought a big juicy steak, red cabbage slaw, cranberry juice, and crusty whole grain bread.

I went to my loft, ate dinner, and studied maps on the Internet, looking for street views. None of the satellite photos available showed the compound, which allowed me to pinpoint the location by its very absence.

This was just the occasion to wear my new black leggings, a black tank, a jacket with lots of pockets, and black tennis shoes. I put my hair in a bun and shoved a lot of bobby pins in it in case I needed to escape from handcuffs. I pulled on a black beanie, which made me look as if I had a giant tumor on my head.

My plan wasn't very good, but it was the only one I could think of that wouldn't endanger anyone else.

When darkness came, I drove the truckasaurus toward the south end of the City, and after some searching I found the sewer pipe where I'd left Average Joe's keys. I had to reach into muck, but they were still there.

I drove to a block of shut-up warehouses near the Professor's facility. I parked between two buildings, with the truck facing toward the street, and left my keys in the ignition so I could make a fast getaway.

After putting on my backpack, I jogged on dark and empty streets until I saw my destination. A few lights were on at the perimeter gate and on the second floor, where I thought the Professor had his living quarters.

There was an olive green post office drop box across from the property. I watched as the guard patrolling the grounds walked back into the building, and then I dashed to the drop box and hid behind it.

Several minutes later, I heard the engine of the nightly delivery van, and then I saw its headlights.

When the van turned into the facility's driveway, I ran so that I was hidden behind it on the passenger side. The gates slid open, and I kept pace with the van as it crossed the lot and entered the garage. Once inside, I dropped to the cement floor and rolled under a vehicle.

I heard the van's engine stop, and then clanking as the driver opened its doors. While he unloaded his cargo, I crawled to the car parked closest to the lab.

Waiting is hard. One of the cat clones found me under the car and curled beside me. I pet its soft fur while the minutes passed. I heard the delivery van driver say "See ya," then doors closing. The engine started and the van drove off.

I peeked out from under the car. The garage was empty. I crept out and found the Professor's car. When I clicked the transponder key to unlock it, the beep echoed in the garage, but no one came. I unlatched the trunk but didn't raise it, and left the driver's-side door slightly ajar.

Then I made my way to the autopsy room door and pressed myself flat against the wall in the shadows. To stay calm, I thought about *Don* Pedro's story and the chapters I had yet to write.

My tension made my wait seem interminable, but then the door opened and the lab tech stepped out. He held a pack of cigarettes in his hand and began walking to the garage exit.

I slipped through the autopsy room door, before the automatic doors slid shut.

The scene was more gruesome than I recalled. I was momentarily transfixed by the glass cases of limbs and organs bobbing in the viscous yellow fluid.

I opened the heavy metal door of the chill room and the frigid air hit me. Cricket and Ford Poindexter were still lying on gurneys, their medical machines beeping and buzzing around them.

I didn't know if *Don* Pedro's weavings would work after so long a time, but I took them from my backpack. I detached the tubes from Cricket, lifted her small, cold body, and rolled her in the fabric.

The jealousy I'd once felt seemed stupid and petty.

Then I removed the tubes from Ford and wrapped him in the fragrant shroud. I'd intended to take Señor Pickles, too, but something stopped me.

I put the Poindexters together on one gurney and pushed it out of the chill room.

I went to the computer at the lab tech's desk. I might not know how to fix a computer, but I had a talent for screwing them up. Too often in my temp jobs I'd accidentally sent an embarrassing personal message to the entire company.

I took the flash drive out of my pocket and inserted it in a port. A few seconds later, I'd sent the toxic file to everyone in the company with the tantalizing subject title "Hawt zombie azz in sexxxy axtion!"

To help get things started, I opened the worm file. A button popped up that said "Run?" and I clicked "yes." A second later, the screen started flashing with files being automatically opened and, I hoped, irrevocably corrupted.

I glanced at the clock on the wall. I'd been in the lab for three minutes. I rolled the gurney to the door that led to the garage, hit the button to open it, and looked out. The garage was empty, so I pushed the gurney to the Professor's car.

I placed the bodies in the trunk and gently pressed down until I heard it click locked when I heard a familiar sound, the *shsh-shsh-shsh* of corduroy pants.

The Professor came across the garage and said, "I had an alarm set on the bodies because I expected you to return." He looked at me with a satisfied smile. "Your recovery is excellent."

I leaned back against his car. "How did you know I wouldn't go to the police?"

"Because they don't take vampire abuse very seriously. My men are now stationed outside the building." The Professor took his hand from his pocket and held up a dark plastic device. "If you even move to hurt me, they're instructed to slaughter you."

"Sounds unpleasant for the both of us. Can you suggest any alternatives?"

"Give me a few organs to work with and I'll let you live. A kidney, a lung, and an eye to start."

"Can I think about that and get back to you?"

"My time is valuable and I need to get Ford and Cricket stabilized before degradation sets in."

"In that case, no, I will not let a mad scientist use my organs for evil."

"Your sense of self-righteousness compromises your already limited intelligence. You're a stupid girl with a delusional sense of your value to the world."

That's when the building rocked and huge boom sounded. I thought it was an earthquake when it started, but the building shaddered from above, not from the ground. The Professor looked around, bewildered.

"I'm not stupid," I said. "I'm a Miracle of the Saints." I jumped in the driver's seat of his car as a second explosion jolted the building. A frightened cat was crouched nearby, and I grabbed it and tossed it to the backseat, slammed the door shut, and turned on the ignition.

The garage gate opened and a few uniformed men stormed inside, and I could see others scrambling around the lot.

"Get me out!" the Professor yelled at me, and then one of the garage walls exploded and chunks of concrete rocketed out. A hunk of cement struck the Professor's head and knocked him off his feet.

He was a man with too much brilliance and no moral compass. He was a danger to the world and I couldn't take the chance that the military contractors might save him. I hit the gas and ran over his body, crushing his skull, and I screeched out of the garage.

More explosions sent shattered glass hailing down on the car. I glanced back and saw orange flames blazing out from every level of my prison.

The entrance gate opened for a black SUV turning into the asphalt lot, and I streaked around it, missing it by inches, and careened onto the street and away.

Shots were fired as I escaped, but the car windows were bulletproof, and they spiderwebbed without breaking. A black SUV tore after me, but I could drive in the dark faster than anyone else. Almost anyone else.

As soon as I evaded my pursuers, I returned to the truckasaurus, put the cat in the cab, and transferred Ford and Cricket to the back. I drove the Professor's car to the bay and sent it over the barrier, watching only for a moment as it sunk in the dark water.

I ran back to the truckasaurus and was safely driving away when I heard the helicopters in the distance, their propellers beating the air, and their searchlights piercing the night.

nineteen

Fly Me to the Loon

Wil had woken up nine days after being shrouded, and I hoped I had that much time before the Poindexters returned to this plane of existence.

I packed away most of my belongings and put them in a long-term storage locker. I rented a security deposit box for the gifts from Ian . . . except for the disco ball earrings, which I tucked into my makeup bag.

I found an old three-bedroom bungalow for lease near the desolate desert town of La Basura. The house was on a side road, miles away from other houses, and I figured that strange greenish inhabitants could go unnoticed there for some time.

I rented my loft to Juanita, the leader of My Dive's house band. Then I said *hasta la vista* to my Stitching & Bitching group, one of whom was happy to adopt a striped cat; she also took my unfinished knitting project, the blue-gray scarf and yarn.

I told Nancy I was going on a long-term writing sabbatical, which she thought was loony and said so. "It sounds too serious for you. I give you a month max before you realize that a life without nonsense is not worth living."

"It's good to have ideals like that," I said. "You'd have to be doubly silly on my behalf until I return."

At dusk, on my last day at my loft, I gazed out the windows. Ever since I met the vampires, this seemed like a special time, the time to gather and talk, to share our days and our affection, *espíritu de los cocteles.*

My life with Oswald at Casa Dracula had been like a favorite novel I'd read when I was young, and now that I read it again, I had a more mature perspective on the characters and themes. My friends had been right all along, but my journey back to Oswald was one that I needed to take.

Mercedes came by with Cuban ham sandwiches and strawberry Nehis. We stood at the wobbly kitchen table, the only piece of furniture left, and ate silently. When she had crumpled up the wax paper wrappers and put them in the paper bag, she said, "I heard an interesting rumor from Los Hackeros."

"Does it involve alien abduction?"

"No, but it's right there with other conspiracy theories. Word is that a notorious military contracting firm has just folded because their computers suffered a massive attack that spread to their main data center and all their international locations."

"Really?" I said, cheered.

"Los Hackeros say that only a genius could have had the espionage skills needed to infiltrate that organization and design such a comprehensively malicious worm."

I grinned. "Sounds like another one of those urban myths, like vampires and werewolves and Elvis sightings."

My friend smiled back at me and then said, "There's got to be another way. You can't just leave forever."

"It's not forever. It's just until Ford and Cricket wake up and figure out what they want to do . . . and what they can do. Ford's pretty easygoing, at least he was when he was alive, but I expect some truculence from Cricket. She liked the high life, and society's not too keen on zombie socialites."

"She should be grateful to be alive. Where are they anyway?"

"In the truckasaurus. I got a locked cover for the bed and put them there with a note, some magazines, and bottled water and fruit in case they wake up early."

"There's got to be another way," Mercedes repeated.

"It won't be bad. I need to finish this fauxoir, and if *Don* Pedro gets another book deal, he'll want to hire me again. I've got several Tolstoy books, and I imagine Ford and Cricket will take up a lot of my time."

"I'll visit when I can."

"You better." I looked at my friend and said, "You know that to me you are everything that is good, don't you? You are honest, and brave, and brilliant, and you bring beauty and music into this world, and I love you. I wish I could have given you half of what you've given me."

"What are you talking about?" she said. "You introduced me to Pepper and the Grants. If not for you, I wouldn't have the sandwich shop, or half the bands that I've signed, or all the crazy energy you give me, or my business partner."

"Ian. You can say his name." I hugged Mercedes and tried not to be sad, but then she began crying and I couldn't stop myself.

"You'll need a place to stay when you come back. You can stay with me and Rosemary."

I laughed and said, "I know. Your casa has always been my casa."

We hugged several times before Mercedes actually left. The loft seemed as sad and empty as it had the first time Oswald had shown it to me, a thing stuck in the past.

I had the small pile of items I hadn't already packed in the truck: the sports bag, my chic green zebra-print suitcase, the Tolstoy novels, books about desert horticulture, and my backpack.

I crawled into a sleeping bag on the floor and tried to think positively about the future. It wasn't what I had planned, but it could be fabulous if I just made up my mind to be happy.

When I awoke, it was dark and I knew someone was watching me. I turned my head and saw Ian sitting on the zebra-print suitcase.

He was dressed casually, in a fine-gauge graphite gray sweater, dark jeans, and black boots. Something had happened while I had amnesia, because he *still* looked like the most gorgeous man I'd ever seen.

Ian smiled sadly and said, "Hello, darling."

I was tangled in my long T-shirt, so I sat up rather ungracefully and brushed my hair out of my face. My heart was pounding from the shock of being awakened, from being near him. "Hello, Ian."

"I came to talk to you in my capacity as a member of the Council."

"You could have knocked."

"I thought you might not open the door. You haven't called me since you've recovered your memory." He took a key and set it on the floor. "I won't do it again."

"That's good, because I won't be here," I said. "Did Mercedes tell you I was leaving?"

"Yes. She broke her rule about keeping out of our relationship," he said. "The Council has cleared you of all charges in Wilcox Spiggott's death and we would like to thank you for helping to apprehend his murderer."

"Sure, anytime. I apologize for accusing you of killing him."

Ian shrugged and I thought of the powerful shoulders moving beneath the soft fabric.

"It was a reasonable suspicion. I certainly considered it," he said. "I understand that you have accomplished what Professor Poindexter did not—you are able to raise the dead. Well, I have always found your presence uplifting."

"Ha, ha, and ha, Ian," I said, and when he smiled it made me feel . . . wonderful. Ian always made me feel wonderful. "You bought that house so you could meet Ford and, through him, his father."

"Yes. I'd heard through various acquaintances that Poindexter had been contracted to reanimate corpses for warfare."

"You weren't skeptical about such a story?"

"When there is profit enough, man achieves things that seem impossible," he said. "I hadn't counted on Cricket's too-avid interest in me. I tried to channel her behavior, but you see how badly that turned out."

"Of course, it doesn't answer *why* you wanted to befriend a man misusing his genius to create a zombie army."

"I didn't want to befriend him. I wanted to find him and stop him."

"You found the facility and set the explosives."

"I expected to use a more subtle approach, but I let my emotions get the best of me. I believed you were safe at the ranch with Oswald."

"I thought you were still with Ilena. Perhaps we should coordinate efforts in the future."

We sat quietly for a minute and then I said, "You were right about me. I killed a guard to escape Poindexter's compound, and I killed Professor Poindexter when I saw him because . . . because the absence of any good can be evil. He was evil."

"I take no satisfaction in being right." Ian sighed. "I am entirely at fault for putting you in harm's way so many times."

"A large cast played out this particular tragedy. We chose our roles. We can't go back and change things," I said. "I tried to. I think Wil was my trial amnesia, my effort to return to the sort of girl I was *before* . . . And after I killed the guard, I didn't want to be myself anymore."

"So you went back to Oswald."

"Lily thinks I went back to Edna. I felt safe there. The ranch represented something to me, too: a home, family, love."

"Do you still plan on marrying Oswald?"

"Why does it matter to you?" I molted from the sleeping bag and crossed my arms over my chest. "You already told me that you never wanted to see me again. You described your passion for the woman you love, but you've never told me *who* you love."

"I was talking about the most exciting, beautiful, amusing, infuriating, irresistible woman in the world, the only woman I've ever loved." He stood and came close to me. "I was speaking of my coy mistress."

"Why don't you just tell me directly, Ian?"

"I was waiting for you to tell me first."

"The classic Mexican-vampire standoff," I said, and took a step back. "You had Cricket and you still have Ilena, and you blew up a building."

"If I'd wanted Cricket, I would have had her and the situation would have been so much easier because no one would have known. *You* wouldn't have known. But I don't want anyone but you," he said. "As for those who died at the facility, I have no pity for merchants of death."

I wanted to believe Ian. I did believe him. "You have too many secrets."

"I would tell you my secrets if I trusted that you would not run away."

"I'm not running away. I'm taking responsibility for the innocents who got caught in the trap you set for Poindexter."

"Milagro, what if I could provide an alternative safekeeping for Ford and Cricket, so that you do not have to exile yourself like a succulent missionary nun, abstaining from all of life's pleasures to act as a caretaker?"

When Ian took my hand in his firm, sturdy hand, a pleasurable fizz ran through me as quickly as an electric shock. He said, "Tell me that you love me."

I looked into his dark eyes and said, "From the first moment I saw you. My heart knew, but my brain's wiring is a little off. I interpreted the signal as sex, sex, sex. But my heart meant love, love, love."

Ian bent to kiss my neck and must have felt my pulse racing. "I love you, Milagro de Los Santos. Tell me that you'll marry me and never leave me."

"You can't have any more secrets from me, and I'll fight you if I think you're doing something wrong, and I won't share you with anyone, ever."

"Anything, everything, whatever you want," he said as he put his arms around me. "No other men for you, either. No running back to Oswald, or tormenting me with liaisons."

"What about flirting?"

"That's like asking, what about breathing?" His teeth nipped my skin and my blood rose up, wanting release, wanting him.

"Yes, Ian Ducharme, I'll marry you."

I put my arms around him and smelled his skin, warm and spicy, and felt the heat of his breath on my ear as he whispered, "I shall tell you everything, such extraordinary things, my own girl."

He pulled me down to the sleeping bag with him, and I

looked into his face and asked, "Do you remember the first time we made love?"

"Vividly. You were a revelation."

I pulled off his sweater, and thought, *He is mine*, thrilling at his broad chest, the dark hair that ran down to his belly button and farther.

"You were so delectable." His hands went to the hem of my shirt, and he lifted it over my head. He grazed my collarbone with his fingers, making me ache with want.

I took his hand and brought it to my mouth, biting until my teeth broke his skin. The rich, salty, intoxicating blood that flowed into my mouth made me shudder with pleasure, and while my mouth was on him, Ian was kissing my shoulder, my arm, my breast.

When I released his hand from my mouth, I gasped, "I've never liked that kitchen table."

He was strong and I was strong.

twenty

Get Me to the Club on Time

A great playwright once said that if you introduce a Margaritanator 3000 in the first act, there will be strawberry margaritas by the third act. And so it was that my frozen drink maker was commissioned by the My Dive bartenders to augment their own equipment on my wedding day.

Mercedes, dressed in a simple navy suit, seemed unusually nervous as she paced in the lobby of her nightclub.

"Chillax, cutie," I said, although I was fidgeting with the bouquet of ivory roses from my garden at Casa Dracula.

"I can't. I keep thinking of all the trouble you'll cause here now that you're going to have part ownership."

"Oh, my God, I hadn't thought of that! Now do you regret asking Ian to stop me from leaving?"

"A little," she said with a smile. "But I'm selfish. I couldn't stand the idea of you inflicting your craziness on other people."

"That's the nicest thing you've ever said to me."

Pepper, resplendent in a navy blazer, kilt, and biker boots, came in the lobby and said, "You ready?"

Mercedes and I looked at each other and I said to her, "Am I doing the right thing?"

"Do you love him?"

"Completely, utterly. From the moment I met him."

"I'm crazy about him, too, Milagro. He's got his quirks. What guy doesn't?" Mercedes glanced fondly at Pepper.

"He's a righteous dude," Pepper said, with a nod that sent the tiny metal skull beads on his beard dancing.

I took a breath and smiled. "Okay, Pepper, we're ready."

Juanita was at the piano and when her trumpeter played the first pure notes of "At Last," our guests in the club fell silent. Juanita joined in next, singing, and then the rest of the Rat Dogs began playing.

Mercedes went down the aisle between the small cocktail tables and took her place onstage. I followed, wearing her grandmother's scarlet satin cocktail dress, ruby drop earrings, and an antique gold and ruby tiara.

As I walked through the crowd, I saw the Grant family, Nancy, Mercedes's family, the Stitching & Bitching crowd, the bikers, the heiress, the tabloid writer, my masseuse friend, the foxy shape-shifter, and Ian's family and his other friends. They all smiled at me and I felt so lucky to have them in my life.

And when I arrived by my groom's side and looked into his dark eyes, I thought, *Love, love, love.*

Ian, wearing an exquisite black suit and white shirt, smiled his dangerous smile, and my heart was so full, I thought it would burst. When he took my hands, I felt the thrill that no one else gave me, and I knew he felt the same thrill.

The doorman Lenny's wife, a minister, conducted the brief service. Ian slipped an ancient gold and ruby band on my finger, and it looked exactly right.

The minister said, "I now pronounce you husband and wife,"

and Ian kissed me, sending shivers down my back. Everyone clapped and many hooted and hollered and the party started right away, just the way we'd wanted it to.

Champagne corks popped, guests started chattering, and the band began playing. My new father-in-law, compact and distinguished Augustin Ducharme, in tails and a sash with medals, kissed me on both cheeks, saying, "Our son is a lucky man!"

Lala Ducharme looked both chic and matronly in a pink Chanel suit. She held my hands in her small ones and said, "We've been waiting for this day ever since Ian told us about you. I know you will be a good wife."

"I will do my very best."

Friends handed me off from one to another, kissing me and wishing me well. Nancy said, "You look incredible, and I knew you'd get to wear a tiara. My envy is boundless. You should keep it on for the wedding night. Do you have a title now, too?"

"I've always had one. It's Miracle of the Saints."

"I'll find out and get calling cards for you. The more hyphens the better."

"I'm keeping my name, and a toaster would be fine."

"I knew you would have this kind of wedding. The only thing I was off on was the bongos and bad poetry."

"You know me too well, Nancita."

Ian's sister, Cornelia, came at me with her thin arms open wide, like a spider in haute couture. "Dearest!"

"Cornelia!"

She smirked and said, "You see, I told you I would be at your wedding to the man you loved."

"You certainly did, Cornelia, although I was annoyed when you sabotaged my engagement to Oswald."

"It was from love, Milagro. I couldn't wait until you were my

297

sister. I have the best brother in the world, but I've always wanted a sister."

"Me, too."

I was pulled away by Gabriel, who said, "You look ravishing, Mrs. Dark Lord."

"So do you, Gabriel. Will we see you and Charlie next month?"

"Yes, and while we're in Lviv, Charlie will be looking at a chalet to convert to a hotel."

"We'll go sightseeing together, Gabriel."

"I think our lives are inextricably tied, girlfriend," he said, and kissed my cheek.

Although I got sidetracked, I set my course for Edna, who was chatting with Gigi Barton and her guest. Kisses went round and Edna said to me, "You have never looked so radiant."

"I never thought I'd marry Ian."

"You were the only one, Young Lady. The rest of us knew it the moment you two crocodiles met."

"You could have saved me trouble and told me."

She gazed at me with her gorgeous green eyes. "I think that you have become a lady at last, Milagro."

"Don't say that, Edna. I want to believe that I can do better."

"Don't expect an argument from me," she said. "I've figured out your superhero power."

"You have?"

"Look around you."

I did, and said, "All I see is people waiting for the roast pork to be served and the dancing to begin. What's my superpower?"

"You open people to passion. There's my grandson Sam with his wife and child, and that wouldn't have happened without you. Gabriel wouldn't have met Charlie if you hadn't caused problems. Mercedes and Pepper are an oddly right couple. Nettie and Wilcox are together as they wish."

Suddenly, everywhere I turned, I saw couples who had come together in connection to me.

The crowd quieted a little as Thomas Cook approached, looking more beautiful than his photographs.

Edna said, "I never would have met Thomas if not for your shenanigans."

Thomas kissed my cheek and said to Edna, "I told Milagro she was a happy ending sort of girl."

"You were right, Thomas," she said with a smile. "You have a deeper understanding of character than people give you credit for."

"I'm not just a stunning face and amazing body."

The besotted actor pulled Edna away and I saw one more couple I'd brought together, Oswald and Lily. In a slate gray suit that intensified the silver-gray of his clear eyes, he looked like the successful professional he was. Lily was lovely in a shimmery lavender dress and a wrap around her ivory shoulders.

They held hands and came to me. "Best wishes," Lily said. "I'm so happy for you."

"Thank you, Lily, and thanks for bringing the roses from the ranch."

"I'm learning more about them," she said. "Oh, and I've got some questions about planting for late summer blooms."

"I'll give you a call and we'll talk."

"Maybe you could come up sometime," she said, and then Oswald glanced at her. "Or we can have a just-girls lunch until things are more settled."

"That would be fine. I'll save up my gardening catalogs for you."

"Great. Excuse me, because I've got to try a margarita," Lily said.

Then she left us, and I was staring at Oswald and remembering so many things.

My former fiancé looked solemn. "I've never seen you look so happy and beautiful. You got the wedding you wanted—the club, the music, the food, the dress . . ."

"This is more my style than a formal wedding. You know that."

"Yes, but I kept hoping you'd change."

"Funny, I kept hoping that about me, too. Ian once told me, 'You're Milagro de Los Santos, why would you ever want to be anything else?'"

"He was right. Goddamn Ian Ducharme. Before, during, and after, it was always Ian."

"Why did you try with me, then, Oz?"

"Because you're so damn hot and I was in love with you. Why did you try with me?"

"Because you're the perfect partner for a sincere and serious young woman, but I'm not that woman," I said with an apologetic smile. "I never knew when I met you what my life would be—secret cabals and vampire maniacs, werewolves and incubi, zombies and mad scientists."

"And amazing sex," Oswald said, and touched my hand. "We had a wild ride, didn't we, babe?"

"It was astonishing," I said. "Thank you, Oswald, for everything—for all the incredible memories."

"If we could go back in time . . ."

"But we can't," I said.

One side of his mouth went up in the crooked smile that I would always love. "If we could, I would do it all over again, in a heartbeat, because I wouldn't have missed any of it—I wouldn't have missed *you*, Milagro, for anything in the world."

"Someday, Oz, we'll be the best of friends."

"Sure we will, babe."

When Oswald kissed my cheek, I took in the scent of his

herby sunblock, and I felt an ache deep within me, such grief. Because it's painful to see something die—a beloved grandmother, a favorite pet, a kind friend, life changing a passion for a fabulous man.

Oswald and I gazed into each other's eyes, and I thought he must feel the same bittersweet pang.

And then I turned back to my guests.

There was dinner and toasts, and after that Ian and I had our first dance as a married couple to a romantic bolero. I said into his ear, "Do you remember the first time we danced together?"

"Vividly," he answered. "You moved like a dream. A sweaty, lusty wet dream."

"I thought we danced *too* well together."

"Is there no pleasing you? I shall try to rise to the challenge."

"Not in front of the guests, Ian."

"If you insist."

"Where's Ilena?"

"She decided not to come."

"I can't say that I'm upset. But thank you for letting me invite Oswald."

"The sooner he marries Lily Harrison, the more comfortable I'll be," Ian said. "I have a wedding present for you."

"Is it in your pants?"

"Not in front of the guests, Milagro," he said in his low, sexy, rumbly voice, and I wished that the guests would all go away so I could be alone with my husband.

Our second band of the night was Pepper's new rock group. Mercedes's father joined the biker on bagpipes, and the wall of sound pulsing through me was exactly what I loved about music.

I took off my shoes and danced with my girlfriends, before Ian picked me up and carried me out, while our guests shouted congratulations.

A black Mercedes pulled up, and Mr. K got out and opened the door for us.

"Good evening, sir, ma'am."

Ian said, "Good evening. Home, please."

I said, "Mr. K, please tell me that I'm not a 'ma'am' already."

He smiled and said, "As Lord Ducharme has instructed us, you will be exactly who you will be, Milagro."

"Thank you, Mr. K."

We got in the backseat, and Mr. K closed the door.

I leaned against Ian. "You didn't have to carry me out."

"You would have stayed there all night, and I couldn't endure sharing you any longer."

As Mr. K started the car and began driving, I said, "It was the best wedding ever, Ian."

"We still have the family ceremony in Lviv. My mother has been planning it for years."

"I'm trying to make that traditional vampire wedding fruitcake, and it looks all kinds of dreadful. Mrs. K promised to help fix it, but it may be unfixable, wrong at the molecular level, as Nancy would say." I looked out the window. "This isn't the way to the hotel. Where are we going?"

"Home."

I sighed. "Did you buy another house without telling me?"

"You won't set foot in the Modern Tuscan, so I found a place that I hope will be more to your liking," he said. "It's down the street from Nancy's apartment, and you can run back and forth and visit."

"That will be fantastic! Is that the present you mentioned?"

"No, darling."

We'd reached Nancy's tony neighborhood, where Beaux Arts buildings, Victorians, and a few daring moderns had spectacular views to the bay. Mr. K turned into the driveway of a graceful three-story pewter Edwardian with white trim and a long stair-way to the front entrance.

When Mr. K opened the car door, we got out and Ian led me through a black iron gate and up the marble steps. "It's a bit empty now, because I know you'll have your own ideas about decorating."

"So if I want to cover the walls in flocked leopard print, you won't object?"

"Not in the least."

Mrs. K opened the front door with a bright smile. "Congratu-lations! Come in, come in."

Ian picked me up again and said, "Welcome home, Milagro," and carried me over the threshold into the foyer.

It was silly, but in the good way. "Thank you. Now let me down so I can see this place."

I walked into a long living room with French windows look-ing out to a balcony. The house had been remodeled in a clean, airy way, from the white coffered ceiling to the simple marble fireplace, so that it was neither stuffy nor stark. "Ian, it's beautiful. Are you sure this isn't my present?"

"No, come along." He took my hand and led me down the hall past a dining room, closed doors, and to the kitchen with its gleaming new appliances and hardwood floor. "I'll leave it to you to decide where we put the mirror ball."

"Is this an appliance-related gift?" I said. "Because, if so, it should match my chartreuse Margaritanator 3000."

"It's not an appliance."

"Is it the yard?"

"No, but the yard does need a great deal of care. Perhaps you can recommend a garden designer." Ian opened a back door and the first thing I saw was a laundry room. The second thing I saw was a small fuzzy thing coming at us with an abundance of wig-gling and tail wagging.

I bent over and picked the puppy up. Her amber eyes gleamed and she squirmed and began licking my face. I loved her right away.

"Is she a clone?" I asked.

"I wouldn't presume to dabble with God's work. She's just a rescue dog who reminded me of your dog, Daisy."

"She's wonderful. I love her." I looked into the puppy's face. "I think you'll be Sweet Pea, because that means bliss and that's what I feel."

With a puppy in the house, there would be whining. But no matter how much I wheedled, Ian refused to let the dog sleep in our bedroom on our wedding night.

Mrs. K heard us from the kitchen and said, "Pardon, but I'm fond of the little thing and she can stay in her bed in our parlor. I'll hear her if she's lonely."

"Thank you," I said, and handed her the puppy.

"Good night, Mrs. K." Ian put his arm around my waist and led me back down the hall.

"I have made one alteration to the house." He stopped at the staircase. "I've had the master suite soundproofed."

"Excellent. Now Mr. and Mrs. K won't come running when I make you beg for mercy tonight."

"That sounds like a challenge," he said with a wicked grin. "I think it's time we went to bed, my own girl."

"Ian?"

"Yes?"

"All this lavishness is fab, but I didn't marry you for your money or because you have a title."

"I know exactly what you want from me. It's in my pants." With that he hauled me over his shoulder and ran up the stairs while I laughed.

Ian carried me into a sumptuous ivory and moss green bedroom and lay me on the bed. Candles in silver candlesticks flickered their warm light, a bottle of champagne rested in a wine cooler, and there were vases of antique roses in creamy shades.

Ian gazed at me and said, "I thought I might never have you and now that I do, I'll never let you go."

"'Thus though we cannot make our sun stand still, yet we will make him run,'" I quoted. "Kiss me, Ian."

The next day, we took a flight to the Caribbean, and then we were taken by sloop through azure waters to a tiny green island that had been abandoned by terrified and superstitious tourists over a century before. Ian held the legal title only to protect the true owners, a tribe with a name that could only be sounded with whistles.

Wil and Nettie greeted us at the pier. He was wearing board shorts and a guayabera open on his chest, a white stripe of sunblock on his nose, and sunglasses. "Welcome, welcome, Milagro and Lord Ducharme!"

"Hi, Wil, Nettie," I said, happy to see that they looked almost healthy.

Wil was about to hug me when Ian said, "Hello, Spiggott. Do keep your hands off my bride at least for the honeymoon. Then you may resume your flirting, but no more."

Wil looked fondly at his girlfriend. "Yeah, Nettie feels the same way."

"Hello, Nettie," Ian said, and took her hand. "I hope your recovery is going well."

She ducked her head shyly, and Wil said, "The shaman says that normals can take months to recover. I was different because I'm a vampire. *Was* a vampire. But Nettie will be as right as rain in a few more weeks. Meanwhile, I get to chat without interruption."

Nettie slapped Wil's chest, and he said, "Oh, cutie, you know what I like."

I noticed that my friend was a slightly darker shade of greenish. "Wil, you've got a tan! How's the surfing?"

"Kick-ass, great barrels on the flip side of the island, draw you in, spit you out. I've been teaching Matthews a few basics."

"So you guys are getting along?"

"Yeah, now that he's loosened up. He's a changed man. Well, we all are," Wil said. "I'll take you to your hotel."

He helped load our things into a jeep and drove us up a narrow road to a neglected but still grand white hotel among the palm trees.

When we entered the empty terra-cotta tiled lobby, Wil said, "The shaman said that the Poindexters should stay in the village. The tribe is caring for them."

Wil suggested that we all go to the lounge for a drink. We went into a magnificent old bar with mostly bare shelves. Only a few other people were here, greenish hued and relaxed as they raised their glasses toward us and smiled as a greeting. A few were people who had "disappeared" when Ian was sent to solve an intractable problem.

Ian waved toward them and said to me, "We keep things simple here, darling. I hope you don't mind."

"It's lovely," I said. "It reminds me of a campus that's been emptied out for the summer."

Wil went behind the bar and pulled out a plate of sliced mangos and a pitcher of sangria, and Nellie got glasses for us. Wil said, "The local zombies are friendly, but they're basically nocturnal. Been there, done that—now I want to spend all my time in the sun."

When we were seated, I said, "How are the Poindexters adjusting?"

"Good." The surfer grinned. "Anger and aggression, greed, all those things vanish when you change over. I don't know if it's seeing death, or because we're more like plants than people." He looked at Nettie and took her hand.

"We're happy," she said softly, gazing at Wil.

"Everyone should consider becoming a zombie," he said.

I shook my head. "Weren't you the one who was talking big ideas about a progressive vampire movement?"

"I was more interested in getting in your knickers," he said. "You were the one who made the charts and action plan."

"I thought I was helping. I've come to see that maybe it's better to understand a situation before jumping right in to change things."

Ian began laughing, stopped himself, and said, "Sorry, darling."

I picked up the pitcher and filled our glasses. Then I lifted mine in a toast. "Well, here's to this lovely nameless place and its people."

"It's not nameless," Wil said. "The tribe calls it Isla Milagro."

When night came, we visited the tribe, whose name meant the Caretakers, at their village of low huts. They made a feast for us of grilled fishes, vegetables, and fruits, and Ian and I watched the shaman dance around a fire with aromatic smoke from herbs that were used in the weavings.

Cricket and Ford, both wearing woven tunics had wreaths of flowers on their heads. They watched contentedly as they held hands and sat cross-legged on a mat.

Ian and I thanked our hosts and took a walk up a hill. We could hear the faint music coming from a zombie band that played in the empty hotel every night.

I stared at the bright stars above. "There are Castor and

Pollux. I know who told me that now. It was just before I was attacked by Vidalia in werewolf form."

"Your life has had many surprises."

"One of them is that your international bon-vivanting had a higher purpose."

"Not all of it, darling. Some of it was so that I would meet a certain delicious and elusive young woman who also was more serious than she seemed."

"And sillier than she should be?"

"That is what I loved about her," he said. "Once when I was in Sozopol—"

"Which is where?"

"On the Black Sea. We'll go there," he said. "I met an amusing little man who said he was studying folktales and shape-shifting."

"And was his name *Don* Pedro?"

"It was. We went to a dinner with music by a mystic, we smoked opium, and I had just met a captivating local beauty when *Don* Pedro seemed to go into a trance."

"Let me guess. He had an eerily prescient vision."

"Exactly. He told me I would meet a woman with hair as black as midnight, a living miracle, and that she and I would do good for the world, and she would be my partner in life and that I would love her till death and beyond death."

"So you went in search of me."

"Certainly not. I wasn't going to disappoint my pretty companion because of a lunatic's prophecy," he said. "I forgot all about it until years later when the Council sent me to meet a girl who had miraculously survived infection."

"And then you fell madly in love with me."

"I wanted you for my own, but you had the audacity to reject me for Oswald Grant."

"I had a crush on Oswald first. So then you met me again and fell madly in love with me."

Ian smiled his dangerous smile. "It took some time to take *Don* Pedro's visions seriously, especially when you seemed so reluctant to return my affections. I stopped counting the times you broke my heart."

"I wasn't sure you had one, Ian."

He took my hand and placed it on his chest. "I do, and I entrust it entirely to you."

"I promise to care for it." I kissed his warm hand. "How many of *Don* Pedro's stories are actually your own adventures?"

"We have the rest of our lives, together, and I think I shall save those stories for other nights. You and I will have so many adventures."

Laughing, I said, "Ian, I think I can dedicate my life to going to parties in order to save the world."

"I never doubted that you could, my own girl. Shall we go for a swim?"

"Go ahead, *mi vida, mi corazon, mi amor,*" I said, because he was all those things to me: my life, my heart, my love. "I'll meet you on the beach."

He kissed me and strolled off, leaving me alone but not lonely as I looked into the star-spangled sky.

Before meeting the vampires, I was a girl with dreams. I dreamed of being in love with a fabulous yet worthy man and being loved in return. I dreamed of having my stories published. I dreamed of having a home. I dreamed of being surrounded by friends and family. I dreamed of making a difference.

My stories were dreams, too, of a world that was bigger and more fantastical than what seemed prosaic reality.

And all those things had come true for me. I was loved by a fabulous, amazing man who could laugh with me. I had success as an author, albeit under *Don* Pedro's name. Oswald's family had become my family, and now I also had the Ducharmes and all my friends.

I'd made a difference. I'd united couples, created gardens, and thwarted the dangerous ambitions of madmen, death merchants, and extremists, while always finding time for friends and fun.

As for my home, the earth was my home, and, like Ian, I was a citizen of the world.

Death and happy endings were only the transfer points of an amazing journey. My story had just begun.

I walked down the hill to the beach. The white sand sparkled in the bright light of the moon. I pulled my clothes off and ran into the water and into my husband's arms.